The Prisoner of the Castle of Enlightenment

Therese Doucet

D. X. VAROS

Published by:
D. X. Varos, Ltd
7665 E. Eastman Ave. #B101
Denver, CO 80231

Book cover design and layout by, Ellie Bockert Augsburger of Creative Digital Studios.
www.CreativeDigitalStudios.com

Cover design features:
stone wall background By Eky Chan / Adobe Stock
Plant Vines Green, Leaves Bunch By higyou / Adobe Stock
Plant Vines Green, Leaf Four Twisting By higyou / Adobe Stock
Plant Vines Green, Leaves By higyou / Adobe Stock

ISBN: 978-1-941072-63-9 (paperback)
ISBN: 978-1-941072-63-9 (ebook)

I

I HAD FOUND a measure of happiness, sitting on the edge of the well in the evening, watching the Alpenglow paint the peaks across the valley in shades of rose and marigold. Once I had wanted to drown myself in this same well. That was after my husband died and my father sold off all the books in the shop my husband and I had kept. I saw my path to freedom disappear then, just as the paths on our mountain sometimes vanish in the space of a few seconds from rock falls, or avalanches during the heavy snows.

The well water below was black-green in the shadows of the encircling stones, and cold air rose from it like the breath of spirits passing to and from the underworld. I could have weighted my pockets with rocks, could have plunged into the icy water and freed myself from worry and care, taking my body back for myself once and for all. People thought I grieved the death of my husband, Guillaume Bergeret, a lay pastor of our Vaudois faith who'd kept the bookshop in Annecy to support us; but it wasn't true. The pastor's soul and mine were always strangers to each other, and I could never bring myself to call him by his Christian name or use *thee* and *thou* with him, even after two children were born to us and grew into a pair of lovely, willful wood sprites.

Valentin's shouts and Aimée's giggles echoed from around the bend in the trail through the trees to Father's house, where we'd lived since the pastor died in his bed in Annecy. The pastor would have expected me to scold them, for clearly they were building a fort instead of gathering sticks for kindling as I had asked them to do. But I, too, neglected my chores to savor the warm, clear early June evening, the cries of the hawks and doves through the fragrant rustling pines mingling with the children's voices and the cattle bells clanging from the grassy slope beyond.

I caught a glimpse of our housekeeper, Edmée, hurrying up the path. She spoke to Valentin and Aimee and they fell silent, before scurrying back down the hill to the house. I stood up quickly to dust off my skirt, filled my buckets, and hooked them back onto the yoke. Then I set them down again as Edmée came into sight on the path, panting and out of breath, her face pink.

"Violaine! Your father's returned. Here, I'll take those buckets, you go."

I left the buckets to her and set off at a run. I'd long since forgiven my father for selling the books. It simply never occurred to him that I would prefer taking over the bookshop to marrying again, or that I'd even be capable of running the shop on my own. Father had already sold everything and packed the stock off to the buyer before I had any chance to lay out my plans to him. He had no way of knowing about the poems I had hidden in the pages of the *Book of the Rose,* which he sold along with the rest, or that it was the book I loved more than any other.

Now perhaps he'd brought the *Book of the Rose* back to me – the one thing I had asked for when he'd left three months earlier, after the snows had melted. My older sister, Hortense, hadn't been shy about asking for a pearl brooch and earrings like the fine Catholic ladies wore to church in Annecy, and for brocade fabric and lace to make a dress and collar that would be the envy of the other matrons in her village. Françoise-Angélique, my younger sister, would never think of such luxuries for herself, but since the midwife had told her she would give birth to twin girls in April, she had asked for linens and lace for the christening dresses and silver cups and spoons for the babies.

My *Book of the Rose* was an old, tattered volume, but the poems I had hidden in its pages were the tear-spattered outpourings of my heart. Its story of knights and roses and courtly love had kept me company through many a desolate night, when I lived through the sagas in my mind to forget the misery of my circumstances. My soul had come to inhabit that book, and more than two years had passed since I'd lost it. But Father was hopeful he could recover it, for he was going to stop in Annecy on the way home from his travels.

I reached the door of our house, out of breath, and found Father seated at the table with Aimée on his knee. His graying mouse-colored hair was windblown, and his face had grown thinner. Valentin stood next to them, his dark curls hanging over his eyes, tall enough at ten years old to reach his grandfather's shoulder, looking on as his little sister chattered. When Father raised his eyes to meet mine, there was a terrible expression in them, a hollowed-out, haunted look. He didn't return my smile but put Aimée off his knee and rose to accept my embrace and kisses on each cheek.

"Father, are you well?" I asked. He looked away instead of answering. I tried to fill the silence. "But you're home at last. We missed you so much. How was the journey? Did you come all the way from Annecy today?"

He nodded and sat down again. Dust from the road had gathered in the folds of his stockings, and his fingers twitched nervously in his lap. "I had some business to finish in the city this morning, and then I came straight on."

I hurried to fetch him water and the soup Edmée had made for our supper. Edmée returned from the well with the buckets I had left there, and I filled the kettle and set it on the fire to brew a tea of verbena and balm. "You must have made good time," I said.

He frowned and prodded at the thin soup that was mostly vegetables. "Not bad. The roads were clear, and I had a fresh horse."

Valentin's eyes snapped wide open. "What about Claudette?" he asked. He and Father's old mare Claudette had been great friends ever since Valentin could walk.

Father smiled, though his eyes were tired. "Never fear, she's coming along with the buggy tomorrow. I stayed overnight with a gentleman who lent me a faster steed to speed me on my way."

"That was kind of him." I lit candles for the table from the fire. "Was it a friend of yours – another Vaudois?"

Father shook his head. "Not one of us, no, though I think he might become a friend."

I wrinkled my brow and bustled around the table to make sure the children had taken their share of the soup from the pot before I served myself.

"Violaine," Father said, "Sit down. Let Edmée do it."

I couldn't remember that he'd ever spoken to me like that before – telling me to sit and rest. Usually he expected the women around him to stay busy. Something awful must have happened. I hoped whatever it was had only to do with money and wasn't something worse.

I took a seat and pushed the onions in the soup around with a slice of hard black bread while the children and Edmée ate theirs quickly. He spoke of the weather and of the places he had visited. He had journeyed south, to Chambéry, Grenoble, the Dauphiné valleys, Montpellier, and then back up northward, through Briançon and the province of Piemonte, to Genève, and at last Annecy before coming home. When the soup had all been eaten, Edmée took the children to put them to bed in the back room, and I washed up. Father still hadn't found the nerve to tell me what was troubling him. My heart pounded a little. We sat with our tea, and I poured him a glass of *génépi*; perhaps this would loosen his tongue.

4

He took the liquor gratefully, drank it down in one swallow, and poured himself another. I blew on my tea to cool it.

"It was all a failure," he admitted at last. "I haven't made a single wise decision since your mother passed away. God is punishing me for my sins and foolishness."

I thought by this talk of sins he meant Edmée. At first I hadn't wanted to see that he'd taken up with her after our mother died. Edmée still had a husband, a worthless drunkard who lived near my sister Hortense in the hamlet of Nant-Pierre, a league away. But much of the reading I had done in the bookshop in Annecy had changed my thinking, and I no longer judged Father or her for finding comfort in one another.

"What happened?"

"I'd thought my investment in the trading company was lost. Then in Briançon I got word that the ships hadn't been wrecked as we'd feared and were on their way into the harbor. So I extended myself further than I would have otherwise, with new letters of credit. I expected I'd be able to negotiate settlements on the old debts and pay off the new ones quickly, but when I arrived in Montpellier, my creditors had anticipated me. They'd devoured the lion's share of the profits without my being able to negotiate anything. So now I owe more than when I started, with worse rates and shorter terms. At least, so I thought until I came to Annecy. I don't know what to do. It could be our salvation, or it could be a disaster worse than all the others put together."

"The gentleman in Annecy had some proposal?"

Father let out a long sigh, and tears welled in the corners of his eyes. "I knew I wouldn't be able to bring Hortense her pearls, or Françoise her silver, but I thought I could still try to get your book back. I'd corresponded with the gentleman who'd bought up most of the stock from the pastor's shop about the payments, so I had his name and address in Annecy. It was a Monsieur du Herle, and he'd bought the books on behalf of a marquis."

"A marquis bought the books? All for himself alone?"

"The Marquis de Boisaulne, yes, for his private library."

I propped my chin up on my hand and sighed. "Wouldn't it be nice, to be so rich?"

"I'll admit, I hoped asking about your book might give me an opening for a business proposal of some sort." Father drummed the fingers of one hand on the table, frowning at the memory. "The Marquis wasn't at home, but Monsieur du Herle received me and invited me to stay for supper. He remembered the shop of Pastor Bergeret very well, and buying up the stock for the Marquis's library. He even remembered the *Book of the Rose* being among them." Father looked me in the eyes. "I'm sorry to tell you, but it's a far rarer and more valuable book than I think you realized. The most precious of the whole collection, in fact. He thought it quite a bargain at the time, as he might easily have paid as much for the one book alone as he had for the whole library."

My mouth drooped in disappointment. I could readily believe my old book was a rare find after all, with its beautiful capitals and illustrations, and the antiquated spellings and obsolete words. "So you couldn't afford to buy it back."

"Well – I'm getting to that." Father hesitated for a moment, and then continued more slowly, his mouth set like that of a man about to step barefoot into a pile of burning coals. "Monsieur du Herle also remembered you. Perhaps you'd know his face if you saw him again. It seems that for a time he was a frequent visitor at the shop."

I nodded, feeling chilled. "I don't remember the name, but the pastor used to hold gatherings in the evenings for gentlemen who'd come to talk about religion and political philosophy. Women weren't allowed, of course, but I'd come in to serve drinks after the children were in bed, and sometimes" – I lowered my eyes to the table – "I'd linger in the room or listen at the door. Monsieur du Herle was probably among them."

Father wrapped his hands around the still-warm cup of tea. "I suppose the pastor meant to do his part to spread tolerance. I'd expect no less. He was a brave man and courageous for our faith, even when it put him in danger."

"It's strange, though, to think any of his guests would have remembered me. That was so long ago."

Father looked at me sternly, as if I'd told a lie, pretending to be unaware of the effect my face and figure might have on men. Perhaps I had. I felt sick to my stomach, for I thought I already knew where this conversation was going.

"Monsieur du Herle asked after you," Father said. "He asked if you'd remarried. I told him you hadn't. He paid me extravagant compliments about you, and said he well recalled how lovely and charming you were, how quiet and decorous in your manner."

I searched my memory for some recollection of M. du Herle. Had any of the men at the pastor's philosophical gatherings been handsome? I remembered being too shy to look them in the eyes. I only recalled dark coats and hats, perhaps a set of whiskers here, a pair of spectacles there, a dress sword buckled to one side if any of them were particularly elegant. There'd been the occasional colorful waistcoat and wigs of many shapes and sizes, some powdered, some plain. Had there been a pair of light gray-blue eyes that followed me around the table once or twice as I poured out coffee? Had that been M. du Herle? Most of all I remembered the gentlemen's voices through the keyhole, and the ideas that tantalized me, hovering just at the edge of my understanding in fragments I tried to piece together, and how I'd longed to be seated at the table to hear all that was said, and to speak back with my own thoughts that were always brimming up in me. I had no one to confide them to otherwise, apart from the occasional sheet of paper in quiet moments.

"I was beginning to think he meant to ask me for your hand," Father said, "but he didn't. He said he thought you'd please his master, the Marquis. And not –" he added as I started up out of my chair in astonishment – "and not as a wife."

He fell silent for a moment, and his words sank in. I felt as though someone had wafted a shovelful of manure in front of my nose and I sat back down. "But –"

Father pressed on. "He said his master, the Marquis, sought the companionship of a young woman. I said it seemed to me that there must be no shortage of young ladies of that sort in Annecy, and surely if he knew the pastor, he must know we're God-fearing people. I said you would never consent to such a thing, and frankly I was deeply offended at the suggestion."

I breathed out a sigh of relief. "Was he angry with you?"

Father shook his head. "He understood perfectly. Then he explained the Marquis's circumstances. He's been estranged from his wife for many years. He married young, not realizing her character. He's not free to marry, as long as she still lives. But he wishes to make as honorable an arrangement with us as possible under the circumstances. You and the children would be provided for, even if you separated from him at some time in the future. There would be a signed contract. Monsieur du Herle visited the Marquis's lawyer this morning and had it drawn up, and I've brought it back with me."

Heat rose along the sides of my neck with my growing sense of horror. "Father, what madness is this? You agreed that I'd become a ... a *prostituée*?"

"Keep your voice down," he said in a forceful whisper. "It's nothing of the kind. You turned down every match Edmée or I tried to make for you. No suitor from our villages was good enough for you. You thought yourself above them all, because your husband let you learn Latin and Greek and read all the books in his shop. You've shown not a scrap of gratitude and treated them all with disdain."

"But I – they weren't ..."

"How am I to find the money for an apprenticeship for Valentin, when I can barely even feed us? Do you know we're in danger of losing the house and the livestock? If I can't find a way to hold on until my investments pay off, we'll lose everything. We'll be beholden to the charity of your sisters, whose husbands can barely feed their own families."

I gaped at him, blinking. "You're seriously considering his filthy proposal then? You want me to agree to it? This Marquis, whoever he is, has never spoken one word to me, and you didn't even meet him, did you? You have no idea of his character. Suppose he's unkind to the children?"

He slumped back tiredly in his chair. "You wouldn't take the children. He would provide for their upbringing and education, but they would have to go to live with Hortense, or Edmée could go on caring for them here. We could even send Valentin to school in town. The Marquis is proposing quite a large quarterly sum. Hortense would be happy to have the help, I know."

I shook my head. This couldn't be anything but a terrible dream. I was just becoming used to this life, where I could only read in secret, if at all. I had resigned myself to the loneliness of village society, of living among people who were good-hearted but unlettered, whose minds and speech were a foreign country to me. Now Father wanted to sell me like the pastor's books, to abandon me to the mercy of some dissolute nobleman, probably thirty years older than I was, who was buying me sight unseen on the word of his agent who'd taken a vague liking to my face nearly three years ago. And Valentin and Aimée! I had never been apart from them for more than a few weeks after the pastor had become ill from his time in prison, when they went to stay with Hortense and their cousins. It was unthinkable.

"Listen," he pleaded, "I understand this sounds like madness to you, but Monsieur du Herle testified up, down, backwards, and forwards, to the Marquis's good and honorable character. You'll live in luxury, the envy of every village girl. Besides, you won't be so far away. You'll go to live at the Marquis's hunting lodge in the forest, where he spends most of his time. He has houses in Annecy and Paris too, but Monsieur du Herle said he doesn't mix with society. The Marquis means for our arrangement to be perfectly discreet, so there'll be no shame for our family or harm to our reputation."

9

I raised my eyebrows. "Do you think the villagers won't find out?"

He gave a weak shrug. "I don't know how long we can truly keep it a secret, but the arrangement he's proposed would keep us afloat until I see some of my own money again. Otherwise –" he leaned back and squeezed his eyes shut – "it's possible I might be called before a magistrate and end up in prison. That's the point things have come to. If I go to prison, we won't just be shamed, we'll be beggars. I know I'm asking a frightful sacrifice of you."

I closed my eyes. "This is monstrous. I'm not some rare book you can simply sell to get out of debt."

"There's more, I'm afraid. More than all I've told you so far. The Piedmont Easter –"

"What about it? That was a century ago. Surely you don't think –" My mind raced through the possibilities, and I remembered the winter nights before the fire when the pastor used to tell stories of the bloody massacres of the Piedmont Vaudois. The stories had made little Aimée weep and Valentin's face turn sickly green, conjuring visions of infants skewered with spears, children torn to pieces in front of their parents, girls and women violated, and the survivors driven into the upper valleys in midwinter, forced to build houses in the snow while more of them froze to death.

"I never knew this," Father said, "but Monsieur du Herle showed me the documents, and it's beyond dispute. All these years, our villages have bordered on the domain of the Marquis's family. We remained hidden and safe while the southern Vaudois were tortured, pillaged, and slaughtered, all because we were under the old Marquis's protection."

"What – do you mean to say the Marquis helped us? The *same* Marquis?"

"It appears the lords of Boisaulne had a long tradition of tolerance, and they gave us sanctuary without our even knowing it. The present Marquis has never alerted the parish or the governor to the fact that we don't pay tithes, or that our villages are more than just a couple of scattered farms by the *alpages*. If it weren't for him, we'd be burdened with the same wretched church taxes as the Vaudois in the south. Your husband was arrested for selling anti-clerical treatises and political *libelles* and helping smuggle them across the borders of Savoy into France. If I were called before a magistrate ... it might take very little to spark an inquiry and new persecutions. It's not a good time to lose an influential neighbor's favor."

I felt faint. The hour was growing late, and my mind was clouded with weariness. "Did Monsieur du Herle threaten us? That our villages would lose the Marquis's support if I didn't agree to be his ... his kept woman, his *femme entretenue,* I guess you'd call it?"

"You're twisting my words all out of proportion. He made no threats. He simply told me the history, as a way of explaining that the Marquis is trustworthy and that we have reason to be grateful to him and to believe he's acting in good faith."

I was so tired that I couldn't hold back my tears any longer. As angry and wretched as I'd felt when I was sixteen and Father told me I had to marry the pastor and live with him above the bookshop in Annecy, this betrayal was a thousand times worse. I knew well enough now what marriage was, that it meant one's body was not one's own. Beyond that, it meant living to serve a husband who saw you as housemaid, mother, and child all in one. It meant hiding your feelings and thoughts and wishes, and that everything you did and said had to be guided by what pleased and didn't anger your husband. Now not only would I have to have to bear those burdens again, but my children would be taken from me and I would be ruined as well.

Father was crying too. "I know it's nothing like what you imagined for yourself. It's not at all what I wanted for you, either. I just can't see any other way. I must leave the choice up to you, but consider all that depends on it. Won't you at least meet the man? We still have some time to think it over before Monsieur du Herle arrives tomorrow to fetch you."

"Tomorrow!"

"*Shh*, please, just sleep on it for now, and we can talk more in the morning."

Father got up heavily from his chair and lumbered through the door to his room at the front of the house. I went to the back room I shared with the children, but I didn't undress. I sat on the edge of the bed for a long time, waiting until I could be sure Father would have fallen asleep next to Edmée. Then I went back to the main room in the darkness and found a couple of empty sacks. Silently, feeling my way in the dark, I packed a kitchen knife and what food I could find: hard bread, cheese, some carrots and scallions, a flint and some candles. I returned to the children's room and packed a few clothes. Then I woke Valentin and Aimée and told them we were running away.

II

GOD WAS MERCIFUL and Aimée didn't cry when I woke her and explained that the three of us were in danger and had to leave at once. I didn't worry for Valentin; he was frightened but obedient. Moonlight outside filtered down through the tall pines to light our way, along with the lantern and candles I'd stolen. I opened the door of the barn attached to the side of the house and found the horse belonging to the Marquis de Boisaulne, the one M. du Herle had lent to father. The stallion was white with a silvery mane and gentle. He didn't shy away from my touch, but ate a carrot greedily from my hand.

It was fitting that my would-be enslaver's horse would aid us in our escape. In two days' time we would be in Genève. I could sell the horse and tackle for perhaps as much as five hundred livres. We might live in a cheap boarding house for a year on that money, but our funds would run out eventually. Instead, I would visit the offices of the publishing houses from whose catalogs my late husband used to order, and I would set up my own accounts with them. The illicit works that landed the pastor in prison fetched the best profit, so I would specialize in those. I'd start as a traveling book peddler, like the ones who used to compete with my husband's shop. I wasn't afraid of the mountain paths that skirted the customs offices on the borders between Savoy and France. If I were stopped, no one would suspect me, a woman traveling with children. When I had saved enough, I would open my own shop as a widow, under a false name in some town or other where no one would know me. I wouldn't be a burden on Father anymore.

The horse was fine and strong enough that the two children and I and our sacks all fit on his back easily, riding astride in the dark. It was less than an hour at a careful, slow walk to the hamlet of Nant-Pierre and Hortense's farmhouse. Usually my younger sister, Françoise-Angélique, was the one I confided in, but her twin baby girls were barely four weeks old, and her health had been delicate since the birth. I would have to take my chances with Hortense and hope that, for once, she would take my side.

I brought the horse into Hortense's barn and tied him up with the other animals, while the children waited. The poor things were fainting with weariness. We found the side door to the house unlatched and went in. I lit a candle from the embers in the hearth, and by its light I found two old woolen blankets in a chest. I made an uncomfortable bed for us on the rug before the hearth, and we fell into an exhausted sleep.

I woke several times through the rest of the night, my dreams troubled and my limbs numb from the hard floor, but Valentin and Aimée slept soundly. I was lying awake and alert when Hortense discovered us at dawn. She cried out in surprise before I sat up and she recognized me.

"Violaine, what on earth?" she said softly.

I put my finger to my lips and pointed to the children still sleeping. I slid out of the blankets and stood up. "Come," I whispered, "let's go into the barn. I can help you with the milking and I'll tell you everything."

Arm in arm we went through the door of the kitchen into the barn that adjoined the house, and while I helped her milk the cows and goats, feed the pig and the chickens, and gather eggs, I told her the story and my plans for Genève. I begged her to lend me enough to pay for food and lodging for the next few days, to tide us over until we could sell the horse. She said little at first, only listening, asking questions, making me repeat myself, and shaking her head. I could have wished for more sympathy and outrage from her. She didn't like the Genève plan one bit, it was clear. But she agreed to speak to her husband, Pierre-Joseph, on my behalf.

We went back inside to give the children and Pierre-Joseph their breakfast and then served ourselves. Aimée and Valentin joked and squabbled with their cousins, Ronald and Jacquot, and left with them to take the cows to the pasture. Hortense repeated all that I'd told her to Pierre-Joseph. I had left out nothing, sure of being in the right. I hoped to leave soon, for the daylight was wasting and I wanted to get to Genève before anyone could come after us.

"Well, that takes the cake," Pierre-Joseph said finally. "Running off like a scared chicken, straight into a fox's den. You'd get eaten whole in Genève. What makes you think I'd put up money so you could shame your family and end up dead in a gutter?"

Before I could respond, Hortense added, "Really, it's monstrously selfish, Violaine. How could you even think of doing that to the children? Father must be at his wit's end to accept an offer like that. Then you torment him and make it all the worse by running away, when it was all your fault in the first place."

I was almost too astonished to speak. "My fault?"

"You refused three different marriage offers, all made in good faith, and from perfectly good families, all of them. Any one of them would have eased Father's mind, and you and the children would have been settled. He might not even have had to go on that accursed journey if it hadn't been for you draining his money and being a constant source of trouble."

"And if I understand right," Pierre-Joseph added, "if you don't go, we could all be punished with new taxes like the southern Vaudois, or worse, who knows? And you want to steal a horse too, and break the law like an outright criminal, and drag us into it. All while your father's just trying save us."

"I always knew you were prideful," Hortense said, "but this is beyond arrogant. How bad could life be if you're the companion of a marquis?"

"But we wouldn't be married," I said. "Does no one care that I'd be living with a man in sin? Would anyone even still speak to me here in the villages if they knew?"

"Pearls and silver cover a multitude of sins," Hortense said wryly. "But you said yourself, Father intends that no one will find out. You and I both know Father's done nearly the same thing himself, keeping Edmée with him. He's as kind to her as to a wife, and she's been as good to us as a mother. Do you think you're above them, too good to live as Edmée does?"

Of course she would have to bring that up. I twisted away from them in my seat, folded my arms tightly across my chest, and looked down at the floor. "Of course not, but this is different. No one knows this man at all. I'm being sent off like a lamb to the slaughter."

She puffed out her breath in exasperation. "You're always so melodramatic about everything. That's your problem. You imagine the worst, but it might not be so bad. I don't believe Father would have agreed to it if he didn't think you'd be well-cared for. I know it's not what you want to hear, but I can't support you putting Father, yourself, or the rest of us in danger. It's no easy thing, but for the good of all us you ought to accept the arrangement. Better to be dishonored than to starve or end up in prison."

In tears again, I felt a tug at my sleeve. It was Aimée, who burst into tears herself at the sight of me crying.

"Maman, I don't want to leave here. Couldn't we live here with Tante Hortense forever?"

Hortense squeezed her into a hug and pulled her up onto her lap, comforting her. Outside, I could hear Valentin's joyful shouts as he played with Hortense's boys. I felt defeated and hopeless, and for the first time, I began to imagine giving in, walking willingly into this nightmare from which I could see no immediate escape. My mind revolted at the truth, but I forced myself to face it. Aimée and Valentin could be happy here. What life would it be for them, living on the road with me trying to scrabble out a living as a book peddler in the mountains and towns, keeping one step ahead of the police and the customs agents? Not to mention that for committing the crime of horse theft, I could be imprisoned or sentenced to labor in a workhouse. Even if I stayed out of prison, I'd be entangling myself in risky financial investments, just as my father had done.

I shuddered and imagined the alternative. Shut up in some old aristocrat's hunting lodge in the woods, with no one to protect or rescue me if he turned out to be wicked or violent, subject to this man's whims, however depraved and cruel – to being shamed, degraded, and abused. I'd read certain books in my late husband's shop, books he had stocked not only illegally but also hypocritically, given his piety – books he sold only to customers who ordered them in advance or asked for them by name, that cost double or triple the price of ordinary ones. Those books, titillating as they were, had given me an alarming impression of the proclivities of aristocrats and clerics.

Or perhaps ... perhaps the Marquis would be kind. Perhaps the stories I had read were only that, stories meant to shock and arouse, obscene exaggerations. Perhaps I would only need to perform the ordinary duties of a wife, and would merely have to endure it, as I had endured Pastor Bergeret's weekly attentions on Sabbath evenings, and then I would be left alone. I might even have servants to do the household work. And perhaps he wouldn't be as old or ugly as all that. Perhaps we could even have conversations – he must be an educated man, after all. And if he truly were cruel, I could simply run away and then face whatever consequences might follow. He could hardly keep me prisoner there forever, could he? I could at least meet him, as Father had begged me to. In the end, he might not even like me and might change his mind once he had met me.

"I'm going out for a walk," I said. "I need time to think, alone."

They traded glances and watched worriedly as I went out, but didn't rise to stop me. My feet took me around the side of the house to the barn door. How I wished I could saddle the Marquis's magnificent white horse and ride away into the woods, gallop far from all this trouble and confusion, high up into the mountains, and live in a cave like a hermit. I wouldn't last long once winter came, but never mind, let the cold take me for all I cared. I started to compose a poem in my mind about how I would return to haunt my family as an angry shade, one of those spirits that wailed when the wind whipped through the valleys during the winter storms.

But when I reached the barn door, I found Pierre-Joseph had tied it shut with a tightly knotted cord. I'd have needed a knife to cut it open. I had packed a knife in one of my sacks, but it was inside the house. Just then the sound of clopping hooves and neighing horses came from the lane. I peered around the side of the house and saw that it was Father riding our old mare, Claudette. Another man rode beside him on a black horse. Pierre-Joseph and Hortense came out of the house, spoke to them, and pointed them toward me. They rode up to where I stood, and Father climbed down from Claudette with a jump to embrace me. Out of the corner of my eye, I saw the other man climb down out of his saddle slowly, averting his gaze from Father's emotional display.

Violaine, how could you?" Father said, low enough that the other man wouldn't hear. "Edmée and I were so worried when we woke up this morning and found you gone." He drew back to look me in the face. "But Hortense says you've come to your senses? She believed she'd persuaded you."

I drew in a deep breath, my heart pounding. "Yes, I'll go to the Marquis. I'll do as you ask." I couldn't bring myself to apologize for running away, nor to return his embrace.

18

"This is Monsieur du Herle," Father said, putting a hand on the shoulder of his companion. "He's come to accompany you there."

M. du Herle cleared his throat and looked guilty and uncomfortable. He had light gray-blue eyes, almost silver, just as I remembered from the shop. They were fixed intently on me now, as then. The Marquis's pimp, I reminded myself. His procurer. For an involuntary instant I found myself trying to decide whether he was handsome. He was a lean man of about thirty years, of medium height. His clothes were well-tailored and elegant but muted and dark in cut and color. The fine silver-handled dress sword of a gentleman hung at his waist in a richly worked silver scabbard. The skin on his cheeks was clean-shaven and slightly pock-marked; he had high cheekbones, a narrow chin, light reddish-brown hair under his hat, and a slightly bulbous nose. Both his ears were pierced with ebony rings. No, he wasn't strikingly handsome, but it wasn't an unpleasant face to look at, and I liked the modest turn of his lips, as though he were about to deny a compliment.

"Good afternoon, Madame Bergeret." He bowed and I was struck by a certain shyness in his gesture. "If you're ready we could leave at once and arrive before dark. If you need anything from your father's house we can have it sent on later, but the manor is well-provisioned, and I think you'll find all you need there. The Marquis wishes you to be comfortable."

He didn't bother to pay me any of the extravagant compliments my father had told me about or make a speech. If the Marquis had any sort of honorable intention, if he wasn't some deformed hunchback, why did he not come to meet and fetch me himself? Perhaps that was precisely the reason for all this bizarre mystification and for subjecting me to such an alarming proposal by proxy. Perhaps the Marquis was a cripple, or clubfooted, or hare-lipped; some physical deformity had made a recluse of him, so he had shut himself up in that remote hunting lodge with no company to relieve his loneliness. I wanted to ask M. du Herle if this was so, but the question died on my lips. I was fearful of offending M. du Herle or making an enemy of him right away. All I could do for now was place myself in the hands of Providence and hope M. du Herle's respectful tone and quiet voice boded well. If it was nothing but a physical deformity to worry about, if the Marquis was a good man in an ugly body, then ... perhaps all would yet be well. I had always prided myself on seeing beyond appearances, on not judging books by their covers, prizing wisdom, learning, and the beauty of the soul above jewels or wealth or material comforts.

I badly wanted to believe in this possibility; the thought comforted me. With his fine silver sword, M. du Herle easily severed the knotted cord that Pierre Joseph had used to tie up the barn door to prevent me from running away with the Marquis's horse again. If M. du Herle knew of my attempted horse theft, he politely refrained from mentioning it.

He said very little as he saddled up the Marquis's horse for me, apart from telling me my white steed's name was Zéphyr and his own black mount was called Hadès.

Valentin and Aimée rushed out to say goodbye to me, Hortense trailing after them. Hortense had somehow explained things to them. Maman was going away on a brief journey, but it wouldn't be long before she returned for a visit, and we would see each other again very soon. Aimée cried plentiful tears nonetheless. Valentin tried to act manly and to keep from crying, but hugged me tightly and kissed me on each cheek six times. A small smile played around M. du Herle's mouth as he looked on. Then his face resumed its serious expression as I mounted Zéphyr. He didn't flinch or protest when I explained that I preferred to ride astride rather than side-saddle, as I had little experience with horses and felt safer that way. I was allowed to bring nothing with me, not even the sack with the knife in it.

"We're off then," said M. du Herle. "We'll send word when we've arrived safely."

Why couldn't my father accompany us? Why hadn't he insisted upon it? These were questions I was too afraid to ask. I felt like a girl in a fairy tale, bewitched by a wizard's spell. Would I turn into a swan at dusk? Had some magic stolen my voice so that I didn't scream or shout protests? What power did this M. du Herle wield, that he had gotten his way despite his reserved manner, his deep but quiet voice, and his sparing words? As far as I understood it, not one of us had even laid eyes on this Marquis de Boisaulne, who for all we knew didn't even really exist, though he must have put his signature to the contract with my father, and a lawyer must also have witnessed it.

At first, M. du Herle and I rode side by side on the lane as it climbed uphill.

"Let me know if you need to stop and rest," he said. "Otherwise we'll just stop in the village before we get to the manor."

"There's a village?"

"Not a large one, more of a hamlet. Part of the domain of Boisaulne. They call it Maisnie-la-Forêt."

"But you're not from there?"

"My estate is in Picardy. In the north of France."

"Have you been in the Marquis's employ a long time?"

"A long time, yes."

"You know him well then, I suppose?"

"Fairly well."

After a time the lane narrowed and we began a series of switchbacks, M. du Herle riding ahead of me. I didn't mind; it made it less awkward to ride in silence, and he clearly meant to discourage me from asking questions. Perhaps I ought to have kept trying, but I felt too hopeless and wrung out from my tears, too exhausted from my sleepless night, to understand or to make conversation anyway. After another hour or two, M. du Herle led us onto a side path I wouldn't have noticed otherwise. It was more of a game trail than a proper horse path. Now and then I saw red deer leaping away from us down the hillside. Later we followed a small herd of chamois, the goat-antelopes whose skins makes the softest of leathers. The horses stepped over piles of their droppings along the way. I could only hope we'd see no signs of wolves, lynxes, bears, or wild boars.

After another hour I was forced to ask for a stop, because I needed to relieve myself. M. du Herle dismounted, stretched his limbs, and pointed toward a patch of the woods where rocks, thick trees, and bushes provided some cover. He turned and looked in the opposite direction, crossing his arms over his chest, as I made water behind the trees and came back. Then he took his turn going off into the trees, while I watched the horses and let them munch on leaves and grass.

As he climbed back into Hadès's saddle, I noticed M. du Herle wore a signet ring turned inward on the fourth finger of his left hand, as noblemen did when they were married. I didn't know whether to feel reassured by this or not. He still turned his silver-blue eyes on me from time to time in a way I didn't find comforting. I doubted that a man who respected wedding vows would be acquiring me and bringing me to his master in this manner.

The shadows of the pines, elms, and alders we rode through grew thicker and longer with the approach of evening, and M. du Herle urged the horses to a canter until we came out of the forest. We forded a stream and met a lane wide enough for a buggy or a wagon to travel along. With a glance at me to see if I was all right, he kicked Hadès's flank, and the horse broke into a gallop, Zéphyr matching his pace one length behind. We reached Maisnie-la-Forêt a little before sunset.

The village was a cluster of houses in a clearing above the stream our road had been following, with farms and pastures radiating out from it. There was a tiny chapel on a hill at one end, and in the center a wagoner's shop, a communal oven and bakery, a tavern, a tanner and furrier, and a scattering of market stalls.

We dismounted and tied the horses to a post in front of the wagoner's shop.

"I need to speak to the owner inside," M. du Herle said. "Do you mind waiting here? If you're hungry or thirsty you can go to the tavern and they'll serve you. You only have to tell them you're with me."

I nodded and he went in. His tone was still polite, though we'd ridden in silence for much of the way. I should have been starving, for I hadn't eaten since breakfast, but I had no appetite. I wandered toward the tavern anyway. A young woman sat knitting in front of it, next to a few baskets of cherries.

"Good day, Madame," the woman said. She had positioned her chair to catch the last of the day's sun.

"Good day to you too. Are the cherries for sale?" I knew I ought to eat something, if only to keep up my strength, and they did look ripe and free of worms.

"I was just fixing to take them back inside, but I'll let you have a pound for three *sous*." She grinned at me.

"Oh no, I just wanted a few."

"Ah well, that's all right, have some. I saw you ride in with Monsieur du Herle. I take it he's brought you with him."

"Yes." I put a cherry in my mouth, chewed, and spat the pit into my hand to throw on the ground. The fruit was juicy and sweet, and I felt a little of my appetite returning. I took a handful.

"Is the Marquis de Boisaulne's hunting lodge far from here?" I asked after I'd chewed another cherry and spat out the pit.

"Not at all. Just another mile up the road and across the bridge. You can't see it from here. The road curves up and around and it's hidden back among the trees. Where've you come from?"

I told her a made-up name instead of the village I was from, and she squinted. "It must be on the other side of the mountain from us. We don't usually go across the river."

"Why not?"

"No one wants to be mistaken for a poacher in the Marquis's forest. He's a great hunter."

"Is he?"

"You'd think so. Monsieur Fréret, the wagoner, delivers letters and milk and eggs to the manor each day when anyone's staying there, and a load of supplies each week. But they never need meat. He brings back animal carcasses all the time – they're left for him in the courtyard. Sometimes with the meat still on them, sometimes just the skin and bones."

"Oh," I said, repulsed at the thought of bloody piles of dead animals and pelts.

"We're allowed to hunt and cut wood and forage all we like this side of the river," she said. "But with all that Monsieur Fréret brings back in his wagon from the manor we don't need to that much."

I shuddered. "What's the Marquis like?"

She shrugged. "Oh, we never see him. He likes his privacy. We only deal with Monsieur du Herle. He comes once or twice a month to settle the balances and see if we need anything. Monsieur du Herle's quite reasonable and good to us. It used to be we didn't have a doctor, and you'd have to go down the mountain if you wanted to see one. Now Doctor Guillon comes every Wednesday from Thônes and stays overnight with us in the tavern. He does a good business here. The Marquis pays for his lodging and fees."

"That sounds kind of him," I said. We both fell silent for a few moments while I ate more cherries. She introduced herself as Madame Jacquenod, and I told her my family name of Bergeret. If no one from here ever went to the other side of the mountain, I supposed I didn't need to fear for my family's reputation.

She gave me a guarded look. "It's a long time since I saw him bring a woman through here."

I swallowed and felt the prick of tears at the corners of my eyes, and blinked quickly. Of course there had been others before me. "How long did the last one stay?"

"I never saw any of them leave," she said seriously. "They must go out another way than they come in."

"I'm nervous." The words came out of me almost against my will.

She shook her head pityingly, and there was another long silence. Then she said, "In my grandmother's day there were tales.

Livestock or even children going missing. My brothers used to frighten me with stories of an ogre who lived in the forest across the bridge." She chuckled. "They called him the alder-king, the *roi des aulnes,* and they said the Marquis's lineage bore the ogre's blood in its veins from many centuries earlier, when he took the local nobleman's daughter to wife."

I felt the hairs stand up on the back of my neck. I was struck with a sudden chill, and for a moment my teeth chattered.

Madame Jacquenod looked embarrassed. "But it's nothing to trouble yourself over. I suppose there's just another road that goes out from behind the manor that the Marquis and his guests use for privacy, that's all." She wrinkled her brow in concern. "But if they're ever unkind to you there, we're just a mile away."

A little boy toddled out of the tavern, planted himself in her lap, and demanded supper. Madame Jacquenod fed him a cherry and smiled at me.

I smiled back. "Is there a regular market day here?"

"Tuesday morning and all day Thursday. I'm usually the last to leave when our trees are yielding. We have cherries, plums, and walnuts growing behind the tavern."

"Then maybe I'll see you there."

"Yes, perhaps we'll see you then," she said, although her tone was noncommittal. "We'll certainly have green walnuts by Saint John's Day."

M. du Herle came out of the wagoner's shop and looked about until he caught sight of me. "Good evening, Madame Jacquenod," he called. "Madame Bergeret, are you ready? We ought to be going. It will be dark soon."

III

*I*N SUMMER, DARKNESS fell on the mountain with surprising swiftness. The days were long and you'd be fooled into thinking you had an hour or two of light left to go out for a walk or do some chore. Then all at once the sun would slip down behind the jagged line of peaks and valleys, the trees would block out the stars and moon, and you could hardly see your own hand in front of your face.

By the time we reached the bridge over the stream beyond the village it was frighteningly dark. I could hear water rushing beneath our horses' hooves, but couldn't see it, and feared stumbling over the edge of the bridge and plunging into the rocks and water below. Why had M. du Herle not brought a lantern at least? Then up ahead of us, I saw a dot of twinkling light. The horses knew their way and headed toward it. It grew larger until we reached it, a lantern hanging from a hook set into the wall, next to a gate wide enough for a carriage to pass through.

M. du Herle dismounted and searched in his saddle bag, found a key, and unlocked the gate.

"We're here," he said. "Welcome to the Château de Boisaulne."
He lifted the lantern from its hook and took it with him. By its light,
we entered through the gates and came into a broad drive and
outer yard, with another pair of lanterns flanking the gate to the
inner courtyard beyond. M. du Herle led us around to the side,
where there was a stable. We took Hadès and Zéphyr inside.
Several other stalls were occupied by horses breathing and
snorting in the dark. There was also a buggy and a large carriage,
plain and painted black, with only silver trim for decoration and
no noble family crest.

We came back out into the yard and M. du Herle unlocked
the gate to the inner courtyard.

"How old is the manor?" I ventured to ask.

"It's difficult to say." The gate creaked open. In the darkness
I couldn't gauge the height and length of the stone walls of the
house within. "There's been a building here for as long as anyone
can remember," he told me as we proceeded up a walk toward a
large wooden entry door. "The oldest part of the château still
standing is the great hall, where you'll have your supper. When the
lands of Boisaulne were given to the Marquis's ancestors as a
noble domain, that was all there was. More rooms were built on
the first floor in the days of Duke Charles Emmanuel I, and the
second floor was added then too. The Marquis's grandfather built
a third floor above them and the eastern wing. The Marquis has a
chest with some of the old artifacts that have been found and
passed down. Spearheads, Roman coins, amulets, bone carvings,
and the like. All in all, I'd say the site goes back to ancient times."

He turned another key, and we went in through the entry
door. M. du Herle closed and locked it behind us. The house was
as dark inside as outside, but M. du Herle's lantern cast a circle of
illumination around us, and I could see we were in a small
antechamber with a staircase leading up. A few paintings hung on
the walls, and there was a sofa, a table, and a couple of chairs. M.
du Herle picked up a sealed letter from the table, unfolded it, and

read it by the light of his lantern. He slipped it into his pocket and stepped forward down the hall.

The passage opened into a cavernous stone-walled room with a long dining table and a dozen chairs. At the far end was a great fireplace with a fire roaring in it and two upholstered armchairs facing it, with a small table between them. A candelabra illuminated the far end of the dining table, which was laid with a single covered serving dish. We moved to the end of the table, and M. du Herle took the cover off the dish. Steam wafted up, carrying the scent of roasted meat. My mouth watered. I was suddenly ravenous.

"Good," M. du Herle said, "here's your dinner, then. I hope you don't mind venison. It's served often here."

"But there's only one plate."

"Yes. I'm afraid I have to leave you now. The Marquis has been detained, and I need to return to Annecy immediately tonight to take care of a matter there."

"What, tonight? But we just got here. You'll ride in the dark?"

"I'll take a lantern, but I have to go. It's urgent. I'm sorry to leave you alone on your first night here."

"You're leaving me alone?" I looked around the room as if the walls or corners might reveal someone to help me, but all I saw were shadows and stark angles. My stomach twisted in fear.

"You're not really alone, though you may not see anyone else for a few days."

"A few *days?*"

"The Marquis should be back in a few days, and then you'll make each other's acquaintance."

"But why ... why wouldn't he be here to meet me?"

"Might I suggest you use the time to your advantage, to settle in on your own and explore a little? You'll find your way around, have no fear. The Marquis has trained his servants to be exceedingly discreet, well-nigh invisible. If you need anything, just leave a note on the table by the fire and you'll find matters addressed quickly."

He pulled out the chair by the table for me. "Now eat, before it gets cold. I really must go. Don't be afraid, whatever you see. You're perfectly safe here and until the Marquis returns, you're the mistress of the manor. Consider the place your own and make yourself comfortable."

I sat down in front of the plate of roast venison and vegetables. He bowed to me and turned to leave.

"Will I see you again?" I asked.

He nodded. "I'll return. I don't know when, but we'll see each other again. Goodnight, Madame Bergeret. Until then."

I watched him go, hating him for his enigmas and silences, his coldness, the effrontery of bringing me here only to leave me at once, the rudeness of not explaining why on earth I'd been brought here only to be ignored and abandoned. I was seized with terror. What was the meaning of it, this dark, empty, silent place? Though Hortense had mocked me for saying so, I felt more than ever now like a sacrificial victim, a tribute offering led down into a labyrinth and imprisoned there to be devoured by the Minotaur. Why would they leave me alone if I wasn't about to be attacked and eaten by some cruel beast, the ogre of Madame Jacquenod's fairy tales?

For a long moment I hesitated over my dinner, torn between hunger, anger, and fear. I thought of Perséphone, tricked into eating six pomegranate seeds in Hadès's realm and never able to leave again. Finally hunger won out and I ate, cleaning my plate, sopping up the gravy with the marvelous soft white bread, nothing like the hard black country bread I was used to. There was a carafe and goblet on the table, also – had they been there before? Was it my imagination, or had they been placed there by some unseen hand while my attention was turned to my food? I was thirsty, so I poured myself wine from the carafe and drank.

"I'd have preferred water," I said aloud. Wine made my mind dull and my body leaden. When I drank it I would fall asleep too quickly and then wake too early with an aching head. Ordinarily, I drank it only on festival days. With a start, I turned and saw that a pitcher of water now stood where the wine carafe had been a moment before. In amazement, I poured from the pitcher into my cup and drank. The water was cool and sweet, as if drawn from a mountain spring.

"What place is this? Am I really under an enchantment?" Talking to myself out loud made me felt less alone. There was no answer, not even an echo. As my eyes adjusted to the light, I saw that the high walls were hung with massive tapestries that depicted hunting scenes and absorbed the sound. "Or more likely I'm just going mad. That's what you've driven me to, Marquis. Are you happy with yourself? But I suppose I'm to be eaten soon, so you hardly care about my sanity."

My eyes were drawn to the fire, searching as if I could find the Marquis's face in it. Could I discern an ogre's visage in the leaping flames, laughing at me?

I looked down and my dinner plate had been replaced by a smaller plate of fine porcelain, laden with pretty sugary bonbons in pink icing. "Are you trying to fatten me up?" I asked. I brought a bonbon to my lips and my teeth pierced its coating with a delicate crunch. It was delicious. "My compliments to the chef. If this was my last meal, at least it's been a good one." I looked at the fire again and imagined its flames nodding to me.

When I was done, I licked the sugary crumbs from my lips and wiped my fingers on my napkin.

"I don't even know where I'm sleeping tonight," I complained to the fire. "Monsieur du Herle was in such a hurry to get away from me, he didn't so much as show me to my room. I suppose he didn't want to witness me being torn limb from limb and eaten by his friend, the ogre-marquis. I imagine he wanted to be well away, in case a mere widow wasn't enough to satisfy the monster's appetite."

The fire laughed back at me, its boughs snapping and sending up sparks.

"I feel a draft." I shivered. "Can you make it warmer for me?" Was it my imagination, or did the fire rear up and begin to glow brighter? I began to feel warmer. And for better or for worse, I didn't feel alone. I stood up from my chair and approached the fireplace. "You must have known Monsieur du Herle wasn't staying, or he must have known, or else there would have been a place set for him too."

I turned around slowly several times in front of the fire. When I was thoroughly warm, front and back, I seated myself in one of the upholstered chairs. Idly my gaze drifted to the little table between the two chairs, and I sat bolt upright in surprise. There was my *Book of the Rose*.

I pulled it off the table and hugged it close to me before setting it down on my lap. It was just as I remembered. I opened it to the middle and leafed through the pages. My poems were still there, each one exactly where I had hidden it. I read a few of them again, going back and forth as usual between feeling pleased with what I'd written and ashamed of its triteness, the awkward turns of phrase, the ink blots and misspellings and the places where I'd crossed things out. I ought to recopy some of them, I thought, and burn more than a few. I turned to the first page and found a folded, sealed letter addressed to me from the Marquis de Boisaulne.

I broke the seal and opened it. It was written in a rather ordinary, legible hand. A beast with claws couldn't have managed this handwriting, I thought to myself absurdly.

"My dear Madame Bergeret," the letter said, "please forgive my not being here to welcome you. I can only imagine that the manner in which I arranged for you to come here must have seemed strange, if not alarming. Please know that my aim in bringing you here was not what you might have assumed, but only to provide you with greater freedom, rather than depriving you of the least amount of it. This is true to such an extent that I did not even wish to impose my presence upon you, until you should expressly state a desire for it.

"You must wonder why you have been singled out for such admittedly peculiar treatment. I will confess that on a stroll through Annecy some years ago, your late husband's shop caught my eye. I've long prided myself on collecting a tolerably extensive library for this retreat of mine here in the woods. I entered the shop and you were there, shelving books and helping customers. You answered several of my questions, displaying familiarity with the books I was looking for and expressing intelligent opinions about them. You will no doubt not remember this, for my face is a most forgettable one and it must have been the most ordinary experience in the world for you, one repeated many times a day. However, your beauty and wit made an indelible impression on me.

"When M. du Herle was next in Annecy to manage some of my affairs, I asked him to look in on your shop for more of the books I wanted. M. du Herle learned that your husband hosted occasional philosophical evenings in the shop and he attended several of them. I then had to send M. du Herle to Paris for some months, but when he came back to Annecy he looked in on your shop for me again. He found that it had closed its doors because of your husband's passing, and learned that your father had advertised the sale of its stock. M. du Herle wrote to me and asked whether I wished to buy out the stock, and I authorized him to do so.

"Glad as I was to acquire such an array of books for my library at an excellent price, I was gladder still to think that by doing so I might also provide assistance to the pretty and clever widow who had made such an impression on me. Then when the books arrived here at the manor, to my joy and astonishment I discovered among them this valuable antique illuminated copy of the *Book of the Rose*.

"I found your poems among its pages, each one signed with your name. I read and reread them many times over and imagined them in your voice. Of course I had no thought or hope of ever seeing you again. Circumstances have made it such that I almost never go into society anymore, so even if we moved in the same circles, we'd never encounter one another. It struck me as an extraordinary, nigh miraculous turn of events that your father should come to the door of my house in Annecy years later, seeking to arrange a meeting with M. du Herle to recover the *Book of the Rose*. It seemed to be the hand of destiny intervening to bring me into the path of your orbit yet again.

"From your poems I dared imagine your marriage had not been a happy one, and that you had longed above all for freedom and self-determination, rather than a husband to obey and serve. For this reason, I also dared hope your father might be persuaded to accept a contract that obligated only my support of you and your companionship, rather than matrimony, which I am not free to offer in any case. However, the extent and tenor of this companionship is entirely a matter of your free choosing.

"Until such time as you might wish to meet me, I remain, at a distance, ever your humble servant and friend."

In place of a signature there was the imprint of a signet ring, with a *B* for Boisaulne set into the antlers of a stag's head.

I set the letter down. My first impulse was to say aloud to the fire, "I want to meet you." Of course I wanted to meet him. Wasn't that why I'd come? But now that I understood there was the possibility of not meeting him, I hesitated. I had thought I had no real choice in the matter, with few alternatives other than running away to live in a cave on a mountaintop. Now it seemed I had a choice after all, the choice of solitude. Apart from the Marquis's silent and invisible servants here in the manor in the woods, that was. Suppose I never wanted to meet the Marquis, my would-be benefactor, as his letter claimed? In that case, would he banish himself from his own hunting manor for good and give it over to a near stranger? Suppose I wished to leave? Could I simply walk out the front door at sunrise and wander where I pleased in his woods, or return to Maisnie-la-Forêt and throw myself on the mercy of Madame Jacquenod and the other villagers?

I read the letter several more times, searching for clues as to the type of man who would have authored it. A lonely man, estranged from his wife for some years. A man who didn't expect to be desired by women. An idealist and a romantic, perhaps. An imprudent, reckless man, who cared little for society's conventions. A kind of misanthrope who shunned ordinary company. A man with some degree of madness. A hunter who left piles of animal carcasses and skins for the village wagoner to take in exchange for milk and eggs. A man who believed himself kind, but behaved with cruelty.

My late husband fit the last description. He was devoted to God but ruthless in his piety. He had let me teach myself Greek and Latin so I could study scripture and books of devotion, but he was livid when he discovered I'd gone on to read secular works as well – novels, philosophical discourses, the books of La Mettrie, Helvétius, and the Baron d'Holbach, and even some of the "bad books" such as *Thérèse Philosophe* and *L'Académie des Femmes*. When he found the cache of books I'd hidden in the back of a cabinet, he had surprised me with a flurry of slaps and blows, and had left black marks on my upper arms, so tightly had he gripped them before shoving me away in disgust. He had never entered a room without my heartbeat quickening in fear. Though he seldom struck me, he was forever instructing me about my faults, my idleness and frivolity, my rebellious temperament, my covetousness, immodesty, and unchaste desires. On Sabbath evenings there was never any pleasure for me in his embraces under the blanket, and when I admitted to him that his attentions were painful after Valentin's birth, he still wouldn't let me alone, but instead quoted the verse of scripture about the curses the Lord laid upon Eve. Yet everyone had called him a kind and good man, and he had always thought of himself as generous, patient, long-suffering, and good.

The Marquis, too, seemed to see himself as a generous man, and believed what he had done to me was for my own good, spying on me and obsessing over me, disrupting my life and taking me from my children, putting my family's reputation at risk and making a whore of me, at least in the eyes of the world. He surely thought it would only be a matter of time before I called him to me and submitted out of gratitude. No, I was not at all sure I wished to meet him – ever. I couldn't help but be curious, of course, about what sort of person this madman was who had inserted himself into my life and dragged me into his, but in equal measure I was afraid to know.

"I need to think," I said to the fire. "I need to rest. I need to go to bed. Where am I to sleep tonight?"

From the periphery of my vision, watching the slowly diminishing fire, I sensed the room grow suddenly brighter behind me. I turned and saw that lights had been lit in the anteroom from which M. du Herle and I had entered. I stood and went out to the entry hall, where many candles flickered in a candelabra. The stairs, too, were now lit by candles in silver sconces affixed to the wall at intervals, in the shape of hands holding torches, leading me upward. But opposite the stairs, where I had expected to see the heavy wooden door through which we had entered, there was now only a wall. No wonder the Marquis de Boisaulne had gone mad. I soon would too from the strangeness of this place, if this wasn't already a sign that I had lost my grip on reality. I ran my hands along the wall where the door should have been and rapped on it with my knuckles. My fingers discovered no hidden latch or false surfaces, and my knocking revealed no hollow places.

Even if the door had been there, I wouldn't have gone out into the cold and dark of the forest, where wild beasts must be roaming and hunting in the night, wolves, bears, boars with sharp tusks, and perhaps an ogre too, the *roi des aulnes*. I would just have liked to know the door was still there. But I would think more about all this in the morning. For now, my task remained finding a bed to sleep in. I followed the lights up the stairs, passing a dark hallway that led off from a landing. I went up another flight of steps to the floor above, where more candles in sconces led me down a wide corridor to a door slightly ajar, with light coming from within. I went through the door and found a chamber, warm from the coals and embers glowing in its fireplace. It held a large curtained bed piled with plump cushions and pillows and covered with a silk coverlet, with a clean white lace-trimmed chemise laid out on it for me. Next to the bed on a little table was a candelabra, a vase of fresh white flowers, a carafe of water, and a goblet. I undressed, wondering if the fire or some invisible servant was watching me. I laid my clothes over a chair, pulled the chemise over my head, and unpinned my hair, letting it fall down over my shoulders. I left my hair pins on a vanity table that had no mirror, sparing me the sight of my worn and haggard face. I blew out the candle and crawled into the warm and comfortable bed, where I fell fast asleep.

IV

IT WAS MORNING, and I was awake and hungry again. I drained the carafe of water on my bedside table and lay back on the pillows, fingering the soft bedspread and taking stock of my surroundings. Sunlight streamed in through the large window. It was a spacious, charming room, furnished in the style of illustrations I'd seen depicting modern rooms in Paris, with nearly everything one could wish for, self-contained like a little cottage. A brocade sofa squatted next to the fireplace, a kettle already over the fire. There was a little tea table with two upholstered chairs and a tablecloth, and shelves on the wall above it with china and tins. A large wardrobe stood beside the vanity table, and there was a screen in one corner next to a chest of drawers. Getting up to investigate, I found the screen concealed a passage to a small bathing room with its own fireplace, a long oval tin bathtub, and a pretty ceramic basin and ewer glazed with a design of flowers, as well as a closestool and bidet, of which I availed myself. When I came back to the main room, a dressing gown lay on the bed, and slippers had been set out on the floor. I put them on.

The only things missing were books and a writing desk. There must be a library, since M. du Herle and the Marquis had both spoken of it. Today's mission would be finding it.

My window overlooked a walled garden, and beyond that the forested mountainside, without a village or hut in sight. The scent of hot bread made me turn around. In the time I'd been gazing out of the window, the fire had been built up and a tray of bread and conserves and a pot of tea set out on the table. My stomach growled, and I sat down and took generous helpings.

How strange this all felt to me, the life of a lady, full of comforts and luxuries, with everything pretty, clean, soft, and right to hand. To sleep in, with no cows or goats to milk or feed by lantern-light before dawn, no meals to prepare for anyone, no pots to scrub or dishes to wash, no sweeping or dusting, no chores like carrying water, fetching wood, or washing clothes. Not even a bookshop to clean and open and keep accounts for. One could get used to this life. Except that I missed the sweet faces of Valentin and Aimée, their warm bodies cuddled up to me in the bed, having someone to exchange morning greetings with, and describing what we'd dreamt.

I've heard that wealthy ladies in the city wear a dressing gown most of the day, and only dress in the late afternoon or evening, before they dine with guests or go out to concerts, balls, or operas. But apart from the first month or two after giving birth to each of my children, I had always been accustomed to getting dressed as soon as I woke, to be ready for the day's work. So when I had finished my breakfast I went to the wardrobe. My clothes from the night before had vanished. The chemises, petticoats, and stays I found in the wardrobe pleased me with their delicate lace trims. I put on underclothes, wishing for a mirror now in which to admire myself.

"I could use a little help with the lacing," I said out loud. To my astonishment, I felt tugging at the laces, and when I felt behind my back, they had been tightened and tied.

It was more difficult to find a gown. The fabrics were all too rich and delicate, and I was afraid I would ruin them. I had to remind myself repeatedly that so far I had been asked to do no work here that would make me dirty them. Still, I picked out the simplest of them to put on, one that looked like it was meant to be a day dress, cut in a flyaway style, loose and pleated in back and open in the front, with a matching stomacher to cover my stays.

When I was ready, I took a deep breath and opened the door to my room. The passage into which I stepped was dim, the only light coming from a few open doors along it. I went down the hall, looking into the rooms. A few of the doors were locked, but this floor appeared to be mostly private apartments with furnishings and windows like mine. Including my room, I counted ten doors. The stairs went up and ended at the locked door of what seemed to be a garret.

Downstairs I found the landing that had been dark the night before, still forbiddingly shadowed. I ventured forward into the dark corridor and passed two facing pairs of locked double doors, but the next set of doors opened when I pushed down on the handles. I caught my breath.

Here was the library, a room twice as big as the spacious chamber in which I had slept, with every inch of the walls covered in cases and shelves of books except for the great fireplace and mantle, over which hung a large tapestry of a stag surrounded by greenery and flowers. Scattered sets of chaises, tables, chairs, candelabras, and lamps took up the room's interior. The windows were curtained with drapes drawn back to reveal shades of translucent muslin.

"Well done, Marquis," I said aloud. "You've arranged the décor here well. You knew you needed the drapes to protect the books from sun damage."

As I began to explore the shelves, I recognized a number of volumes from my late husband's shop. There was a wide selection of theological volumes, from Papist devotional books to Saint Augustine's *Confessions* and scholastic philosophers such as

Aquinas, books on the doctrines of Jansen and the Molinists, and even a few old tracts on the Cathars and Vaudois. There were Jesuit, Calvinist, and Lutheran works, and an exhaustive collection of treatises on atheism and religious skepticism, as well as illuminated Bibles, books about the saints, books of hours, and grammars of Hebrew, Greek, Latin, Assyrian, and other languages.

I saw shelves of scholarly books: philosophy, history, and geography; botany, physics, mathematics, anatomy, astronomy; books of magic and arcane learning, treating of spells and potions, poisons, and summoning, of demons and angels, mysticism, and freemasonry. There were books about musical notation and tuning, hymns and chants. Frivolous, silly, gossipy books about the lives of members of the royal courts of Europe, of nobles and high-ranking clerics. These were libelous books, illegal and dangerous to own in some countries, that used to fetch a good profit in the shop. There were political treatises, futuristic stories of utopias and dystopias, fables and nursery rhymes, and at last, *belles lettres*, essays, memoirs, novels, fairy tales, and poetry.

I was well-satisfied with the Marquis's collection, but as sometimes used to happen when I browsed the books in my late husband's shop, the dizzying sense washed over me that I would need a hundred lifetimes to read all these books. I was spoiled for choice and didn't know where to begin, so I pulled out five books and piled them onto the table before the fireplace: a romantic novel about knights and ladies, a comic play by Molière, a luridly illustrated book about demons, a botanical guide to the flowers of the Genevois region, and a memoir about exploring the wild lands of Canada by a French soldier of fortune. I read in front of the fire until a grandfather clock struck three in the afternoon. By then I was starving, and my head ached.

I set my book down and went back out into the corridor. If I could find my way back to the great hall where I'd had my dinner the night before, there might be a chance of finding something to eat nearby. There were the stairs again, the entry hall, still without the door to the outside that should have been there. There again

42

was the great hall, with a place set for one at the end of the long heavy wooden table with its twelve carved wooden chairs.

The invisible servants of the manor had left me a plate of cold food, which I fell upon greedily.

"Thank you," I said aloud when I had eaten my fill. "I'm sorry to be late for my dinner. I was caught up in my reading."

A torpor had stolen over me from the long morning of reading, the day of sitting still when I was accustomed to moving and working. Ordinarily at this time in the afternoon I would be only just be sitting down for the first time in the course of my daily chores, to give the children their lessons. I felt restless and dull at the same time.

"Could I possibly take a walk in the garden?" I asked the invisible powers that were. "I saw it from my window, but I haven't seen a door leading out to it."

There was no answer. I supposed they – whoever *they* were – feared I'd run away if I found the door that led to the outside. They weren't wrong.

I got up and went back out of the great hall the way I had come in, out to the anteroom. I crossed it to go back upstairs to continue exploring the second floor. But as I placed my hand on the polished black wood of the stair railing, I stopped and stared at the back wall. It was a room meant for passing through, and it was easy to miss the small detail of such rooms. My impression of it the night before, in the light of M. du Herle's lamp, was of nothing but paintings on the walls, a sofa, and a table or two with vases on them. Now it seemed to me that one of the round carved wooden rosettes set into the dark paneling on the back wall was in fact a door handle. I went to investigate and found that indeed, there was another set of double doors, paneled just like the wall around them and set so neatly and precisely into the wall that their outline was all but indistinguishable from it. Two of the carved rosettes could be rotated in place to open the doors.

They opened easily and soundlessly, swinging forward into the next room. It wasn't so much a room as a long gallery, with candles in sconces along the walls interspersed with alcoves and narrow decorative tables. The candles weren't lit, but light came from the end of the gallery – natural light, daylight. The light grew brighter as I moved forward and at the end I found a pair of unlocked doors made of panes of glass in wood frames, that led outside.

Standing on the steps outside the doors, I breathed in deeply. It was a beautiful day, the sky cloudless aquamarine and the air warm with just a hint of the chill mountain breeze stirring at its edges, redolent with the scent of flowers in bloom. From where I stood, expanding semicircles of stone steps descended to a gravel path bordered by patches of flowers, bushes, trees, and vines. They led to a far back wall where a fountain cascaded down from the opening of a spring set high into the stones above.

For several hours, in the pleasure of exploring the garden, I forgot I was all but a prisoner in this place. The garden seemed to grow and change as one walked down its paths, like an enchanted labyrinth. I found a small grove of fruit trees, and along the far wall of the house what appeared to be a charmingly designed kitchen garden with beds of herbs, vegetables, and berries. There were bowers, arbors, benches, birdbaths, a couple of smaller fountains, and a true labyrinth of hedges in which I nearly lost myself. An arch was set into the middle of each of the three stone walls that enclosed the garden. The left arch was gated in with high iron doors that were shut and locked, and I thought it must lead out to the stables. To the right was an open arched gate that led into an outer park of forested paths, enclosed by more stone walls. The small back arch under the fountain of the spring appeared to have been bricked in, and seemed almost to back up against the side of the mountain itself.

Someone with a keen eye for beauty had created this paradise. Was it one of the Marquis's ancestors, or the Marquis himself, or some gifted gardener among the manor's invisible servants? If I agreed to meet the Marquis, I could ask him. I could talk with him about the books in his library, ask which ones he'd read and what he thought of them, and which ones he thought I might like. Places have character, souls, it could be said, that often reflect something of the people who live in them. From what I had seen of this place so far, the manor, its library and gardens, there was a yearning to it, for knowledge, for beauty, for the transcendent – however old or ugly and deformed the Marquis himself might be.

At the same time, I felt a very practical mind had a role in the manor's design. Doors often didn't open, or even appear, until they were needed. The food I had eaten had been filling and good, and certainly superior to the country fare I was accustomed to. Yet so far it hadn't been more than I could comfortably eat in one sitting, nor too rich. There were no mirrors, suggesting a lack of vanity. The tapestries and paintings were of scenes from nature, of plants and animals, myths, or hunting scenes, but I had found no prominently displayed wall of family portraits. There was a certain modesty and restraint amidst the opulence.

Still, as I trailed my fingers in the water of the fountain under the spring, I feared that if I agreed to meet the Marquis, it would be like opening a Pandora's box of undreamt-of troubles, griefs, and complications. Once I had met him, I couldn't un-meet him. The fairy tale or the nightmare, whichever type of story it was into which I had been cast by some unseen author's hand, would become real then. And how would I even tell him I was willing to make his acquaintance? Should I tell it to the fire in the great hall? M. du Herle had said I could leave notes for the servants, and they would attend to my wishes. Perhaps I could write a note and ask for a meeting with the Marquis.

Still divided in my mind, I stood, clasped my hands behind my back, and headed back down the main path of the garden toward the glass-paned doors into the manor. The sun was setting, and my stomach rumbled. I wanted to wash up in the basin in my room, if I could find it again, and perhaps change out of my sweaty underclothes or my dress, which had become dusty from wandering amongst the greenery. As I went back into the cool dimness of the corridor and found the stairs in the entry hall again,

I wondered whether I would ever meet another living soul here, if I didn't agree to meet the Marquis. Would M. du Herle return as he had said he would? Was my choice between the Marquis and solitude? Did he mean to wear me down that way – to wait until I couldn't bear the silence and the loneliness any longer? I shuddered at the thought of being not only a prisoner in this great gilded cage, but one consigned to solitary confinement unless or until I gave in.

I found my room tidied and the bed made, with fresh underclothes and a velvet gown laid out for me. However preoccupied I had been with my fears, I had to laugh at the absurdity of it.

"Very well," I said. "I'll dress up for no one and pretend to be a fine lady. Why not? It's no stranger than anything else I've done in the past twenty-four hours."

In response I sensed a certain winking of the light in the room, as if whatever presence had been observing me was laughing back. As I undressed and washed up in my small bathing room and dressed in the fresh new clothes, my unseen maid seemed less shy in helping me here and there with hooks and buttons. I was changed in a trice, but what to do with my hair, which felt sweaty and frizzy and bedraggled? I wished again I had a mirror to primp in front of, to subdue what felt like unruliness and disarray on top of my head. I sat down on the chair at the vanity table and surveyed the collection of hair pins, ornaments, jewelry, powders, and cosmetics. I felt a gentle hand smooth the side of my hair and jumped in fright. I turned around quickly, but of course no one was to be seen. Shaking my head, I turned back to look in front of me.

"If you can make something of my hair," I said, "you're welcome to try. Just, please, no wig." I'd noticed an elegantly-dressed wig sitting on a stand next to the table. "I had to wear one for my wedding," I explained, "and it was so hot and itchy." Then it happened – the ghostly hands undid my hair and combed it out, so gently it hardly pulled or hurt at all, and then piled and pinned

46

it atop my head. I felt a little tap on my shoulder, and this seemed to be the signal that my coiffure was complete. I felt my hair with my hands and wondered again how I looked. I stared curiously at the cosmetics, which had been strictly forbidden by the faith in which I was raised, although my sisters and I and the other girls of our village used to rouge our cheeks and lips sometimes with the juice of red berries. I dipped my finger into a pot of rouge and applied it sparingly to my lips and cheeks.

"Is it too much?" I asked.

The light winked again with laughter, and I took that as a no.

"Now I'll faint with hunger if I don't go down, like it or not."

At the table in the great hall, another hot supper waited for me, delicious and filling. Again I finished my meal alone. Were silence and solitude really so bad? If only I could see Valentin and Aimée and hear how they'd spent their day. I imagined them playing happily with their cousins. Had they cried for me?

Apart from these thoughts, I confessed to myself that this day of exploration alone had felt peaceful and luxurious. If only I could be assured that the children were well, and knew I could go home and visit at will, I shouldn't have minded a few more days like this one.

When I had finished my meal, I went back to the *Book of the Rose*, still sitting on the small table before the fire where I had left it the night before. Inside the front cover I found another note.

"My dear Madame Bergeret, I hope your first day here was a pleasant one. Would you care to meet me? Your most sincere and humble servant." Again, the imprint of the signet with the stag's antlers.

A quill and ink and a fresh sheet of paper had been left out on the table, presumably for my reply. I thought for a long while, staring at the fire, and then I wrote: "M. le marquis de Boisaulne, I hope you will forgive me if the answer is 'not yet.' I have been very comfortable and well-treated here so far. But I miss my children and worry over their welfare. All is strange to me here and I confess myself bewildered and unsure of what to think of the circumstances in which I find myself."

I could think of no polite closing words I could be sure I wouldn't later regret, so I left the note unsigned and with no valediction. Part of me wanted to vent fury at my benefactor, or jailer, but since I didn't know which he was yet, I bit back the angry words gnawing at my tongue. I reflected that whatever I said couldn't be unsaid, any more than a meeting with him could be undone, and therefore it behooved me to be prudent.

I returned to the library to fetch my pile of books for reading in bed, and as I sat down to examine them again, I heard music begin to play. At first it was only a violin. Then its lone melody was joined by a violincello, string bass, and harpsichord. It was slow, soothing music in a minor key, plaintive, but with lighter moments of playfulness. It sounded close by, as though it came through the wall of the room next door. I stood and walked toward the wall of the library where the music was louder and noticed that what I had taken for a broad alcove in the wood-paneled wall was, in fact, another set of hidden double-doors with handles that turned and opened inward into an adjoining room.

At first I didn't realize it was a music room, dumbfounded as I was by what I beheld: an ensemble of instruments in the corner, playing themselves. The violin was suspended in midair, and its bow slid backward and forward across the strings, seemingly of its own volition. I watched for a long time, but the shock didn't wear off. Until now, I had thought myself possessed of a certain degree of education. I was pleased with the neat arguments of Voltaire, Diderot, La Mettrie, and the Baron d'Holbach, in their books that condemned superstition and irrationality, and with the Englishman Sir Francis Bacon's idea of a scientific method. But no experimenter could ever have arrived at this result by looking through the lens of a microscope or telescope, or by mixing vials of liquid chemicals, or documenting the humors of fauna. There seemed nothing to do but accept that there was no logical explanation, any more than there had been for the food that had appeared out of thin air, or the gentle hands that had arranged my hair.

Having resigned myself to wonder, I looked around the room as the music played on and slowly understood that it was devoted to various kinds of instruments and shelves with folios of sheet music. The paintings on the walls were still lifes depicting instruments and musical manuscripts, as well as fruits, flowers, skulls, and candles.

It appeared, then, this was to be the evening's entertainment provided for me by the Marquis, or by the manor and its invisible servants – whatever will it was that guided and directed things here. At first I felt it somehow impolite to do anything but sit down facing the instruments, my hands folded across my lap, listening attentively. Then my mind began to wander, and when there was a pause in the music, I went back to the library, leaving the doors to the music room open. A new piece began to play, and the sound was nearly as good from the library as within the music room.

I took off my slippers, curled up on the sofa, and returned to my books. I set aside the romance and the Molière play I had begun to read that morning and turned to the book on demons. I didn't believe in demons – at least, I thought I didn't. But I liked looking at fantastical illustrations and found it interesting to read books that purported to be compendia of arcane knowledge. As a child, of course, I had believed in a whole host of these imaginary beings, angels, witches, devils, fairies, ghosts, and spirits, who populated the Bible stories my mother read to us and the tales she told to get us to go to sleep. Over time I had lost the faith of my childhood and had come to see myself as a Deist, like the *philosophes* whose books I admired. As I flipped through the pages of this anonymous author's *Dictionnaire des démons et des esprits maléfiques, illustré par la main d'un savant de toutes les matières alchimiques et démonologiques,* I stopped at an entry that recounted the old legends of Doktor Faustus and his bargain with the demon Méphistophélès to sign away his soul in exchange for youth, beauty, riches, and the pleasures of the flesh.

Méphistophélès was presented as a dapper gentleman clothed in the last century's finery, hairy, horned, and hooved like a goat, with a forked tail. Had the Marquis also made some kind of a bargain with a devil, to obtain a place so full of magic and the aid of his invisible servants? I shivered and turned more pages. I stopped again when I came to a page depicting the legend that Madame Jacquenod in the village had alluded to, the *roi des aulnes,* the king of the alders. The Erl-king, or *Erlkönig* in German, sometimes also called the Elf-King in English. I'd thought it was only a local legend. The illustration was chilling, a tall, gaunt but muscular figure, like a man but wearing a mask made of the skull and horns of an enormous stag. He carried a bow and hunter's horn in his gloved hands, and his long fingers were coated in dripping blood. Around him rose tall forbidding trees under a full moon.

No doubt the legend had been invented by some past nobleman who wanted to discourage villagers from poaching in his forest. Still, I shuddered. I closed the book and went upstairs to bed.

I fell asleep quickly in my luxurious bedding but woke again in the middle of the night. Somewhere else in the manor, perhaps a floor below in the library, a clock chimed midnight. The fire in my room had gone out completely. I wasn't cold, but the darkness felt curiously intense and unrelieved, like being shut up in a cabinet. Not even the faintest glow of moonlight or starlight came in through the window. Yet a breeze stirred across my cheek with the softest of caresses. I listened intently to the silence, and within it, I seemed to hear someone, or something, breathing. Seized with terror, I lay perfectly still, hoping against hope it was only the blood rushing in my ears. At last there was the slightest sound of the floorboards shifting, as if from a soft tread of feet, and my door opening and closing. It felt as if whatever presence I had imagined there had gone. I breathed out, only then realizing I had been holding my breath. Gradually the racing of my heartbeat slowed, and I unclenched my muscles. My vigilance gave way to drowsiness, and I relaxed into the soft pillows and fell back asleep.

V

MY DAYS IN the manor fell into a pattern much like the first day. I woke, broke my fast, read in the library, and walked in the garden. There was a concert each night in the music room, and I discovered that if I left out a set of sheet music, the invisible players would play it. Every evening I found a letter from the Marquis tucked into the cover of my *Book of the Rose*. Since I had told him I missed my children, he began to make a regular practice of assuring me they and the rest of my family were well, based on inquiries he claimed to have made. I had his permission to write to my family if I wished, but I hadn't done it yet. Let Father and Hortense wonder whether I was well or even still alive, since they had thought so little of bargaining away my honor and freedom. Let them explain to Aimée and Valentin why we had been so cruelly parted from each other. Always, every night without fail, the Marquis asked if I would meet him. Always I answered, *Not yet*.

Some nights I woke to the chiming of the clock at midnight and sensed someone was in my room and lay fearfully awake until whoever it was had left and closed my door.

I ceased to wonder at certain marvels of the manor as time passed. I became used to the silent and invisible hands that helped me with my hair and clothes and served my meals. But the garden inspired awe each time I explored it. I found new species of flowers and birds, and insects with iridescent wings like tiny fairies, spiders of many colors and sizes, frogs, mice, chipmunks, squirrels, hares, foxes, and small golden fish that darted through the murky waters of the little pond. Even shy red deer ran through the forested park. In the absence of any visible human presence, I came to think of all these creatures as my companions and friends. At the same time, I never ceased searching along the garden walls for an exit. I found none. The gate to the stables was always locked, and the walls were too high to climb. None of the trees grew close enough to them for me to climb over by way of their branches.

I continued to make new discoveries in the rooms of the manor as well. The place gave the impression of being larger on the inside than it looked from the outside. Cabinets, doors, closets, and even whole rooms seemed to appear and disappear, and then reappear in different places. One day I found a chest full of maps, embellished with pictures of dragons and monsters from faraway lands. In a cabinet I came upon a trove of astronomical equipment, a set of curious movable brass rings set inside one another that showed the paths of the stars and planets, as well as a telescope and maps of the heavens. I discovered galleries full of small paintings, sculpted figures, porcelain vases, and enameled plates, colored in stunning deep jewel tones. Hidden doors abounded, artfully concealed in the paneling of walls or behind tapestries. Some were locked, others open, and some were locked one day and open the next. Sometimes I couldn't find doors again that had almost certainly been there the day before.

It wasn't any one thing that prompted me, at last, to answer yes to the Marquis's nightly question. I was lonely, true, and felt a great deal of curiosity about him, and I had grown less fearful as I accustomed myself to the manor and its oddities. But perhaps more than anything, it was exhausting to see so much beauty and speak of it to no one. I'd had many sorrows in my life, short as it had been: the passing of my dear mother, far too soon; the unhappiness of my marriage, and of losing the faith of my childhood; a stillborn child, the imprisonment and death of my husband, and for so long, the feeling of being wrong in the life to which I had been born. Sorrow I knew how to bear in silence, for the sake of sparing others the burdens I bore, and to avoid shame and condemnation from less compassionate souls. But joy in my breast, and wonder in my heart, and the exhilaration of new learning, new thoughts and ideas springing forth in me, these felt like children that didn't want to be cooped up indoors; they wanted to be set free to sing and shout. Sensible of my own condition as a prisoner, I didn't wish to keep them imprisoned. Though it was a strange imprisonment, to be sure, that contained so many joys. In truth, more and more in the struggle within me between anger at my confinement, the ache of missing Valentin and Aimée, and pleasure in the daily beauties I beheld, it was the joy and pleasure that had taken the upper hand. If only I could be angrier at my jailer, the Marquis ...

At any rate, where it had always felt right to keep silent about my sorrows, and so I had found the strength for silence, it felt wrong to keep silent about beauty and joy. It cost me an effort, and the burden of silence grew greater with time. At first I started to write in my notes to the Marquis such things as, "I found it charming to sit at your fountain today, and I saw a bluebird. The book by Montesquieu about the spirit of the laws is fascinating so far, though I must read it slowly to understand it all."

His responses were formal, modest, and restrained. "I've read the Montesquieu book as well," he wrote back, "and his accounts of other countries and peoples made me want to travel to them, however savage and dangerous they might be. I'm glad you enjoyed the fountain and the bluebird." On another day, I was so proud of a new poem I had written about the legend of Perséphone that I enclosed it with a note to him. He praised it warmly. "The soul always hungers for understanding," he wrote, "and it only takes a little of the sense of being known and appreciated for who one truly is beneath the mask of appearances to bond deeply with a friend, so sweet is that feeling. And when it takes hold, it may run as deep as Hadès's kingdom of death, and may bind one in faithfulness all one's life, as Perséphone was bound to her deathly lover for immortality. To me that's what Perséphone's pomegranate seeds represent in your verses."

As our letters to each other became longer and more amiable, it finally began to seem silly to write when we could just as easily speak to one another. So one evening I wrote, "M. le marquis, thank you for the news of my family and for recommending the *Lettres Persanes* to me. The views of those fictional travelers are most interesting. I wish we could discuss the Montesquieu books in person, and it occurs to me we can. If you would still care to meet, I think I'm ready."

I set the note down on the table with a tremor in my hand, wondering how long it would be before he saw it, how long until he appeared, where and when I would first see him.

I woke again at midnight. It was strange to me how pitch dark it always was at that hour. The moon was nearly full outside, I knew, but none of its light came in through the shutters. I supposed the darkness, and the presence whose breathing I had heard at my past midnight awakenings, were both a part of the manor's idiosyncratic magic. It had gradually ceased to frighten me, this presence, whatever or whoever it might be. It had never done me harm or even made its existence definitive. Its watchfulness had begun to feel benign and protective rather than malevolent – if it was there at all, and if I hadn't merely imagined it.

I listened for its breath, holding my own for a moment or two in the hope of hearing better. At first there was nothing. Then a cool wave of air wafted across my cheek, as if the door had silently opened and closed. The slightest creak of the parquet floor. There.

I almost felt relieved that my night-watcher had come, as I had come to expect it.

Then it spoke.

"Are you awake?" It was a man's voice, whispering. He used the polite, formal pronoun, and I replied in kind.

"Monsieur, le marquis? Is that you?"

"It's me. Did I wake you?"

"No. But ... what are you doing here, in the middle of the night?"

"You said you were willing to meet me at last."

"But I thought perhaps I'd see you tomorrow, or in a few days. Not that you'd come to my bedchamber in the dark, in the middle of the night."

"I was impatient for our meeting."

I sat up in bed and leaned against the pillows. "Couldn't you light a lamp or a candle, so I can see you? It's so dark."

"No. No lights or candles. You mustn't see me. I can only meet you in the dark."

"What? What do you mean?" I rubbed my eyes, as if it might dispel my night-blindness.

"It's a precaution, for your sake and mine. It's for the best. You'll have to trust me on that."

"But – then I'll never see your face?"

"Not for now. Not yet. You're not missing anything, I assure you. I'm nothing much to look at."

"Are you ashamed of how you look – is that why? Are you disfigured in some way?"

There was a long silence. Then he said, "Suppose I were to tell you I'd been cursed. That I was an ordinary man who'd been transformed into a horrible beast?"

"Is that the truth?"

He laughed softly. "I don't know. Perhaps. I don't know what I turn into when I go to sleep and lose consciousness. Who knows what I become when the moon is full?"

I was reminded of the unsettling and vivid dreams I'd had in the past of flying, falling from a precipice, making love, or committing violence. "I suppose no one really knows what happens when they're asleep."

"Exactly. Sometimes I dream I go hunting. I have a reputation as a great hunter, you know. The wagoner from the village comes to deliver our supplies and finds animal skins and slain carcasses in the outer yard. He takes them back to the village and I suppose they're butchered there. It gives the village meat and leather, and they prosper in the fur trade. All very well and good. But in fact I don't like hunting. I've never liked the idea of killing living things for sport."

I drew up my knees under the covers and clasped my arms around them. "So you hunt, even though you don't enjoy it?"

"That's the thing. I don't know how the animals get there. It's assumed I'm a great hunter, that it's I who slays them, but I have no recollection of doing it. Perhaps it's a monster who lives in the forest and rules over it, who hunts by night. Perhaps the monster is me."

I shook my head. "You're confusing me. This place is so strange. I don't know what to think. I used not to believe in magic, but I've seen so much here I've come to believe in it after all."

"May I sit on the end of your bed?" he asked.

"Yes," I said, before it occurred to me what a mistake this might be. For a moment as his weight settled on the side of my mattress by my feet, I was fearful again, but he didn't move or speak. At last I was emboldened by his stillness to say, "Let me feel your face. I want to feel if it's the head of a beast or not."

"Very well."

I reached out into the darkness until my right hand found his shoulder. He leaned closer as I felt with both hands: the fabric of his coat, the cravat around his neck. The fabrics were soft and fine to the touch. The coat was embroidered satin and his cravat was muslin. His chin was clean-shaven. He wore no wig, and there was no powder in his hair. Otherwise he seemed to be dressed as a no-bleman might be for a dinner or a ball. I reached further and felt his lips, his cheeks, his nose, his eyes, and his forehead. I could form little impression of his looks merely from touching him, but it felt like an ordinary face to me, not that of a hairy, horned, horrible beast.

"I think you're a man, not a beast," I said. I drew back my hands and let them rest in my lap on the bedspread.

"There's an old story that an ancestor of mine was an ogre. The *roi des aulnes*, they called him. An immortal monster who haunts the forest to this day. Sometimes he took the form of a stag, and at other times appeared as a monstrous man wearing the mask of a stag's skull. He seduced a great-great-great grand-mother of mine. My nurse told me the story many times when I was a child. It's also said the youngest son of a former marquis, another ancestor of mine, was lured away by the monster into his underground lair. The boy disappeared after going into the forest and never returned. A century later some traveler reported coming across the bones of a child. He'd dug up a mound in the forest thinking it might be buried treasure. The story says the traveler heard fairy bells, and almost followed them down into a tunnel at the base of an alder tree. He was saved by a magic potion that protected him and turned the sound of the fairy bells into the growling of wild animals."

"A woman in the village told me the story about the ogre. It made me a little frightened of coming here. More than I already was."

"You needn't be afraid. I'd never wish to do you harm. There may be dangers in the forest and outside of it, but I'll do my best to keep you safe."

I fell silent, because I didn't believe him. How safe could I be if a man could come into my room in the middle of the night? Especially one who believed he might be wholly or in part a murderous beast, or descended from one?

"Was your day a pleasant one?" he asked.

59

"How could it be otherwise? I lack for nothing here, except the freedom to leave."

"Do you wish to leave?"

"No," I found myself answering honestly, surprised to feel the truth of it.

"No?"

"I only wish I had the freedom to leave if I wanted to."

"Ah." There was a pause. "Tell me about your day," he said at last, and so I did. I told him of the spider's web I had seen in the garden with sparkling drops of dew like diamonds on it. I told him about two caterpillars that seemed to be having a conversation and then a fight. How I started to write a poem about it, and then looked in the library for books of poetry, because I was curious whether I'd find any that had been written about caterpillars. I told him the story of Valentin befriending a caterpillar and following it all around the garden of our house in the village the previous summer. The Marquis laughed, declared it charming, and told me he remembered reading a verse about a caterpillar, and would try to find it again later if he could recall the author.

I liked his laugh. I liked the sound of his voice. It was somehow familiar to me. I tried to place it.

"Monsieur le marquis," I said, "you wrote that we met each other before, in the bookshop in Annecy."

"Yes."

"I didn't recall our meeting. But if it's true, then why all this mystery? Why this meeting in the middle of the night? Did something happen to you in the meantime?"

"I couldn't flatter myself you'd remember me. As I said, I'm unremarkable in the extreme. Call it a peculiarity of mine, if you like. I prefer the darkness. I'm comfortable in it."

"But ..." I struggled to formulate my question inoffensively. "If you took such an interest in me as to ... as to come to this arrangement with my father ... it must have been at great effort and expense. Doesn't it trouble you, not to see me?"

"Oh, I can see you. Another peculiarity of mine. I see unusually well in the dark."

I laughed. "I don't believe you. How many fingers am I holding up? Tell me."

"None. Your hands are folded in your lap. And if you don't mind my saying so, you look very charming in your nightdress."

I gasped. "How ...?"

"I told you. I'm the great-great-great-grandson of the beast who hunts in the forest at night. For all I know, perhaps I am him. Oh, who knows? I grew up thinking it was nothing out of the ordinary. Apparently my father had the same ability, and his father before him. Only later did I realize other people were blind where I could see."

"And ... do you see well in the daylight too?"

"Well enough, but I prefer the night. And shade and shadows during the day."

It still seemed incredible to me, but I set my skepticism aside to continue. "But then, you have me at a disadvantage. You can see, me but I can't see you."

He laughed. "I do indeed."

"Can I ask a question? Have you ever come into my room before, in the middle of the night?"

He hesitated, and at last said, "Yes."

"I woke up a few times. I thought someone was here. I was terrified at first."

He didn't reply.

"Then, have you been here at the manor the whole time? You weren't detained elsewhere, as Monsieur du Herle claimed?"

"I come and go. I prefer to be here, but sometimes I need to take care of affairs away from the manor."

"I see."

I heard the clock chiming again downstairs. Could so much time really have passed while we had been speaking? I let out a great yawn.

"I should let you sleep," he said.

I answered with another yawn, though I tried to suppress it.

"May I visit you again tomorrow evening?" he asked.

I considered it, wanting to be sure of my answer. "Yes."

The bed creaked and the mattress shifted as he stood. "I'm bowing to you, Madame Bergeret, though you can't see it. Sleep well, and may your dreams be sweet."

The door opened and shut. He was gone. At least, I thought he was; in the darkness I could be sure of nothing.

VI

WHEN I WOKE in the morning, my first thoughts were of the Marquis, the feel of his clothes and face and hair, the sound of his voice, the words we had exchanged. They persisted in my memory instead of fading like the memories of my dreams so often did; yet they seemed absurd and illogical enough to have been a dream. After breakfast in the library, my mind turned to philosophy, and I decided to research the subject of dreams and self-deception. I unshelved treatises from René Descartes, John Locke, and Pierre Bayle.

In the book by M. Descartes, the philosopher wrote of sitting before the fire in his dressing gown with a piece of paper in his hands, so sure of the truth of his impressions. And yet, *how often has it happened to me,* he wrote, *that in the night I dreamt that I found myself in this particular place, that I was dressed and seated near the fire, whilst in reality I was lying undressed in bed!* Ah, you see, M. Descartes, this is the very problem. Meanwhile, M. Locke, if I understood him rightly, believed we felt certainty in trusting the evidence of our senses, and this certainty was as great as it needed to be in order for us to make proper choices in the world in which we found ourselves. *And if our dreamer pleases to try,* he wrote, *whether the glowing heat of a glass furnace be barely a wandering imagination in a drowsy man's fancy, by putting his hand into it, he may perhaps be wakened into a certainty greater than he could wish, that it is something more than bare imagination.* Very well then, I had felt certain I was awake at the time. I had heard the man's voice and felt his skin, and perhaps in a sense I did put my hand to the fire in doing that. But what about the other things I had seen here that were impossible, illogical, magical?

I still doubted the reality of the night before. Not only that, I doubted the substantiality of the Château of Boisaulne itself, and the whole history of my being there, for it seemed nothing more than a fantastical fairy tale. However, M. Bayle reminded me that the grounds of doubting were themselves doubtful, and therefore we ought to doubt whether we ought to doubt. Moreover, I found empirical evidence to support a conclusion from inductive logic that last night's interview was reality and no mere dream, for when I went downstairs for my noon meal, there on the little table before the fire in the great hall, where the Marquis and I had become accustomed to leaving notes for one another, he had left me a book of naturalist drawings and observations about all the varieties of caterpillars and butterflies. Underneath it were two books of poetry and a note telling me to look at the pages he had marked. Each had a verse about caterpillars, one comical, the other serious. In his note, the Marquis expressed the hope that he hadn't given me too great a fright with the manner of our first meeting. He looked forward to seeing me again that evening.

Shyness overtook me at the thought of meeting him again in my bedroom, in the dark. It seemed exceedingly strange that an aristocrat who had troubled to buy my company at such a cost hadn't availed himself of the opportunity to try to make love to me. I was relieved he hadn't and that my worst fears weren't realized. But had I been granted only a temporary reprieve? In the end, it was I who had placed my hands on him and he who had submitted docilely to my touch. Would he think it was his turn tonight?

All day long, I found myself storing up questions to ask him, since it occurred to me he had let me do most of the talking the night before, apart from the strange stories of the beast who hunted in the forest and the unsettling revelation about his having watched me in the dark. I wondered too whether he hadn't touched me because he wasn't so attracted to me after all. Had I disappointed him? Or was I merely one of a number of women he had acquired in this same manner, so that he simply felt no urgency where seduction was concerned?

Nonetheless, the anxiety and excitement I felt at the thought of speaking further with the Marquis weren't entirely unpleasant. There was a sweetness to the gesture of the caterpillar books that touched me, beyond the pleasure I had felt so often in reading his letters to me.

I sat in the garden to make notes on my new poem, which I envisioned as a silly satirical epic for Valentin, "The Clash of the Caterpillars." My eyes teared up a little as I thought of Valentin and Aimée and how much they would have loved playing in this garden. I could almost hear their voices echoing from the stone walls as they shouted to each other in their games, like two fey, mischievous ghosts. If only the Marquis could meet them. How could he help but love them as dearly as I did? And then perhaps he would allow me to have them here with me. Perhaps I could ask him about it when he came to me that night.

My concentration was miserable, and after an hour or two I had only written the title at the top of my sheet of paper. The sun had made me drowsy, so I went back inside and took a nap in my bedchamber through most of the afternoon. After supper I paced up and down in my room, arguing with myself about whether to undress for bed. If I went to sleep in only my chemise, knowing the Marquis would see me in it, might he not mistakenly regard it as an invitation? On the other hand, I certainly didn't wish to lie down and go to sleep in my stays.

I compromised by wearing a pretty robe over my chemise, which I tied with a sash for more modesty. I settled into my soft feather bed with a book, but I must have dozed off quickly, for the next thing I knew, I was woken by the chiming of the clock. The candle had burnt out or had been extinguished, and all was dark again.

I stretched and yawned, filled with a sense of warmth and well-being. I realized the Marquis was seated on the edge of my bed again.

"There you are," he said. "I wondered if I ought to try to wake you. You looked beautiful, lying there in the dark."

I struggled to gather my thoughts and wake more fully. In my confusion, the first question on my mind rose to my lips. "Monsieur le marquis ... do you ..." I murmur.

"Do I what?"

"Do you mean to make love to me?"

He laughed. "This is one thing I like about talking in the dark. People are more honest."

I blinked, more alert now. "It's like being drunk on wine. Forgive me."

"It's a reasonable question, my lovely Madame Bergeret. Do you wish me to make love to you?"

This was not a question I had anticipated. "I ... I don't know." What was it about talking in the dark that unmasked me this way and made it so much more difficult to dissemble?

"I was honest with you in my first letter. Another way of explaining why I brought you here is that I didn't think a woman of your education was suited to a life of poverty. I wanted to rescue you from it, with no obligation on your part other than staying here. But if you mean to ask, am I attracted to you? Would I like to stroke your black hair, to feel the touch of your hands on my lips again, to see you without your nightdress, to give you what pleasures a beast's love can afford? The answer must be yes."

I lay motionless, frightened and aroused by his words. Perhaps there was safety in a change of subject. "May I ask, how old you are?"

"Four and thirty. And you?"

"Six and twenty."

"Ah."

"I was afraid you'd be much older. Is it true you're estranged from your wife, as Monsieur du Herle told my father?"

There was a silence that somehow felt sullen. Then he said, "But we were going to speak more of Montesquieu's books, weren't we? Tell me, what did you think?"

Had I made him angry? I tried to remember what I had thought of Montesquieu. "It seems to me perhaps he idealizes the English form of government too much in the *Spirit of the Laws*. I don't know how free any people can really be under a monarchy. The nobles might be free, but the poor work so hard, what he calls 'political freedom' can't mean much to them. He's a baron, isn't he? He must have grown up rich and likely doesn't understand what it is to be poor."

"Indeed. It's a good point about freedom for the poor being different from freedom for the rich. Perhaps I'd go even further and say freedom can be a great burden if it isn't granted along with freedom from want."

"Hmm. Anyway, I think a justly governed republic would be better for the common people, if the rulers and lawmakers could see to it that things were fairer. I don't know why some people should have so much, just because they were born noble, while others starve."

"Things are beginning to change, though, here in Savoy. There's been talk of doing away with the old seigneurial rights and privileges, and I think it will happen. I don't see it as a bad thing. The villages will be enfranchised. They can buy lands back from the old hereditary estates, so it's not as if we noblemen will lose our holdings without getting something in return. Things won't be so unequal, when those who work hard can rise more easily in the world."

"But the people I met on the way here seemed to be doing quite well, I must say. The famine seems not to have touched Maisnie-la-Forêt. When I passed through with Monsieur du Herle, the buildings looked in good condition, and there were flower gardens in front of the houses. The people seemed healthy and well-clothed."

"I'm pleased to hear it, and even more pleased you noticed. Monsieur du Herle does a good job as my steward. My conscience could never bear to collect my full seigneurial dues, so generally he takes no more than the minimum we require to maintain the household here. You'd be surprised at how little that is. In return, the villagers take what's been hunted. I like to imagine my old ancestor, the *roi des aulnes,* watches over them and blesses them in return for leaving his part of the forest alone."

"I never thought of ogres being in the habit of blessing people. The prosperity seems to be mostly your doing, though. Madame Jacquenod told me you arranged for a doctor too."

"I thought they ought to have one. I only regret that I can't permit them to gather wood and hunt in the entire forest. But it's always been the tradition of my family to protect the forest on this side of the river, and to protect the villagers from it. There are supposed to be certain trees there sacred to the *roi des aulnes,* and if anyone were to fell one by mistake, he'd come to harm. Or children or animals might go missing. The tradition has it the alder-king is lord of the plants and animals in the forest, the master of life and death, and only he or his descendants, the lords of Boisaulne, have the right to hunt there."

I shuddered. "And you believe in the traditions?"

"It's an old superstition and must be as true as those generally are."

"But do you know what I'm curious about? You say you don't need much to maintain the household here. Yet the manor and garden are so beautiful and full of fine things. Aren't they very costly to keep up, if you haven't even collected your full dues?"

"Many of the furnishings and fine things are from my grandfather's day, or older. I suppose the past lords of Boisaulne had less sympathy for the *petites gens* of the villages. My father, God rest his soul, was a generous-hearted man, they say. I suppose he must have been, since my grandfather's fortune was only a fraction of what it had been by the time I came into my inheritance. But I barely knew the man. I was sent away to school in Paris at six years of age, and my father and mother both passed away not long after. And when I came of age, I did my share in spending what little remained of the fortune."

"You were an orphan?"

His silence was an agreement.

"I'm sorry. I lost my mother, too," I said.

"I know. Your father's done a fine job of raising you, though. He seems a good man."

"Do you really think so?"

"I do. That's why I didn't mind helping him out of his predicament. It wasn't greed that got him into it, but a desire to support his family, and perhaps a nature that was too trusting, and his strict sense of honor. If he hadn't been determined to pay his creditors honestly, he could have found some relief in defaulting on his debts. He only needed more time and wiser counsel, and Monsieur du Herle has provided him with both."

I bit back the bitter words that rose in my heart: *My father sold me to you for gain, into a dishonorable position, and let my children be taken from me, and little care did he have that according to his own religion he'd be making a sinner of me and endangering my soul for all eternity.*

The Marquis said, more quietly, "Perhaps you weren't happy at first about the arrangement he made with me to bring you here, but you must understand, he had your best interests at heart. As do I. Monsieur du Herle can be very persuasive, and he laid out the advantages to your father well. That's why I've employed him to see to my affairs. I hope you won't have ill feelings toward your father. He meant well and chose wisely. I noticed you haven't asked me to pass on any letters to him."

I maintained a resentful silence. What did the Marquis know of honor or wisdom or my best interests? He was arrogant and patronizing, like my father, like Pastor Bergeret. Men were all alike.

"Were you very angry at your father?" he asked at length.

I was exasperated by his thick-headedness. "Of course I was. Wouldn't you be, in my position? I'm still furious. It's demeaning to be sold like a milk cow and kept locked up like a bird in a cage. I'm not an animal. I'm a human being, after all."

"I'm sorry."

"Will you let me go?"

"I promised to protect you, to take care of you and keep you safe."

I could make no quick answer to this.

He said, "I thought you didn't wish to leave. Is there anything you lack that might make your stay here more tolerable?"

My heart beat quickly. "My children. If only I could have them here with me."

"This is no place for children," he said with a vehemence that startled me. More gently he said, "I'm sorry to deny you anything, but no, I'm afraid they can't be here. Perhaps there's some other wish I could grant you."

My heart had fallen and it took me a moment to recover from my disappointment. With little hope I asked, "Will you let me see your face?"

"Alas, I can't permit that either. Isn't there anything else you desire?" There was a touch of desperation in his voice. "There must be something."

I paused to consider. "If only I weren't always all alone here during the day. The animals in the gardens are my only company apart from you. It's difficult never to see another human face."

"Ah! Yes, I'll see what I can do." He laughed. "I thought you might ask for jewels or clothes, or at least more books."

"But didn't you say you were trying to keep the manor's expenses to a minimum? Don't you have to avoid such extravagances?"

"No, no, there's no need for that."

"But it must have cost a good deal to rescue my father from his debts. You said you spent your inheritance. How do you manage it all? Are we living on fairy gold here?"

He laughed again. "You've guessed it. That's the real reason I brought you here, as payment to the Erl-King, who's shared his fairy gold with me. You're the sacrificial maiden."

"But I'm no maiden."

He laughed harder. "I should hope not. No, my dear, it's not fairy gold that sustains us."

"You laugh at me, but it might help explain the strange magic of this place."

"I'm not sure how to explain it. I remember it feeling magical when I visited as a child. Then I was sent away to school in Paris, and it was all shut up after my parents passed away. I thought the magic had been only my imagination. An uncle became my guardian, but I saw more of his solicitors than I ever saw of him. I completed my education in Paris and lived an aimless life for a few years. And, yes, I spent what was left of my inheritance, which had already been diminished by my father's extravagant manner of living. Then, in my straitened circumstances, I made a deal with the Devil."

I remembered the illustration of the legend of Doktor Faustus and Méphistophélès, and my breath caught in my throat. "I wondered."

"No, no. I mean I married, richly and badly. I was four-and-twenty, younger than you are now. Her father approached me. He knew of my predicament and offered me his daughter's hand as a way out. My debts would all be paid, and a generous sum settled on me. He'd risen from being a clerk to a rich financier, and he wanted a nobleman's name for her. She'd taken a liking to me. So all I had to do was make her my marquise and treat her with correctness, and my fortune would be restored twice over."

"I suppose that's not unheard of." I recalled reading many similar stories in the *chroniques scandaleuses* in my former husband's bookshop, noblemen marrying wealthy merchants' daughters to replenish their dwindling funds.

"I lasted a few years with her, remaining faithful and playing the role of the dutiful society husband. Her father kept his end of the bargain. Then, thanks to a tip he gave me, I had a great coup on the stock market, the Paris Bourse, and increased my holdings enormously. After profiting so greatly, I proceeded to make a monster of myself by neglecting my wife and avoiding her as much as I could. We continued to keep a house together and I occasionally attended the balls and dinners she gave – always drunk, which was the only way to endure them – but otherwise we've lived separate lives. There never was such a cad in all of Paris, in the eyes of her family. So you see, our wealth and the villagers' prosperity all stem from my villainy. Be glad I don't inflict on you the horror of having to look upon such a creature."

It took me a moment to absorb all this, painful as it was to hear. "But if that's so ... you must have had some reason for behaving as you did. What was the cause of the estrangement between you?"

He was quiet for a long moment. "You asked about the magic of this place. After I married, I found I could will myself here. I think it was my desperate longing to be far away, to be alone. My will was so strong, and perhaps the Erl-king's blood in my veins was potent enough, that the manor seemed to respond to my wishes. It's almost as though we live here in a place formed by my thoughts, in a world that's a reflection of my dreaming."

Against all logic and sense, I tried to make out his form, the outline of his face, through the impenetrable darkness. "If that's true, it's a beautiful world. If this place were a reflection of your soul, I'd think you had an exquisite one."

"All I've wanted was someone to share it with. Now you're here at last, real and no dream. But I must tell you, my wishes and dreams aren't the reality or substance of me. My actions are. My wishes have a good deal of darkness in them, too. That includes my wishes for you. Don't you see the world I've created around you now is all dark, pure night?"

My breaths came shallowly, and my muscles tensed, waiting for him to reach for me. Now he would take his due, I thought.

We breathed in the dark, but he didn't stir. A tension pulled taut between us, like a straining cord. I had the wish to feel his face with my blind hands once more. I knew he wouldn't object, but I asked him if I might.

"In the dark, you have all that I am," he answered.

The difference this time was that when I placed my fingertips on his lips, last of all, he placed his hand over mine and kissed my fingers.

VII

HE TOOK MY hand in his then and kept hold of it, stroking the back of it with his thumb. It wasn't a beast's claws I felt, nor an ogre's gnarled grasp, nor an Erl-King's blood-stained hunting gloves. I thought then that my Marquis was only a strange, kind man who had come to hate himself, haunted by the unhappiness in his past. He was lonely and odd, and he longed for me. After a time he let go of my hand with a final squeeze and bade me goodnight.

After this, he began to visit me often at night. I told him the small observations of my day, its delights and occasional frustrations. We spoke of books, poems, and paintings. I gleaned little of how and where and with whom he spent his days, or where he went on the nights he didn't come to me. The ritual of questioning was reversed. Where before he had asked me in his nightly letter if I would meet him, now I was the one who asked him the same questions without fail. Would he reveal himself to me? Would he show me his face, at last?

I traced the outlines of his face like a benediction, with the loving hands of an Isaac seeking to know his eldest born, to give him the birthright that was his. At first the Marquis would only kiss my fingers and hold my hands. One night he went further, kissing my wrists and the soft underside of my forearms. I sensed in his shyness he was afraid of doing more.

I came to love his quiet way of speaking. There was something calm and self-possessed in it, despite his restraint and reticence with me. I came to love his enthusiasm for anything that gave me joy or pleasure, and his sorrow over anything that pained me – even when what pained me was what he himself had forbidden me. So one night, instead of feeling his face, I took it between my hands and kissed it. His forehead, his cheeks – first one and then the other. His mouth.

Did my kiss transform him and free him from whatever curse made him walk in the dark? Does a kiss turn a beast into a man, or a man into a beast? In this case, more the latter, for he kissed me back with ferocity, with ravening hunger. He opened my mouth to his and I felt his teeth (a man's teeth, neither sharp nor cruel, but teeth all the same). Those teeth bit my neck after kissing it and buried themselves deliciously into the crook of my shoulder. My embroidered satin robe and my chemise were taken away, and he removed his clothes and stretched me out naked under his warm skin, pinning me down, looking with his night-sight into my unseeing eyes that looked back in helpless fear and surrender. They inspired no mercy in him. He moved down the length of my body, opened my legs, and ate me until I was near utter abandon. I had read of such things in the hidden *mauvais livres* in Pastor Bergeret's shop, but it never would have entered the Pastor's imagination to treat me in this way, like a succulent fruit. When my shuddering, trembling, and moans had reached a pitch that satisfied him, he drew back, kissed me again, and thrust into me.

I too was transformed by his kisses into an animal unrecognizable to myself, more beast than woman. Only a small part of me was aware that my fingernails raked his skin. I wanted this to go on and on, I wanted ... I wanted ... and there it was, unexpected, the shivering convulsion, and I cried out. Still it went on and on, and then at last he pulled out. He spilled his seed on my stomach.

He fell against me, spent and sweating, and rested. I reached out my hands to feel over his body and assure myself it was in the form of a man, two arms, two legs. The only fur was over his damp groin, where it should be. His *sexe* was a man's. I cupped it gently, affectionately in my palm. Then I ran my hands over my own body to reassure myself that I, too, was still human and hadn't become furred and four-legged, or feathered and winged, or scaled and finned. I was still myself, but I felt changed, made new in learning the act of love was capable of giving me pleasure. It needn't be a painful chore. Instead, under my lover's hands I had been awakened, sated, saturated with delicious perfumes of musks and flowers.

"Violaine," he whispered. "My Violaine, jewel and flower and fruit of my darkness." For the first time he used my Christian name and the intimate pronoun *tu* instead of the colder *vous*.

"What should I call you now?" I asked him, using *tu* as well. *Monsieur le marquis* seemed too formal if he was going to call me Violaine.

"You can call me Thérion."

"Is that your Christian name?"

"No, it's a family name. My Christian name is Prosper-Aloyse, but no one ever calls me that."

"Doesn't Thérion mean 'beast' in Greek? Like the beasts in the Book of Revelations?"

"Exactly, I'm the Beast. The Anti-Christ who ushers in the end times in scripture. It was a joke amongst my school friends when I was younger, so that's what they all called me."

"Mmm. Thérion. My Beast. I like that."

I fell asleep with his kisses in my ear.

When I woke it was light, and he was gone.

After I'd had my morning coffee, I found a new room on the third floor. The eastern end of the passage, with its many doors leading to private apartments like my own, had appeared to end in an alcove with an elegant little inlaid-wooden table, a pretty porcelain vase, and a large painting on the wall above. Now I realized that what I had taken to be wooden paneling on the side of the alcove was in fact, all along, another of the manor's cunningly hidden doors, for it stood open. From the room beyond came the clinking of glass and silverware.

I approached the open door and, peering around the doorframe, was dumbfounded at the vision before me. The place was, I supposed, what might be called a morning room in the books on architecture I had leafed through. Six chairs surrounded an ornately carved and gilded rectangular table in the center, and a buffet on the side was laden with an engraved silver coffee service and trays of food. A fireplace, sofa, and several armchairs lined the walls. It was one of the prettiest rooms I had seen yet in the manor. Everything about it evoked morning, from the paintings of clouds, blue skies, and sunlit green landscapes that hung on the walls, to the blue-and-white fabric of the upholstery and drapes, to the gilt edges of the furniture. Most astonishing of all was that an elegantly dressed woman sat at the head of the table before a gleaming place setting, enjoying a hearty breakfast. Her blue satin *saque* dress, with Oriental embroidery in gold threads over white muslin ruffles, matched the room almost perfectly. Her face, as she chewed contemplatively on a bite of *diot* sausage, glowed with good health and happiness. She had rosy cheeks framed by short blond curls and a few wrinkles around her blue eyes, so that I took her to be somewhere between thirty and forty years of age.

My approach on slippered feet over rugs on the parquet floor had been silent, and a minute went by before she looked up and saw me. She started and dropped her teaspoon with a clatter. Then her face broke into a delighted smile.

"Why, good morning. We haven't met before. I'm Aurore. How nice to see a new and charming face here at Boisaulne."

I curtsied. "Madame ... Aurore, *enchantée*. I'm called –"

"Ah-ah-ah." She held up a hand to stop me. "No 'Madame Aurore' here. It's simply Aurore. This must be your first time visiting the château?"

To avoid a complicated explanation of how I had come to live here, I simply answered, "Yes."

"Well, if no one's told you yet, it's become something of a custom that no one uses their real names here. It's part of the fun. It's like a masquerade in a way. Have you already got a *surnom*?"

I shook my head. No one had ever called me by a nickname before. She rubbed her hands together delightedly.

"Then I'll claim the honor of giving you one. How about simply ... Belle? Because you're so lovely. Will that do?"

I blinked. "But ... you're very kind, but I don't think that would suit me."

She frowned and shook her head. "No, no, you're right. Forgive me." She tapped her lips with her index finger. "If you're here, surely you're a woman who'd like to be more than merely beautiful."

I inclined my head to the side, gratified by her quick understanding. "I like to think of myself as a person who cares more for the beauty of the soul."

"Which is a sign that you must have a beautiful soul. That could be a better *surnom* for you. How about *Belle-Âme*, then? I like it. It's the kind of name I'd give to a girl in a fairy tale. But come, sit down. Have you eaten yet?"

I took a seat in one of the comfortable padded chairs. "I've only had coffee. You're visiting then? As a guest of the Marquis?"

"As it were. Of course, it was Harlequin who invited me. None of us has ever met the Marquis in person. Don't tell me you've seen him? I'm dying to know what he looks like."

"I ... no, in fact, I haven't *seen* the Marquis. I'm also very curious to know how he looks."

"Then I take it Harlequin invited you too."

I paused to consider how much I ought to reveal to this strange new visitor about my position at the manor. In the joy of finding a lover in the Marquis, I had entirely forgotten others would likely think me of the lowest character if they knew I'd been brought here to be his mistress. So I answered, "No, it was a gentleman by the name of Monsieur du Herle who arranged for me to come. He knew my father and my late husband from Annecy."

"Ah, then yes, Harlequin invited you too. That's his *surnom*, just as mine is Aurore."

"Monsieur du Herle is called Harlequin? But is he here then? He's come back to Boisaulne?"

"I should think so. I only just arrived from Paris late last night, by the usual way. I expect we'll see him at dinner tonight in the great hall, if not before. I'm not sure who else is coming this summer. The invitation was a little last-minute this time round. You might meet Séléné, Donatien, Ulysse ... There's a circle of us from Paris, who've been coming the past three summers in a row, mid-July through the end of August. This'll be my fourth time here. The mountains make such a fine escape from the stink and heat of the city. Have you been to Paris?"

"No, never. Did you meet Monsieur du Herle – I mean, Harlequin – in Paris?"

"Oh yes, he's something of a fixture at my *salon*, and at my dear friend Séléné's, too. I organize a regular little gathering on Wednesday afternoons, and Séléné has hers on Thursdays so they don't conflict. Before I started the *salon,* I used to see him at Madame Dufaud's, which was where we first met. You said you met him in Annecy? I hear it's a beautiful town."

"I suppose it is. I was so busy when I lived there, helping my late husband with a bookshop he owned and looking after my children, I didn't get to walk along the lakeshore much, which was the prettiest part. After my husband passed away, we went back to my home village, on the other side of the mountain from here."

"Oh, I see. That's a shame. But do you know, from your accent I'd hardly guess you weren't Parisian. There's only a hint of *savoyard* there. You must have been fortunate in your education."

I was on the alert for condescension in her words, but could detect only sincerity and kindness. With her open, friendly manners, she was not at all what I might have expected of a Parisian lady. I explained to her how, after my mother had passed away, back when my father's fortune was still intact, I had a governess who had tutored my sisters and me and had been strict about requiring us to speak the French she had learned in the convent growing up near Paris. But in our village the people spoke *patouè*, the local dialect.

"But you've come here for several summers," I said, "and you've never met the Marquis de Boisaulne. How does that come about?"

She cast a quick glance around the room, as if fearing to be overheard, and lowered her voice. "I don't know how much Harlequin has told you, but as I've heard him tell it, the Marquis is a relative of his, fifth cousin once removed or something like that. Harlequin manages his affairs for him because the Marquis is an eccentric and doesn't go into society. But he permits Harlequin to invite any friends he wishes to Boisaulne as his guests. Where the Marquis hides himself while we're here, nobody knows. It's all exceedingly odd, but we come because we like Harlequin. And it's magical here. Really and truly. Perhaps you've already discovered that."

I smiled and nodded, and she beamed back at me. "We keep it a well-guarded secret amongst our acquaintances," she said. "Everyone would want to come here if they knew, and it would be spoiled. But tell me, you must have a special talent of some kind, or Harlequin wouldn't have invited you. Do you draw or paint or sing?"

"It'd be a great exaggeration to call it a talent, but I have written some poetry."

"A poetess! I knew it. How delightful. Perhaps you'll let me read some of your verses one of these days. My friends Ulysse and Donatien both write poems, too. With any luck you'll meet them."

"I hope so. And what's your talent?"

Aurore gave me a sad little smile. "Ah, I'm the exception to the general rule of Harlequin only entertaining men and women of brilliance. I'm only good at bringing bright spirits together, to draw sparks off each other while they educate and enlighten me. Unless you count my little fairy tales, *mes contes de fées.*"

"You make up fairy tales?"

"It amuses me, and sometimes my friends are dear enough to listen, and I read them out loud when we're gathered in the *salon*. It's not such a bad way to while away a rainy afternoon. I also collect tales, when and where I can."

"I think you're too modest. Surely that's an art, as much as poetry."

"I enjoy it in any case, and some have told me I ought to find a publisher for my stories. Imagine, what a silly idea!"

"I always found it difficult to make up stories, and my children always wanted me to tell new ones. Do you have children?"

She pursed her lips and took a sip of her chocolate. "That's another rule here, though I find it a little difficult to follow. One isn't supposed to speak of children, or even of husbands or wives, though that one's easier for me. I'm sorry, that probably sounds terrible. It's just, I've barely seen my husband the past several years. He's been very ill and sleeps most of the time. Our valet and housekeeper and his doctors tend to him, and there's little more I can do for him."

"I'm sorry to hear it."

"In truth, he's lived a good long life, nearly four-score years, and I think he'd be only too glad to rest in peace at last. And I – well, I've lived almost as a widow for some time."

"Four-score years? You must have been very young when you were married."

"I was only fourteen and he was four and fifty years old. My grandmother thought it a good match. Well, it made us comfortable. Of course my son and daughter are already grown, so the tales I write down are more for my friends and their children. How old are your children?" She whispered the question, as though she felt guilty about breaking the rule she had just told me about.

"I have a son who's ten and a daughter seven years old now." I blinked to keep from tearing up, but my voice caught a little. "The boy's gone away to school in Annecy, and my daughter is staying with one of my sisters in the village."

"You must miss them." She squeezed my hand. My heart swelled with gratitude for her sympathy. I thought of the Marquis – Thérion, as he had asked me to call him – and how I had complained of never seeing anyone during the day. In allowing M. du Herle to invite Aurore, he had fulfilled yet another wish of mine. I should have preferred a hundred times over to have my children with me, but at least in Aurore I might have found a kindred soul, a friend who understood what it was to be a mother far from her family. Our eyes met and we both smiled – I through the tears that had welled up.

When we had finished our breakfast, we went for a walk in the garden together, and through our conversation and laughter, the broad outlines of Aurore's life emerged. She had been born in the mountainous city of Grenoble in the Dauphiné, where her family had a modest estate. At the age of six, she was sent to Paris to live with her grandmother, who gave her a religious education and arranged for her marriage to a retired army officer. She proceeded to educate herself secularly as best she could by reading in her husband's library, and at the age of eighteen began attending *salon* gatherings at the home of a well-known society lady of sterling reputation, Madame Dufaud. It was at Madame Dufaud's that she had first heard about the woman who would later become her dear friend, Séléné, mainly through the terrible things that were said of her. It turned out the much-maligned

Séléné lived only a few houses away on the same street as Aurore. The rumors of Séléné's wild life had stirred her pity and piqued her interest, so Aurore had taken the rather courageous step of making her neighbor's acquaintance and befriending her, much to her husband's displeasure. When Séléné started her own *salon* on the same day of the week as Madame Dufaud's, Aurore had abandoned the stuffy atmosphere of the Dufauds and became a regular member of Séléné's circle.

At Séléné's, it was a much more interesting group. Instead of proper, haughty women and their dull husbands, who talked more of hunting, court gossip, and the yields of their estates than of letters and learning, Aurore had met artists, actors, poets, musicians, opera singers, dancers, and *philosophes*. Séléné herself wrote novels in between her affairs with a never-ending progression of lovers.

"If you meet her," Aurore told me, "try not to be intimidated by her. She can come across as rather brash at first, but she has a good heart."

"I'm intimidated already," I said with a laugh.

"You needn't be, really. You know, when my husband took to his bed for good and was no longer there to object to everything I did, she actually encouraged me to start my own *salon*. That's the proof of her good heart to me. There isn't a shred of jealousy or competitiveness in her. She only wants to see her friends succeed and flourish as she has. So now we have our gatherings on different days of the week. There's a good deal of overlap in our circles, but she doesn't mind if I have my own friends and exclude a few of hers, whose conduct goes against my morals. I like to think I'm broad-minded, but there are a handful who in my eyes go too far."

I told Aurore about the bookshop in Annecy and the philosophical evenings the pastor used to organize there, where only men were allowed and most of them dressed in dark sober suits and smoked and talked of theological disputes. I still wasn't sure whether she would consider it "going too far" that I had come to live with the Marquis in the way I had, so I told her only about how I had fallen in love with the *Book of the Rose* and hidden my poems in its pages, and how I had thought them lost when the shop was sold, but then they were recovered in the Marquis's library, which had led to my invitation to Boisaulne.

"Ah, I wondered if you might be one of Ulysse's protégées."

"What do you mean?"

"Ulysse. He's my friend who also writes poetry, as I mentioned. He has a bit of a habit of finding young women of talent and taking them under his wing. I don't inquire too closely about what else he does with them. But he rescues them from whatever poor circumstances they're struggling in and launches them into the world."

"Really? And do the young women succeed?" This sounded suspiciously like what my Marquis had claimed he intended to do with me.

"Well, he's very well-connected. Ulysse knows everyone worth knowing, which makes it rather impressive that he's managed to keep quiet about the secret of Boisaulne. So, yes, I'd say they've gone on to be successful. There was a stunning actress from Genève whom he helped onto the Paris stage. Then there was a girl from Lyon who painted the most delicate and intricate designs on silk. A dancer from the Paris Opera ... and before her a rather odd girl who sang in the chorus but had taught herself to compose music. Ulysse helped her get some of her work performed at court under a pseudonym. It was quite the little drama."

"What happened to the girls afterwards?" I asked, as we paused at the side of the path to admire a rosebush with flowers of an unusual lavender shade. "I suppose he didn't marry any of them?"

"No. They went on to other lovers, or they found rich husbands. They generally ended happily, except for the dancer, who was taken with consumption and had to retire from performing. I do wonder – in fact, I remember it was Harlequin who introduced Ulysse to a few of the girls. He invited the actress and the silk girl here, specifically for Ulysse to make their acquaintance. Perhaps he intended you for Ulysse as well? It's possible."

I thought back to the words of Madame Jacquenod in the village of Maisnie-la-Forêt, "It's a long time since I saw him bring a woman through here." Perhaps those were the women she had spoken of, women for this gentleman Ulysse, rather than for his master the Marquis.

"Aurore, can I ask you something? Do you know if there's a back way that goes out from the manor? When you came here, did you arrive by way of the village?"

"Yes, there's a back way. If you come from Genève, or from Grenoble, as I did one summer, you might come through the village. But to go to and from Paris, there's a shortcut that goes out from behind the stable. It goes around behind the house and then down into a little grotto under the spring that feeds into the fountain, though you can't see it from the garden. You've seen how there's magic here, so perhaps you'll believe me that it only takes a few hours to reach Paris with the Marquis's horses. Inside the grotto, there's an entrance to an underground tunnel. If you ride through the tunnel for an hour or two, you end up in the old abandoned quarries under the streets of Paris. The exit from the quarries at the other end is hidden behind a stable at the back of Harlequin's property near the Luxembourg Gardens. Of course, on the ordinary roads, in an ordinary *diligence* or carriage, it might take as long as a week to reach Savoy."

"How extraordinary," I murmured, half to myself.

We returned to the manor and parted ways, Aurore to rest and write letters and I to read in the library.

As many rooms as there were in the manor, the library was my favorite, for through the books even more rooms opened in my mind, and I felt the least confined there of all the corners in my great gilded prison, curled up on a sofa before the fire with a book. After a couple of hours of reading, though, I wanted to stretch my limbs. I went into the music room to take a turn around it, and my eye was caught by small lovely details I hadn't noticed before in the antique instruments and paintings on display. There was a mandolin I hadn't realized was inlaid with a design of flowers in different colors of wood, with mother-of-pearl petals that glowed in the dim afternoon light. I touched its strings, the smooth taut sinews pressing lines into my fingertips. When my eyes had taken their fill of it, I returned to the library. I was no longer alone there. A man stood at one of the windows, pushing the muslin shade aside to gaze out at the view over the garden and mountainside.

My heartbeat quickened. Could it be M. du Herle who had returned? But why did I tremble so at the thought of meeting him again? Perhaps it was that I hadn't laid eyes on a man in weeks, in spite of Thérion's visits in the dark.

I was almost beside him before he heard my soft footsteps on the rug. He stood up from his position of leaning over the windowsill, turned to face me, and leaned back against the sill in a languid manner, as though it were the most ordinary thing in the world for him to encounter strange women in remote châteaux in the forest. I ought to have known at once it wasn't M. du Herle, for I remembered then that M. du Herle had dressed in dark and sober clothes. This gentleman wore a suit of pale lilac embroidered with gold threads and had clearly lavished some attention on his appearance. He raised an eyebrow as I approached and quirked up a corner of his mouth in a half-smile. Though he must have been five or ten years older than I was, his face had a softness and feminine beauty to it, fair and slightly fey, that made him seem young.

"Are you Belle-Âme?" he asked. He looked me up and down. "I think it can only be you."

"Monsieur?" I wasn't sure whether to feel offended or not by the way his eyes lingered over my figure.

"Donatien, at your service." He bowed. "I saw Aurore earlier, and she said she'd christened you with that *nom de guerre*. I should have said simply Belle, myself. You *are* the Savoyard girl, aren't you?"

"Yes, I'm Savoyard."

"So Harlequin's lured a mountain poetess to us. Well done. Enchanting. I've been known to indulge in the occasional bit of verse myself."

"Oh, have you published any books?"

"Me? Oh no. It wouldn't do for someone in my position. That looks too much like work. It'd spoil my reputation, you know."

So he was an aristocrat. Since he already knew my origins, I decided I might as well speak openly. "I don't have a reputation to worry about, but I think I should feel embarrassed to have my poems published. It's not that I'm ashamed of them – well, not of all of them. It's only, I've put so much of myself into some of them. I'd feel ... exposed, I think."

He arched an eyebrow. "Exposed? They bare your soul, you mean. Luckily I've no soul to worry about being revealed through my writing. What I seem on the surface is exactly what I am. But I write my verses chiefly for the amusement of my friends, whenever I'm struck with a fit of thinking myself witty."

We talked about our favorite poems and strolled around the library, pausing at volumes that one or the other of us had read. He favored light and humorous verses and was a great admirer of Molière's comedies. As we moved on from one of the bookcases, he placed a hand on the small of my back. I didn't know the habits of aristocrats, except from books in which they tended to be always either debauched or else romantic heroes. Thérion, with his nocturnal habits, could hardly be a typical example of his class. But it seemed to me Donatien was taking a liberty, so I moved away.

An inscrutable expression came over his face. Then an instant later he was pleasant again. "What do you think so far of the Castle of Enlightenment, our *Forteresse des Lumières*?"

"The ... what? You mean Boisaulne?"

"It's my own little nickname for the place, the Castle of Enlightenment, because the intellectual lights of Paris come here to take in the mountain air. It's a funny place. I've heard the most rational talk here in summers past. It makes me think of what Saint Paul says, *When I was a child, I spoke as a child, I understood as a child, I thought as a child; but when I became a man, I put away childish things.*"

He quoted the passage in Latin, and I translated it out loud into French to make sure I'd understood.

"Very good," he said. "Why, you've studied. I've an uncle who's an *abbé*, who insisted I learn. It wasn't entirely dull, reading in the Vulgate. Extraordinary what licentiousness some of the men and women of scripture get up to. But at any rate, I think of what Saint Paul said, since children and families and all the irrational business that goes along with them are *non grata* here. And there's the other rule, that we don't speak during the day of the things we do in the night."

"I hadn't heard that one."

He waved it off. "You'll hear it. The point is, none of our talk is supposed to be shaped by the accidents of birth or fortune, or the vagaries of fate, since we leave our names and identities behind when we come here. We're stripped down to our naked ideas and intellects – 'exposed,' as you say. And yet, and yet ..." He shook a reproving finger at the fireplace across the room. "There's so little that's rational about the fact that this place exists at all. It's mad and magical. We have these odd rules, and none of us has ever seen the Marquis. He could be any one of us in reality. He could be me, couldn't he? And no one would be any the wiser. So despite the idea that our talk should be enlightening, our ideas all brought out from obscurity and examined pitilessly from every angle, the place and the people in it are shrouded in mystery. There's a dark side to the Castle of Enlightenment. It's my sense of irony that makes me take pleasure in calling it that. You see?"

"I'm not sure I follow."

"Never mind." He laughed. "It's not important."

I examined Donatien anew and tried to imagine him as Thérion, my Beast who came to me in the night. But his voice was different, more purring than Thérion's. Somehow, too, I realized I had been picturing Thérion with an ugly face, nothing like the fair, angular one before me. I excused myself to go back upstairs to my chambers to rest before dressing for dinner. At least now I would have company to dress for.

VIII

AURORE HAD TOLD me she would be in the great hall at eight o'clock. In Paris, people often dined later, she said, but she was an early riser and preferred to dine at a more reasonable hour. I didn't tell her how in the village we often went to bed just as her Parisian friends were beginning their suppers.

I changed my mind repeatedly about what to wear and how to do my hair. At first I put on the most formal dress in my wardrobe, a dark maroon velvet affair with a stiff, narrow bodice and a wide skirt with a train, elevated by paniers on the sides, so beautiful I imagined one might wear it to meet the King of Sardinia or to be presented in the court of France. It set off my dark hair dramatically, but I felt ridiculous and could barely breathe or sit down in it. I would be overdressed, and they would think I was trying too hard. Instead I picked out a green silk gown à l'anglaise with a narrower cut that flattered my figure and brought out the green in my eyes. Then I remembered Donatien's hand on my back and how uncomfortable it had made me, and I was afraid of seeming to want to attract further attention from him. I tried on and rejected other ensembles for being too flowery, too plain, and too severe. At last I returned to the one I had worn the most often to my solitary dinners, a comfortable dress in the loose *deshabillé* fashion, in cornflower blue, embellished with silk flowers in pink and cream.

My indecision nearly made me late, and by the time I reached the great hall there was a whole company of people in it, just sitting down to eat. An empty place was set at the end of the table and I hastened toward it.

"Belle-Âme, you're just in time," Aurore said from her seat in the center of the group.

"Belle-Âme? Is that her *surnom* now?" asked a deep voice to my right. I turned and registered that I was sitting next to M. du Herle.

"It wasn't my idea," I said. "It was Aurore's compliment to me after we made each other's acquaintance this morning."

"It suits you well, I think. It's good to see you again. You've settled in properly here now it seems."

"Yes, thank you, I've been very comfortable." There was so much I wanted to say to him. *You didn't warn me about how it would be here. You didn't tell me I'd be surrounded by magic and luxury, waited on by invisible servants. You didn't tell me I'd be so strangely alone and yet not alone, wooed by a lover who comes to me like eerie and marvelous dreams in the night.* But it seemed out of place to say such things to him then and there. "Were you in Paris most of the time, ever since I saw you last?"

"I've been a little bit here and there and all around."

A gentleman seated across from me cleared his throat, and M. du Herle said, "But of course, there are introductions to be made. Everyone, this is Belle-Âme." The chatter around the table died down as the others turned to listen. "She was discovered in a marvelous antique copy of the *Book of the Rose* in Annecy. She'd placed her poems in the book's pages and then I acquired the book for the Marquis's library."

My cheeks burned as this announcement was met with smiles and nods around the table. He went on to introduce the others.

The ugly gentleman across from me, his wig disheveled and his clothes ill-fitting, was a Scottish historian and philosopher. His pasty face and beaked nose were stamped with the deep lines of an imp's features.

"Everyone just calls me the Scotsman," he said. "Makes things easier since there's no mistaking me, and I'm proud enough of my country I take honor in it." He spoke mostly-correct French, but with harsher consonants and longer vowels than ours.

The woman next to him was Séléné, the friend of whom Aurore had spoken. I regarded her with keen curiosity. Her body was shorter and plumper and her face had plainer, harsher features than I had imagined. Her coiffure of short black curls framing her face accentuated the severity of her looks. She had also rouged her cheeks, lips, and eyelids to a degree that seemed gauche to me, though for all I knew it was the fashion in Paris.

Donatien sat next to her, his lips and cheeks rouged as well, and across from him was Aurore. Donatien and Aurore could almost have been brother and sister. Both of them were blond and blue-eyed, though Donatien's relaxed posture gave an impression of coiled strength, while Aurore seemed so delicate it was a wonder her hands didn't drop from her slender wrists like petals from a rose. On Donatien's other side was a pretty, sturdy-framed girl of perhaps eighteen or nineteen, with long, wavy red hair pulled back in a loose arrangement of ribbons and flowers. Her smile was sweet and entreating, as though she were about to cajole a bird from its cage to sing. Her green eyes were large and bright and her round cheeks freckled and pink. M. du Herle – but I recalled again that I must accustom myself to calling him Harlequin – introduced her by the *surnom* of Clio.

"Clio's the daughter of a fan painter in Paris who created some fine pieces for a woman friend of mine. Her father taught her painting, and as it turns out, she's an exciting talent, even at her young age. I've no doubt that in a few years, if she works hard and has the proper backing, she could well merit being admitted to the Royal Academy."

"La, a new woman painter in the Academy!" said Séléné. "Wouldn't that be a fine thing? It's enchanting to make your acquaintance."

Clio sat across from a gentleman of perhaps five and thirty with a sad, sensitive expression and beautiful deep-set eyes. He wore a short tradesman's wig and dressed simply, without ostentation of any kind, though even from the other end of the table I noticed that his linen shirt was of fine material and had been carefully washed and pressed.

"Here we have a true Renaissance man," Harlequin said. "Not what he does, but what doesn't he do, that's more the question. A composer of ambitious musical works. An inventor of a novel form of musical notation. A student of the science of botany. The author of several influential philosophical essays and a novel. Since this is his first time at Boisaulne, it's still necessary to choose a name for him."

"You're far too kind," the man said. "I try my hand at many things and I'm not particularly good at any of them. I think I'd like to be called Tristan. The legend of him and Iseult was my favorite as a boy, and I always used to think I'd been born in the wrong time and ought to have been a knight."

"I like to think there's no better place than Boisaulne to try being whatever legendary figure one's always wanted to be, at least for a few weeks," Harlequin said. "Last but not least, we come to Ulysse, who's a legendary figure whether he wants to be or not. Aside from being a fulsome, and often fulminating, man of letters, he writes more letters and knows more people to write to than anyone else I know."

So this then, was Ulysse, the man in the crimson coat with the black mustache, long dark wig of curls, and thick black eyebrows. His animated expression reminded me of an actor in a traveling theater, like those I used to catch glimpses of sometimes in the market at Annecy.

Ulysse laughed. "Thank you, my friend. And since you've announced everyone else but characteristically neglected to introduce yourself, I claim that honor." He stood up and recited a poem in a flawed, uneven poetical meter with rhymes that didn't quite work:

> *Mesdames, messieurs,* here we have
> An enigmatic gentleman
> Who goes by the name of Harlequin.
> Is he a trickster, a sphinx?
> What devilry has he got up his sleeve?
>
> He does not show his cards,
> Nor are they written on his face,
> So he's certain to win the game.
> Beware, beware, of Harlequin!
> Don't bet your hand against him.
>
> But he brings us here,
> We're served food and wine.
> We shall have no fear,
> But of the passing of time.
>
> Therefore we drink,
> After this execrable rhyme,
> To the invisible Marquis our host
> And his friend Harlequin.

Ulysse's poem was received with groans, cheers, and laughter. We toasted Harlequin, the Marquis, and Boisaulne. I drank sparkling wine along with everyone else, and after several toasts the room tilted a little around me. The food began to appear on the table and we worked our way through six or seven courses of dishes richer and more elaborate than the simple solitary meals of game, bread, and vegetables I had become accustomed to in the last several weeks. There were aspics, meats in pastries, piquant and creamy sauces, meringues and Chantilly cream and berries. I had a long talk with the Scotsman, who sat across from me. At first I thought because of his ugly imp's face and bad clothes he would be dull to talk with, but he took pains to keep me amused, telling me jokes and asking me many questions. I didn't wish to lie outright about my position there or my relationship with the Marquis, but through simple omission and turning his questions quickly back on him, I managed to evade any discussion of it. My questions were rewarded with stories of his travels. As a young man he had survived a voyage to America and back. He had visited the courts of Prussia, Bavaria, Sardinia, and Spain. This was his first summer at Boisaulne.

Our conversation was interrupted by an announcement from Harlequin, who had been listening in from time to time, in between chatting with Séléné and Aurore. He held up a hand for our attention and cleared his throat.

"Since some of you are new to our little society here, I must explain there are certain rules traditionally followed by those who spend any length of time at Boisaulne. Most of them have been laid down by the Marquis himself, as conditions for my inviting visitors on his behalf. Whatever his eccentricities, it can be said of him that he's a proponent of the ideals of the lights of our age: reason, tolerance, progress, humanity, science, government for the good of all. I for one have no quarrel with any of it, so I hope none of you will find it too burdensome.

"One rule, as must already have become clear, is that we don't use our ordinary names here. In general, a name is given to us at birth and carries with it a weight of history, of place, of fortune, inheritance or the lack thereof. A man can't help the accidents of his birth and circumstances but can strive against them to do good or ill. So, to remind us to act as masters of our own fates, we go by names of our choosing here.

"Another rule is that we don't speak of families here, of parents, wives, husbands or children, for similar reasons. The third rule is that we don't speak in the day of the things we do in the night. In other words, what you do then is your own business, and shouldn't intrude on the friendly dealings we have with each other in our illuminated circle.

"Apart from those rules, I'll just remind everyone that, like the *salon* gatherings held by some of our illustrious fellow guests, the manor is meant to be a place friendly to serious discussions. So we must all be prepared to find our arguments and ideas scrutinized and criticized from every angle, and ourselves held to high standards of logic, rigor, and good faith in seeking the truth in our discussions. That's all. My thanks again to all of you for making the journey here."

Donatien listened to Harlequin's speech with a slight smile. He caught my eye and winked at me. The Castle of Enlightenment. So this was what he had meant.

When the conversation resumed, Séléné turned to me.

"So, tell me, dear, what have you read?"

I froze with a mouthful of meringue. It took me a long moment to chew and swallow and wash the bite down with a sip of bubbly wine. In the embarrassment of it, tears almost came to the corners of my eyes.

"Er, begging your pardon?" I croaked at last.

"I said, what have you read?"

"I, well, goodness. I began with the Bible in French, I suppose ..."

"Are you a Calvinist?"

"No, our villages all followed the teachings of a sectarian preacher. Though there is some resemblance, I'd say, to Calvinism and the beliefs of the Huguenots."

"Theology isn't my *forte*. You must explain it to me a little."

"Pardon me, of course. It began with a monk who called himself Peter Waldo. He praised poverty, simplicity, asceticism, and chastity. He gave away his riches to become a wandering preacher and founded a sect that became known as the Vaudois, or the churches of the valleys. Most of our people lived further south, in Piemonte and the Dauphiné, and they were nearly exterminated in the Wars of Religion. But a handful of villages on the other side of the mountain from here, where I was born, were settled by Vaudois. They had fled north to Genève at one point, and then instead of going back home they went into hiding in the woods by the *alpages*, high up and far from the main roads, where few travelers ever came to know of their existence or their heresy."

Séléné listened with bright-eyed attentiveness. "Fascinating. Do you mean to say that you yourself are a heretic, from a hidden village?"

I laughed. "No. I must admit that after reading some of the tracts of the *philosophes,* d'Holbach, Diderot, Voltaire, and so on, I became more of a Deist in my heart. I can't disbelieve in a Divine Being, but I see him more as a clockmaker who set the world in motion and doesn't otherwise intervene in human affairs."

She nodded. "You and most of the rest of us I think. But if you were raised in a heretic village, how did you come to read the *philosophes*?"

"My father moved to the town of Annecy after I was born and built up a small fortune as a merchant and investor. My sisters and I had a governess when we lived in town, so I learned my letters in French. Then I was married to a lay pastor of our faith, who kept a bookshop in Annecy to earn a living. I used to read the *philosophes* when I was minding the shop and no customers needed help. But the rules – I'm sorry. Mightn't it be allowed to speak of the pastor, though, since he passed away some years ago?" I asked sheepishly, with a glance at Harlequin.

"I should think so," she said in a conspiratorially lowered voice. "I'm a widow too, and not unhappy with my lot. It's been a way to live prosperously and freely. There are few things more fortunate for an ambitious woman than to have a dead, rich husband."

"Oh," I said, recoiling a little. "Was – was he unkind to you, your late husband?"

She laughed. "You have no idea. But that was a long time ago. Thankfully, a hunting accident relieved me of him after only three years. I've been free ever since – well, except for a short spell in the Bastille."

"I'm sorry."

"But lovers are ever so much better than husbands, aren't they? I thought it would be the same because I'd been in love with my husband for a year before I married him. But when a man regards you as his property it's different. He thought my wild past entitled him to punish me, and he was a jealous man. If there's anything I can't abide, it's jealousy."

Donatien had caught the thread of our conversation and listened with amusement. "You did have a rather wild past. He ought to have known what he was getting into with you. You should tell the story to Belle-Âme, it's a good one."

"Which story?"

"Why, the convent of course."

She rolled her eyes, but seeing my wide-eyed look, said with good humor, "Very well. I ran away from a convent when I was fifteen. My parents thought it would provide me with a good education for being married. But it certainly wasn't the education I wanted! I disguised myself as a boy and fled to my sister's house in Paris, which was a much better life for me. Parties and balls, and I could read whatever I liked without having to make up my own stories. Of course since I'd got used to doing it I kept making up stories anyway."

"Oh, that's right," I said. "Aurore mentioned you're a novelist."

"I publish under a *nom de plume* of course. But perhaps you've come across the *Memoirs of the Baron of L---*?"

I blinked. "Why yes. I could hardly put it down. I stayed up most of the night reading the last half. You're the author? Truly?"

She smiled. "You're flattering me. It was just a potboiler."

"Well, well," said Donatien, putting an arm around Séléné's shoulder and leaning in toward me. "So the pastor's widow likes potboilers. I wonder what other kinds of excitement she likes."

Séléné waggled her eyebrows and giggled. Then her face turned serious. "You're exquisite," she said to me. She was drunk. I think we all were.

After supper, coffee was served, and the faint sounds of a gavotte drifted in from the music room upstairs.

"Let's have some dancing," said Harlequin, who had been quiet through most of the supper since his speech about the rules of the Castle of Enlightenment. He led us out to the antechamber and down the gallery hall, which was lit up by candles in sconces. He opened another pair of double doors set into the wall that I hadn't seen before, camouflaged as they were by the gilded and painted marquetry of the hall. The doors opened out into a spacious, high-ceilinged salon with a mezzanine gallery and railing halfway up the wall above us, from which a wide staircase descended. On the side of the mezzanine was another pair of double doors whose existence I hadn't previously suspected, that opened into the music room, so the melody of the gavotte filled the room.

We paired up into couples. Ulysse asked Clio to dance, and she blushed as she accepted, averring that she didn't dance well – clearly a modest falsehood since she danced very prettily.

Séléné bowed to Donatien as a gentleman might to a lady and asked him whether she might have this dance. Donatien, who had watched Ulysse claim Clio with a petulant air, laughed and pretended to curtsey before accepting, but he took the lead on the dance floor. The Scotsman asked me to dance, and Tristan bowed to Aurore in an awkward, stiff manner. Since we were an odd number, Harlequin stood off to the side next to a buffet of drinks and sweets, looking on. His pale silver-blue eyes seemed to follow me with constant, furtive attentiveness.

For the next few dances in a row we switched partners with each change of the music, and each of the gentlemen took a turn sitting out. Harlequin danced with me last of all and didn't seem inclined to speak much when he finally did. There was so much I wished to ask him that it was hard to know where to begin, but I had to seize my opportunity, since he had been talking with the others and avoiding me all night.

"Harlequin," I said as we stepped forward, my hand resting on his arm, "why didn't you tell me more about the Marquis before I came here?"

"You didn't ask."

"I was so frightened."

"You needn't have been." He looked down at me in concern. "You know that now, don't you?"

"Still. You ought to have told me more of what I had to expect." We turned and faced each other, joining hands. "I never imagined I could be so happy here."

"Are you happy then?" For a moment he met my eyes and held my gaze.

"More than words can say. So much it almost hurts sometimes."

He nodded. "Good."

"But the Marquis – he only comes to me at night, in the dark. You must have seen him. Can you tell me what he looks like?" We pivoted around and walked in the other direction, in line with the other dancers.

"Does it matter, if you're happy with him?"

I considered this as we crossed hands with the other partners and went around in a circle before returning to one another.

"So you won't tell me," I said when we rejoined our hands.

"Anything you want to know, you should ask him. You probably know him better than I do by now. I only follow his instructions."

"Hmm." We turned round again. "By the way," I said as he took my hand and led me forward, "I was curious. How did you get your nickname?"

"It seemed appropriate. Harlequin's a clever, resourceful fellow. In the comedies he helps his master unite with his beloved."

"But isn't he also a rogue and a trickster?"

He grinned. "Perhaps I am, too. Harlequin's half fool, half sage. He's a masked, checkered, patchwork man. So he's not unfitting as an alter ego."

We stepped sideways together. Donatien's words from this afternoon came back to me. *Any one of us could be the Marquis, and no one would be the wiser.* The conviction took hold of me that Harlequin was one and the same as Thérion, the Marquis de Boisaulne. It could be him, couldn't it? It must be him, since my heart beat faster at the touch of his hands on mine, and when my eyes met his silver-blue ones, I felt as though I were sinking down into a bottomless sea. Yet there still remained to me enough doubt that I didn't want to embarrass myself by asking him, only to be proved wrong. I would wait and watch until I was more certain. Then I would ask him.

After several jigs and minuets, sarabandes, and more gavottes, I was fatigued and overwarm. With most of the rest of the group I paused to rest and take another glass of sparkling wine. Harlequin and Aurore were the only two still on the dance floor.

The gentlemen clustered around the adorable Clio. I was inclined to be jealous, even if Harlequin had intended to procure her as a mistress for Ulysse. But I thought of Séléné's words, *If there's anything I can't abide, it's jealousy.* I knew I wasn't pretty in the way Clio was, in the way nearly any man in any country of the world couldn't help but find charming. But Aurore had first wanted to call me Belle, and Donatien had said the same thing. I thought that with my black hair, green eyes, and pale skin, my beauty was of a more particular kind, the kind women found attractive, and perhaps also men of darker and more original tastes, as Thérion seemed to be. I wasn't discontented with my lot. I'd rather be myself than Clio.

An arm encircled my waist, and I looked up to see Séléné, who squeezed me and pressed her cheek to mine.

"How are you faring?" she asked.

"This drink is going straight to my head," I said with a laugh.

"Oops. I brought you another glass. I hope you don't mind."

I set down my empty flute and sipped from the full one she offered me, and she sipped from hers, her eyes sparkling with mischief as we watched each other.

"I wish I could be as direct as you," I said. "You're so brave in saying what you think." I was already regretting that I hadn't asked Harlequin more questions. Séléné certainly would have.

"You needn't be timid with me. Say anything you like."

"Well then ... what did you mean about the Bastille?"

"Oh, that. It wasn't my fault at all. It was a terrible thing, so sad. Looking back, I do wonder if there was more I could have done to stop it."

"You don't have to tell me, if you don't want to talk about it."

"No, no, it's fine. A young officer who was in love with me took his own life in my house. He shot himself with a pistol. I cried and cried, and my valet went out to find some soldiers of the *Garde*. When they came in, they arrested me. I was accused of driving him to it by breaking off our affair. It wasn't true at all. I hadn't even realized he was suffering from a private melancholy. He'd given no hint of it and made no threats. I was as shocked and sorrowful as anyone. Anyway, I wasn't in prison for long. Thankfully my friends rallied around and came to my defense, and the investigation cleared me of wrongdoing."

"Goodness gracious," was all I could think to say, drunk as I was.

"Are you done with your wine? Come along with me to the powder room."

I downed the remainder of my drink and let her take my arm and lead me out to the hall. I hadn't known there was a powder room, but another door concealed in the marquetry had been propped open, and it led to a small room for guests with a privy and a dressing table.

When we were done, instead of going back to the salon, she tugged my arm in the other direction, toward the glass-paned doors at the end of the gallery that led out to the garden.

"Let's go outside, just for a little bit," she said. "I bet it's a lovely night. Was there anything else you wanted to ask?"

"Is Harlequin a pimp?"

"Oh ... that would be too strong a way of putting it, I think. He has an eye for feminine beauty, to be sure, not to mention masculine beauty. He likes to see his friends happy, though I've never known him to have an affair himself. If he has, he's been exceedingly discreet about it. Who could blame him? I probably ought to be more discreet myself, but after the Bastille, I sort of gave up."

We were out in the garden now, under a nearly full moon. The air was cool, and the leaves and branches of the trees and bushes swayed gently in the breeze. Séléné had taken a lamp from one of the sconces in the gallery and held it out before us to light our way.

"I think Harlequin likes me," I said, "or maybe detests me. I don't know which. It seems he's always watching me. Yet I feel as though he wants to avoid talking with me."

"More than likely you interest him. You seem just the sort of woman who would. Intelligent, unusual, innocent, and yet sensual at the same time."

"Is that how I seem? But tell me – do you think Harlequin and the Marquis de Boisaulne could be one and the same person?"

Séléné considered. "Since none of us has met the Marquis, I suppose it's possible in theory. Donatien and Ulysse both like to joke that they're really the Marquis, since after all no one's ever seen them together. But with all the busybodies in Paris, one would have to be very secretive indeed to conceal that one was really a Savoyard nobleman. So far as I know, Harlequin has a run-down estate somewhere in Picardy, nothing to speak of apart from the title that went with it, which he doesn't use in any case. Donatien on the other hand, now his family's estate near Dijon is said to be quite elegant with a lot of land attached."

"Harlequin does seem secretive though. Or at least *guarded*. Doesn't he?"

"*Bof.* Enough about him. He's not ever going to have an affair with you, that's all you need to know. Come on, I want to show you something. Have you been out to the standing stone before?"

"The what?"

"The standing stone, at the entrance to the forest."

"Outside the garden? But the gate's always locked tight, and there's no way over the walls."

"Silly, of course there is. But *shhh*, it's a secret."

We'd arrived at the fountain of the spring set into the back wall of the garden. On either side of the fountain were mermaid figures cast in stone and set into the wall. Séléné set down the lantern, grasped the left mermaid statuette with both hands, and pulled down. The statuette shifted forward and downward like a lever, and what had seemed to be a small, bricked-in arch behind the fountain rumbled open, swinging inward to leave just enough space for a person to slip through the gap. She picked up the lantern and we went through the dark entrance. It was a sort of stone tunnel, but I could hear the trickling of the spring above and to the side of us.

Séléné raised the lantern over her head. In the wall of the cavern to our right, the spring coursed along a sort of raised aqueduct, before spilling out the opening to the fountain on the other side of the wall. Trickles of water ran down the sides of the wall and gathered in pools at our feet, draining into another tunnel underneath that led downward to the right. To our left were strange, delicate-looking rock formations suspended from the low ceiling of the grotto, like icicles or dangling tree roots made of stone, interspersed with patches of green, blue, and purple crystals. I drew in my breath in wonder.

"It's beautiful," I said. "Aurore told me there was a grotto."

"Isn't it magical? I thought you'd like it, if you hadn't already discovered it. Those are real jewels, too – emeralds, rubies, sapphires, amethysts, diamonds ..."

We continued forward and the floor of the passage sloped downward and widened. We arrived at a fork, where another tunnel veered off to the left from the main passage and led further down into darkness. Séléné pointed. "Whatever you do, don't go that way, or you might find yourself in an old abandoned quarry under the streets of Paris. I'm not even joking. I've come to Boisaulne that way from Paris, several times before."

We continued along the main passage, which widened still more and sloped upwards, and came out of the cave into the moonlit night. To the side of the entrance of the grotto we'd just come out of stood an upright oblong stone, as tall as a man, like a black sentry.

"That's the standing stone," Séléné said, raising her lantern to illuminate the stone. "My maid in Paris talked about seeing them in the countryside sometimes around her village in Brittany, and in the old sacred places in the forest. She said there are some rather obscene traditions connected with them. They're a remnant of the old heathen beliefs the village priests could never entirely stamp out. They were associated with fertility rituals, and young girls would go and seat themselves atop them for a night, to find themselves lovers, or assure themselves of a fruitful womb."

I blushed a little, strangely aroused by her description and grateful for the darkness as Séléné set her lantern down again. She took me in her arms and embraced me, backing me up against the stone. She nuzzled her lips against my cheek, kissed it, and then began to kiss me on the lips, opening her mouth to mine like a man. Her hands caressed me down my chest and breasts and then she reached down to lift up my skirts and caressed me under them. I pretended to myself I was too drunk to stop her, but a small part of me knew I could stop it if I wished to, and I didn't. She asked me to return her caresses, and I did. It all seemed unreal, like something out of a dream.

When each of us had in turn moaned and shuddered and cried out, she held me half-undressed in her arms for a long time. I thought of Thérion and wondered where he was just then. Would he be angry if he knew I had done this? Had he thought of this happening when he granted my wish for more company? I took heart, remembering the motto Harlequin had laid down in his speech at dinner: We don't speak in the day of the things we do in the night. Perhaps no one else need ever know of this, not even Thérion.

I closed my eyes drowsily for a moment. The sound of twigs snapping under a heavy tread made me open them wide again. Séléné noticed nothing, resting her head on my shoulder. I stayed motionless, watching the path that led out from the grotto entrance into the forest. Was I only imagining it, or did I see the black silhouette of a massively tall and gaunt horned figure moving through the trees toward us? My heart beat a hundred leagues a minute and for a few seconds I was paralyzed with terror, as in a nightmare. Then I shook off my stupor and quickly moved out from under Séléné's embrace, pulling the top of my dress back up and refastening it.

"What is it?" she whispered.

"I'm frightened. Let's go back. Now. At once!"

Before she could respond, I seized her by the hand, snatching up the lantern in my other hand, and dragged her back down into the cave, back along the path through the grotto and up through the arched stone door behind the fountain, into the garden.

"How does it close?" I asked frantically.

"The mermaid, just push it back up."

I scrabbled in the darkness to find the stone mermaid, now jutting headfirst out from the wall as though on a ship's prow. I pushed it back upright against the stone. The gate rumbled back into place as it was before.

I stood there catching my breath, and slowly my heart stopped pounding.

"Did you see that?" I asked.

"See what?"

"The *roi des aulnes*. The Erl-King. Coming toward us from the woods."

"Oh, come, surely not. It was just a deer, I bet, and you mistook it for a monster from a story."

"No, I saw him. He strode on two legs like a tall man, but his head was antlered."

"*Bof.* You've taken a fright somehow. Let's get you into bed."

We made our way through the garden back into the house, where the lights had been extinguished and no more music came from the salon or the music room. We set the lantern back into its sconce in the gallery and at the end of the hall found the anteroom with a low light still burning, like a night lamp waiting for us. By the light of a few of the sconces still lit on each landing, we made it up to the third floor, where we parted ways with kisses on each cheek, I to my chamber and she to hers. The clock struck two as I changed into a fresh chemise and got into bed in the dim glow of the embers in the fireplace.

I fell asleep quickly, my last thought of Thérion and the fact that he had not come to me that night. Or did he come, only to find my bed cold and empty? The beast I saw in the forest – was it him, going in search of me?

IX

I SLEPT THROUGH to mid-morning and took my coffee in the pale
blue and white morning room. The Scotsman had just sat down
when I came in, and Tristan arrived a few minutes after me.
Neither of them commented on my disappearance with Séléné the
night before. They both spoke of what a remarkable place
Boisaulne was, and how charming the party of the previous
evening had been.

Over breakfast, the Scotsman told me he was curious as to
the avenues of education in Savoy compared to his own country,
and so I told him what I could, that it was a country of devout
Catholic faith with a few small pockets of other forms of belief,
with very limited opportunities sometimes in the mountain
villages. I described to him my own education and autodidactic
efforts and, forgetting the rules of the château for a moment,
explained how my son had gone away to school amongst the
Catholics in Annecy and had to hide his Vaudois faith, while my
daughter was being educated by a governess who had come from
Lyon to live with my sister's family on their farm. I didn't mention

that I only knew how my children were being educated because Thérion told me the news he received from my father.

"But I know Annecy well," Tristan said. "I lived there nine years, and much of my own education took place there."

"Did you go to school there?" I asked.

"I studied music there for a time. I was born in Genève, and my father was my earliest teacher. We used to read books aloud together – all through the night sometimes. Then I was sent away to an apprenticeship in a printer's house, where I was miserable – they starved us and we had no rest, and I had no time to read, though I was surrounded by books. So I ran away and crossed the border into Savoy. I'd befriended a priest, though I was raised a Calvinist, and he introduced me to a wealthy lady he had converted, who lived in Annecy. It was agreed she would take me in and provide for my education if I agreed to be baptized a Catholic, which I did. Converting was a practical expedient and didn't matter so much to me. In my heart I've always had my own faith in natural religion, independent of dogma or creed."

"That's quite a story," the Scotsman said. "And then you chose music for a profession?"

"It was a while before I settled on anything," Tristan said. "My benefactress entertained educated men and women who came to visit, and all of her friends were keen to help me find a suitable profession. I gained an interest in botany at her house, since the lady was a great believer in the powers of herbs and had an expert gardener who taught me the varieties of plants and their properties. I didn't see a living in botany, though. Working as a gardener seemed too menial. Then it was found I had a talent for singing, so I studied music and learned enough to make my living as a teacher and copyist and composer."

"A most unusual upbringing," the Scotsman said. "But a good way to feed a wide-ranging and curious mind. You ought to write your memoirs one day. For my part I just went to school in Edinburgh and liked to study, so I kept at it and ended up by writing books."

"Are you thinking of writing a book on education?" I asked.

The Scotsman shrugged. "Oh, probably not a whole book. An essay maybe."

"The challenge of education," said Tristan, "is that men are born in harmony with nature. Our Maker endows us with natural goodness, but society has a degenerating effect on us – on all things, really."

"The view of man in the world fallen from grace," the Scotsman said. "Which some might debate, but if that view were granted, what would you see as the implication for schooling?"

Tristan chewed his bread thoughtfully, swallowed it down with coffee, and answered, "The key thing is that learning shouldn't extinguish the natural light that's in us, but nurture it. Yet it must still prepare us for life in society with its corrupting influences. The aim should be to balance the need of society to form good citizens, by shaping us for civil and cooperative life, against the need for the individual to live for himself by the light of his own good nature and reason."

The Scotsman took a breath and was about to reply when a crash of thunder struck outside. Our eyes were drawn to the window, which now framed black clouds sweeping in over the mountains. Rain began to pour down on the château, its grounds, and the surrounding forest.

"Ah, what a shame," said Tristan. "I hope it doesn't last. I wanted to see the gardens later. I hear they're quite lovely. I'd promised to meet Clio for walk there in the afternoon." He blushed a little as he said it, and the Scotsman looked stern for a moment, then shrugged.

"Who knows how long it could last? One might need an ark to survive this deluge. But I suppose it's as good a day as any to take care of some correspondence I need to write."

"But one can take a pleasant walk inside the château," I said. "It's bigger on the inside than it looks from the outside. In the library alone you could amuse yourselves for days on end. And there are curiosity cabinets in several of the rooms. Scotsman, in fact you might be interested in a chest of local antique artifacts. I haven't found it yet, but Harlequin mentioned there was one, and I think I saw a chest the other day that might have been it. We could look for it and see if it's unlocked or ask Harlequin if he has a key."

"Exploring for treasure," said the Scotsman. "Why not? Could be a right adventure."

We finished our breakfast and set off together in search of the chest. I discovered it half-hidden under a table in a smaller room with cabinets of clocks, sundials, astrolabes, and compasses in curious designs, some with precious stones or metals worked in, some with enamelwork in deep jewel-like colors, some in the form of ships, owls, or dragons. The chest was large and made of heavy dark wood, so Tristan, the Scotsman, and I heaved together to pull it out from under the table. It was unlocked and filled with smaller chests, bags made of cloth and leather, and objects tied up with ribbons or twine, some with labels written on strips of vellum. Just as Harlequin had told me the night I arrived at Boisaulne, the artifacts ranged from coins and spearheads to amulets made of bone or copper crusted over with the green of age. There were wood and stone fragments with carved inscriptions in Latin, and a few that looked even older, in patterns the Scotsman recognized with excitement.

"Extraordinary. They appear to be something like runic symbols. These would have been created prior to the widespread diffusion of Christianity through the region. For all we know even prior to the Roman conquests. They're not unlike the remnants of the old pagan Celts one can sometimes find in ancient barrows in the countryside in the British Isles."

Reverently he pulled out another small box and opened it. I gasped. It was a large round medallion on a plain black ribbon, made of tarnished silver with a figure stamped on it, a man wearing a great antlered mask made of a stag's skull.

"But it's him!" I cried, forgetting myself in my astonishment. "I saw him last night in the forest." I leaned over the box in the

Scotsman's hands to examine it more closely. At the base of the figure, in Latin capitals, the word *CERNUNNOS* was inscribed.

"Who? Who is it? What did you see?" said a deep voice behind us. I turned and realized Harlequin had come into the room and had been watching us examine the contents of the chest. He took a few steps closer and saw what I was looking at.

"Did you go outside the garden?" he asked me quietly.

For a moment I was too stunned to respond. Then I recovered my composure enough to shake my head and pretend to laugh at myself.

"It was just a dream I had last night. I dreamt I saw a figure very like this one, striding through the forest. I was just surprised by it, that's all."

Harlequin regarded me contemplatively.

"I asked a few of the villagers about some of the objects," he said, "whether they could help identify them. The priest was rather frightened of that one. He said it was an old devilish symbol, a forest god who once was worshiped in these parts. I had to promise him it would be destroyed. Of course I did no such thing. I assume Cernunnos was the name of the deity."

Tristan had already gone back to looking at other artifacts in the chest, but the Scotsman nodded and said, "Perhaps from Latin *cornuos,* horn. It might be a co-mingling with the Roman Pan, or a kind of satyr figure."

"Perhaps," Harlequin said.

The Scotsman closed the box with the medallion and returned it to the chest. Later, when no one was looking, I quickly reached under the lid of the box, took the medallion, and slipped it into my pocket. I didn't mean to steal it, but only to borrow it to look at more closely when I was alone. After we'd gone through the rest of the trunk, Tristan excused himself, eager, I suspected, to go in search of Clio to revise their plan for a walk in the garden. The Scotsman withdrew to write his letters, and I was left alone with Harlequin. We walked out to the gallery together.

"Belle-Âme," he said, "tell me truly, did you go outside the garden last night?"

I blushed at his kind tone, patient as though he were a father questioning a lying child.

"I did, but I wasn't alone."

"Who were you with?"

"Séléné showed me the way through the grotto from behind the fountain of the spring, but we didn't even go into the forest. We stayed just outside by the standing stone."

"You must never go that way alone at night. Will you promise me that?"

I nodded. He looked stern for a moment, but then his serious expression relaxed. Slowly he began to laugh. "Did Séléné get to you so soon? You can be flattered, you know, that she made you her very first conquest. Are you blushing?"

I hadn't thought it possible for my face to get any redder. I felt sweat trickle down from under my arm.

"I thought there was a rule," I stuttered. "We don't talk in the day of the things we do in the night."

He pursed his lips, holding back laughter.

"Don't feel bad. Nearly anyone worth pursuing succumbs to her at some point. It just shows you're not ugly or dull. She might seduce someone boring if they're attractive, or someone ugly and interesting, but never anyone both dull and plain."

"You mean to say she has many lovers."

"It's nothing to take seriously. I don't believe she takes it seriously."

"And you? Have you been with her?"

"Me? No," he said flatly. "I'm ugly and dull."

"You're reserved, but not dull. And I don't think you're ugly."

He shrugged but didn't seem unhappy. "And did you enjoy it?"

"I – I'd had so much wine. I'm not accustomed to it." I lowered my eyes, and then gasped. On the white of Harlequin's shirt-sleeve that protruded from his jacket cuff, there appeared to be a large dark bloodstain. "Are you injured?" I pointed to his sleeve.

He quickly tucked the hand with the bloody sleeve into the bosom of his waistcoat. "It's nothing." He avoided my eyes. "The wagoner came from the village to deliver supplies, and there were fresh skins and carcasses in the courtyard that I helped him load into the cart to take back. I must have gotten some of the blood on me. I'll go and change my shirt."

He strode off toward the far end of the gallery, pulled aside a hanging tapestry, and opened a hidden door behind it that he went through and pulled shut after him.

I shook my head, wondering. It struck me he didn't seem to think the Marquis would be angry with me for what I had done at the edge of the woods with Séléné. It was imprudent of me to tell him, but wouldn't he have let me know if he thought I had done the Marquis a grave wrong?

In the late afternoon I was saved from boredom by taking tea and a light meal with Aurore and Clio. I admitted to them I had drunk too much the night before and had a headache. Aurore worriedly felt my brow with the back of her hand, and her motherly touch and manner soothed me.

"I just hope it's nothing worse," Aurore said. "It'd be too much of a shame to fall ill here at Boisaulne."

"I'm sure it's nothing." I closed my eyes for a moment. "I think the tea will help."

"I'm exhausted, too," Clio said. "I'm so glad it rained. I'd made rather too many plans for today, and it was good to have an excuse to stay in my room and set up my painting supplies."

"Do you mean to paint while you're here?" Aurore asked.

"But of course. A day in which I don't do any painting feels wasted to me. And I have to keep practicing what I've learned or else I'll forget the techniques."

Aurore plopped a sugar lump into her tea and passed the bowl to me. "Have you learned painting from anyone besides your father?" she asked Clio.

"I'm to begin an apprenticeship in the fall with a lady painter who takes young women as students. I admire her work a good deal and I think she'll be a fine teacher. I shouldn't like to disappoint her by forgetting too much before then in idleness."

"Do you have enough room in your chamber to paint?" I asked.

"It's a perfect space," Clio said. "If the sun ever comes out again, it'll have excellent light. I'm a bit fanatical about light."

"Donatien calls this place the Castle of Enlightenment, the *Forteresse des Lumières*," I said. "I suppose if there's any place to be fanatical about light, it's here."

Clio laughed "But I hope there's not too much light. I need plenty of shadows too, or else nothing will work. I've experimented with two different ways of painting. One way is you start with a light-colored background, and then you put in the pastels and grays, and over that you add a layer of the bright colors, and last of all the shading, the darker colors, dark grays, and black. Another way, that's harder and uses more paint, is to start with a black background, and paint the dark and then the bright colors over it, and last of all the lightest colors and bits of pure white, as highlights and glints of light. Leonardo da Vinci claimed it was the true way to paint, to begin every canvas with a wash of black, since all things in nature are dark except where exposed to the light. Papa never used that method, but I prefer it. Either way, it makes you see everything differently, in your mind to be always calculating how you'd paint it. In the sunniest meadow landscape, or the fairest skin for a portrait, you see the black. And in the night, your eye picks out the white."

Aurore nodded agreement. "I like the way you describe it. I should like to see your paintings."

"I'd like to paint you – to paint everyone here, in fact. But I wouldn't ask it of you, or the others. It's a lot of dull work, sitting for a portrait, and most are here to amuse themselves, I think."

"I bet any of the gentlemen would sit for you," I couldn't resist saying. "I think you're very admired. They'd be glad to have an excuse to talk with you and pay their regards."

Clio looked at me quizzically, as if examining my remark for any hint of jealousy or malice.

"But I don't think they'd be very pleased if they tried it," she said. "When I paint, I'm all business. I don't like to talk much since I'm concentrating on my work. I find if people talk there's a temptation to accompany their speech with gestures, which spoils the pose."

"Well, I'd sit for you," Aurore said. "I'd be flattered to have my portrait painted."

"What if I read aloud to you sometimes while you sat for it?" I asked. "Perhaps that would help make it less tedious. Clio, would it distract you too much?"

"Not at all. I won't hold you to it if you change your mind," Clio said, "but I'd like that very much. If it pleases you, we could start tomorrow morning. It'll be far more amusing for me than painting still lifes."

"Only don't read me anything too funny," Aurore cautioned me. "Not *The Indiscreet Jewels,* or any books by Voltaire, or Molière plays. Or else I'll come out looking like a gargoyle from laughing the whole time."

"Very well," I said, "only serious and lofty things that give you a faraway noble look in your eye."

She nods solemnly. "Racine tragedies."

"Perhaps a scientific tract of Bouffon, or a d'Alembert essay on mathematics," I suggested.

"If you mean for me to look constipated," Aurore said, "then certainly."

Clio had to swallow to avoid spitting out her tea before she burst out laughing. "But you know, if you'd like a quicker portrait in ink or charcoal, you could always ask Harlequin to sketch you. He's not bad, unless he's trying to make a caricature of someone on purpose."

"Harlequin draws too?" I asked.

"Didn't you know? Of course his style's as different as could be from mine. He doesn't work in oils much but does drawings in ink on paper. His alter ego's rather notorious in Paris. If the authorities found out who he was, I bet they'd throw him into prison in the tower of Vincennes."

"Why? Are the drawings obscene?"

Clio laughed. "No. Well, mostly not. They're political."

Aurore nodded. "My friend's gazette publishes his caricatures. They can be quite cutting toward the ministers and courtiers. It's a good thing he signs them Harlequin, instead of his real name, or there could be trouble. But most of the gazette's authors write under *noms de plume* to be on the safe side. A woman I know whose father is in the book policing ministry told me the gazette is on the list of the most illegal titles, but as long as it's all anonymous, they can't do much more than confiscate the copies wherever they find them."

I remembered the police raid on my late husband's bookshop and shuddered.

Since our tea was almost a light supper and my headache was only just beginning to recede, I skipped going down to the evening meal in the great hall and resolved to go to bed early. I blushed, too, at the thought of seeing Séléné at dinner and preferred to avoid her, at least for the day. I dozed off quickly in my room before it was even quite dark.

I woke again in the night. I lay there a while, trying to fall back asleep, thinking of Thérion and missing his arms around me. I heard the clock strike half past something. If he was coming to me that night, I didn't know how much longer I still had to wait for him. But I was wide awake, restless, impatient, anxious I wouldn't see him.

I put on my slippers and tied my dressing gown around me. The hall was dark, so I lit a candle and took it with me. My pacing brought me to the end of the hall (was it really the end or was there another hidden door behind it?) and I turned around and paced back to the morning room. Back and forth, from one end of the floor to the other I went, several more times, until a sound from one of the rooms stopped me.

It was the sound of someone slapping someone, of skin striking skin. As I came closer to one of the doors in the hall the sound grew louder. Light came out of a large keyhole in the door. I crouched down, peered through the keyhole, and found it gave a full enough view of the inside of the room to see the source of the noise. It was Donatien and Séléné. Séléné was naked except for her stockings and ribbon-trimmed garters. Donatien wore only his shirt, which was bunched up around his waist as he perched on the bed with one foot on the floor. Séléné's hands had been bound to the bed post by cords, and she knelt on her elbows and knees with her face to the wall. Donatien was slapping her bottom with the flat of his palm. With each slap she cried out, with what sounded like pleasure as much as pain. I was horrified, embarrassed, and aroused, and I couldn't look away.

Finally Donatien lay off beating her and began to copulate with her violently from behind. She groaned and cried, begging him for more. I stood up, hot-faced, and went back down the hall, back to my own room, and climbed back into my bed. I curled up with my knees under my chin.

"Oh, Thérion, where are you?" I said aloud.

"I'm here," said a voice from the sofa by the fireplace where the fire had gone out. I might have guessed he was there from how the room had gone completely dark.

"I missed you."

I heard the tread of his shoes across the wooden floor and felt his weight settle onto the side of the bed as he sat and removed his shoes. I sat up and reached out and found his shoulders wrapped in his coat. I pushed the coat off him and began to undress him. At last he was naked, and I pulled off my chemise as he climbed into the bed next to me and wrapped his body around mine. I let out a sob of relief and longing. He kissed my eyes and cheeks and tasted the salt of my tears.

"Violaine, what's wrong? It's only two nights since I saw you last. Are you unwell?"

I told him about the night before, about all that had happened with Séléné, seeing the alder-king in the woods, and what I'd just now witnessed taking place between Séléné and Donatien. As I talked he caressed me, and when I left off speaking, he kissed me and made love to me, more roughly than before. My pleasure in it was intense, and I did as I had seen Séléné do, crying out loudly and asking for more. When it was finished, we lay in each other's arms and he asked me how I had felt with Séléné, and when I had watched her with Donatien, whether I had felt afraid, ashamed, or aroused. I admitted I had felt all of those things.

"I know these people," he said, "or I feel as if I do from what Harlequin has told me of his guests."

I was quiet. One thing I wouldn't tell Thérion was that while he had made love to me, I had imagined him as Harlequin.

He went on, "I told you from the beginning, my purpose in bringing you here was to make you more free. It's for you to choose whether and with whom you make love. I can't begrudge you any pleasure, though it'd be a lie to say I'm not envious of Séléné enjoying your charms. I suppose I take some consolation from the circumstances, that perhaps it was only a passing pleasure – one mad night of dancing and drinking, rather than a strong and deep liaison that might replace me. It would grieve me greatly if it were the latter."

"It was no more than that, I swear it. I'd never want to grieve you. I care for you very much. I was so frightened you'd stay away and I wouldn't see you again, or you'd be angry with me. I was so happy you'd granted my wish to see other people here during the day, but I worried the cost might be losing my nights with you."

"I was going to tell Harlequin he couldn't invite guests this summer, as he has in the past, until you said you wished for friends. I wasn't sure you'd want anyone else intruding on your solitude here – I feared enough to do it myself until you called for me. But Harlequin draws talented and interesting people to himself. I'm glad you're happy. There's nothing I love more than seeing you that way."

"Aurore told me Harlequin had made a habit in the past of introducing young women to that man Ulysse, and that Ulysse takes them under his wing and makes them his protégées. I wondered if that had anything to do with his finding me and arranging for me to come here. I thought perhaps ... perhaps once you'd had me, you wouldn't want me anymore, and I was to be passed on to Ulysse."

He chuckled. "I have my opinion of Ulysse, but I won't try to influence you for or against him. You should be free to form your own judgment as to what you think of him."

"I've barely spoken with him so far, though we danced together a few times. He doesn't seem interested in me, but he has the air of a rake, I think – a man who's larger than life. He paid a lot of attention to Clio. She's an artist, like Harlequin, and very young, but intelligent."

"Yes, I've heard about Clio too. It sounds as though no one ought to underestimate her, even if she looks like an ingénue. But listen, you mustn't doubt, I want you more than ever. You should never imagine I mean to cast you off, just because Harlequin likes to play the role of matchmaker, like an old grandmother from one of your mountain villages."

"Is that really all it is? He's not some kind of pimp or procurer?"

"I respect his privacy too much to tell you all I know of him. Suffice it to say he's one of those men who's kinder to others than he is to himself."

Now, more than ever, I was convinced in my heart that Harlequin and Thérion were one and the same, but something held me back from pressing him on it. If I loved him – and I believed I did – would it be kind of me to unmask this man who for whatever reason felt it necessary to play these games of hiding in the dark? If it was truly him, he must have his reasons for keeping me at the distance of night and blindness. And suppose I was wrong? Would it do me any good to learn he wasn't the man I had pictured when we made love? Didn't it increase my pleasure to imagine him as the one to whom I was most attracted, of all those I had seen? I was aware that I owed this pleasure to the darkness and to his gift of remaining mysterious to me. And so I became a willing participant in my own blinding.

X

I PASSED A pleasant morning reading to Aurore in Clio's sitting room while Clio began work on the portrait. Out of curiosity, I chose a book by Ulysse to read, which turned out to be full of irreverent humor and mockery, so that Clio had to break off her work several times because all three of us were convulsing with laughter. We looked through Clio's other sketches and the paintings she had stored in her portfolio. Though I knew little of drawing and painting, I was struck at once by her gift for bringing out the beauty in her subjects. There were self-portraits and sketches of still lifes – flowers, fruits, insects – and many drawings of her younger brother and of her family's and neighbors' pets – dogs, cats, and a little green bird in a cage. There were sketches of the neighbors too, generally young mothers, alone or with their children. The common thread among the sketches of people was the natural way her subjects were posed and dressed.

Before we went down for our dinner at midday, Aurore pulled me aside and gently touched a spot on my neck.

"You … have a few red marks. Here." She took off the neckerchief she'd tied around her own neck and arranged it on mine. She fussed with it a good long while, trying to pin it just right, and then gave up and asked Clio if she had any ribbons we could borrow instead. When Clio had found some, Aurore wrapped a wide one around my throat and tied it with a bow in back. Only then was she satisfied.

The whole company was present for the midday meal. For a moment or two I thought a new young gentleman had joined us, before I realized Séléné had dressed herself in a man's breeches, stockings, shirt, waistcoat, and coat, all elegantly cut and tailored perfectly to her small, compact figure. She laughed at our surprise.

"I'm much more comfortable like this. You should try it sometime. I like coming to Boisaulne because I can dress however I want here."

In truth it seemed impractical to me, to go without stays and have to unbutton breeches and pull them down every time one had to make water. But I was relieved the general excitement produced by her dress spared me the embarrassment of any reference to our night together by the standing stone. Her neck and chest weren't covered by a handkerchief or ribbon or collar, but there were no blue or purple marks to be seen on her white skin. I supposed hers must be all below the waist. A part of me wished I could ask Aurore if she had ever been seduced by Séléné as I had been, but at the same time I was glad for the rules of Boisaulne that discouraged such conversations in the day. Although, in truth, it seemed the rules were often ignored.

When Aurore, Clio, and I told the others how we had spent our morning, everyone was eager to join in our new project. It was agreed we would take turns reading to Aurore while she sat for her portrait, and whoever else wished to hear the reading could sit in on it too.

Tristan claimed the next slot for reading aloud and offered to read us his favorite novel.

"What's it about?" Clio asked.

"It's the story of two noble souls, a man and a woman in a small town at the foot of the Alps, who fall in love with each other, but society places obstacles in the way of them being together. The woman must marry another whom she respects but does not love with passion. She and the hero surmount the difficulty by forming a spiritual union that allows them to be true lovers even while they're kept apart."

Clio screwed up her freckled face prettily. "Hmm, I don't know. It sounds like a rather sad story, if the lovers never come together."

"It's total tripe," said Ulysse. "I know the one you mean. It's an absurd travesty of a storyline. It takes a rake and strumpet and paints them in lovely colors so she becomes a philosopher and he a prince. I'd rather read a story where a rake is admitted to be what he is and he and his strumpet at least end up happy together."

"There's no disputing tastes," the Scotsman said, "but I suppose with a story like that it comes down to whether one is an idealist or a materialist."

"Does it?" said Séléné. "As if those were the only two alternatives. Isn't there a third way, some more moderate view in between?"

"I've been struggling to find that compromise in my own philosophy, that takes account of the best and truest points of both," the Scotsman admitted. "By nature I'd say I'm inclined to moderation, though I recognize sometimes extreme circumstances require extreme actions."

"Such as?" Séléné asked.

"Well, for example, a case of extreme evil. If you meet a man who wishes to destroy you, unprovoked, it may be the most moral response to defend one's life by any means necessary, including inflicting a fatal wound upon him."

"No one with half a brain would dispute that," Ulysse said. "Though our idealistic Tristan might say it's better to let him kill you."

"Indeed, it might be," Tristan said. "If one's principles are absolutely against killing or violence."

"In that case, it seems your principles would amount to suicide," Donatien interjected.

"Perhaps even suicide might be an honorable course of action in some cases," Tristan replied.

The Scotsman said, "I've argued as much in print, myself. But there are those who'd counter that it's the very definition of evil to disregard the sanctity of life, even one's own."

"And I would agree with them," Aurore said, looking to Clio and me for confirmation. "For my part I can't think of a scenario where I could condone suicide. So long as one is alive, one can always strive to better one's condition, to do good, and to make the best of one's God-given gift of existence."

A part of me wanted to agree with her, but another part remembered the terrible loneliness of the darkest days of my marriage, when I had lost my faith in the God of my childhood. If I hadn't had Valentin, Aimée, and my father to think of, who knows? Perhaps my despair might have overcome me.

As though responding to my thoughts, Harlequin said, "Sometimes, perhaps, a person might take his own life out of cowardice. Far more often I think of those who do, it's because they've faced extremes of despair or anxiety or misery. They're to be viewed with compassion, rather than judgment."

Séléné nodded vigorously, and I remembered the story of her young lover who had killed himself.

"But I'm of Aurore's opinion," Clio said. "It's never right. The breath of life in a human being is a divine, sacred thing."

"What about killing in times of war?" the Scotsman said. "What if the unrest spreads in the capital of France, for example, or if the King of Sardinia orders the Savoyards to go to war with the French or the Swiss over disputed territory? Suppose you or your menfolk were called upon to fight. Would it be just then, to follow the sovereign's orders and defend one's country?"

"Unthinking allegiance to sovereigns is an abdication of moral agency," Tristan said firmly.

"For once we're in agreement," Ulysse said. "Sovereign powers, whether church or state, have their own interests, independent of morality. It may be that sometimes the state's interests coincide with what's moral and right for an individual, but only the individual can judge whether that's so, by consulting his conscience and reason."

"I should say by consulting his heart," said Tristan.

"Ah," the Scotsman laughed, "another topic for another essay. Can we trust feeling as surely as reason?"

"Far more so, I think. Absolutely," said Tristan.

"Reason can be mistaken, but desire doesn't lie." Donatien said, meeting Aurore's eyes. "When you see someone or something beautiful, you know without a doubt you desire it. You don't have to scratch your head over it."

Aurore's cheeks turned pink, and she looked away.

Séléné laughed out loud, and there was a hard edge to her words. "But that's utter rubbish. Desire and feeling depend on perception. And perception fools us all the time. One sees a stag in the woods at night, for example, and mistakes it for a monster out of a fairy tale."

"It's true," Aurore said. "In fairy tales it often happens that someone's senses are enchanted and they fall prey to an illusion. The princess in the tale of Peau d'Âne disguises herself in a donkey's skin to escape from her father, who wants to marry her. In the story of the Path of Needles and the Path of Pins, the wolf deceives the girl and makes her believe he's a safe and comfortable grandmother so he can lure her in and eat her."

Donatien kept his gaze on Aurore and said in a gentle tone, "Fairy tales are only meant to frighten children and terrify pious peasants. When I feel enchanted by someone charming, I can usually trust it's not a wicked sorcerer deceiving me." He smiled at Aurore, and she looked up and smiled back at him shyly.

"There is truth at the heart of those tales, though," Aurore said. "That's why they're told over and over again. People aren't always what they seem and our impressions aren't always reliable."

"Isn't deception the essence of all seduction?" Harlequin asked. "To create an appearance of beauty or love that conceals the mere desire for conquest, for dominance?"

Donatien drew his brows together. He seemed to be considering a reply when Clio interrupted.

"Well," Clio said, laying a hand on Tristan's arm, "you can read that book to us if you like. Perhaps it'd be interesting. In any case, it will give us something to talk about."

After the rapid volleys of conversation over the meal, I wanted to go out for an afternoon walk in the garden, since the clouds and constant downpour of cold rain had finally broken. I wanted to be alone for a while, to think about all that had happened in the past two days since the others had arrived. So I slipped out of the hall into the privy room and waited until the gallery was empty. From there I slunk out to the garden unnoticed, and into the labyrinth of hedges and tall bushes where I could hide if I heard anyone coming. How beautiful the flowers and plants were, washed clean from the rain! I walked down the paths, shaded by arbors and trellises of clematis, honeysuckle, and roses, stopping now and then to watch bees dipping in and out of the cups of the petals. After an hour of walking, I sat down on a bench in the sun across from an elaborately woven spider web. Its maker, the size of a hazelnut and shiny black, clung to the center. The spider's forearms were busy, turning a piece of prey back and forth, back and forth, encasing it in a white cottony cocoon.

I heard voices approaching, Séléné's and Ulysse's. I stood up to dart around the spider's web into the bushes behind it. In this way I succeeded in avoiding the two speakers, but unwittingly stumbled nearly into the laps of a silent couple sitting on another stone bench. Donatien pressed close to Aurore, with one hand at her waist and another laid against her chest. When Aurore saw me, she pulled away from him and jumped up as if stung. He stood up too, and I averted my eyes so as not to stare at the erection under his breeches. He smiled at us both.

"Good day, Belle-Âme," he said. "It's a pretty afternoon, isn't it?"

Aurore wrung her hands, blushing and trembling, and then put a hand to her hair and realized that her coiffure was half undone. Without a word and without meeting my eyes, she plunged forward, nearly breaking the spider's web before I grabbed her arm and said, "Wait," and pointed out the shiny black creature that was a hair's breadth from her arm. She gave me a grateful look and skirted around it, and I followed after her. Donatien stayed behind.

I took Aurore's arm to steady her and we walked arm in arm. "What was that?" I asked her.

She took a deep, shuddering breath. "I don't know ... I ... Donatien was being so sweet and sympathetic to me. I let things go farther than I should have. I've never in my life been unfaithful to my husband, though it's been years since he's touched me."

I walked her to the house, through the gallery, and up the stairs to her own room on the third floor. I didn't know if it was right to tell her what I had witnessed the night before between Donatien and Séléné, since it might reflect badly on Séléné. I didn't wish to harm Séléné in her friend's eyes, or seem as if I wished to create bad blood between them, or to disobey the rules of Boisaulne.

"I'll lie down. I don't feel well," she said. She no longer trembled, but her face was white as a moonflower and the skin around her eyes was drawn.

"Are you sure you'll be all right?"

"I'm fine, thank you. I just want to rest for a little."

We parted with kisses on each cheek.

Aurore, Donatien, and Séléné were all absent from the table at supper. Ulysse, Tristan, and the Scotsman got into a long discussion about whether the soul might be a separate and different kind of substance from the body. Tristan believed it was of a spiritual nature, like love. The Scotsman believed it consisted of the action of ordinary physical substances such as the brain and the other organs of a human being, rather than being a separate kind of substance unto itself.

"When Galileo dropped cannonballs out the window of his tower, he performed the experiment to observe the effects of gravity and the resistance of the air. But no one would posit – and he certainly didn't – that the downward movement of the balls was a substance unto itself. Rather, the state of movement was the balls' potential energy that was being actualized. So it is also with the action of the brain, when it directs the body and its thoughts and movements. It's that action, I believe, that has been given the name of the soul."

Ulysse, for his part, didn't doubt the materialist position. He was mainly concerned with drawing out its implications for morality and ethics.

"If there's no separate soul to save or lose, that means morality isn't spiritual, but rather practical. For the ancients, indeed, morals or *mores* were practices – the way one chose to live one's life, not divine injunctions. Therefore, our morals, our ethical practices, must be determined by our material circumstances."

"But the implications of that are rather monstrous, don't you think?" said Tristan. "Is it justified then for a hungry man to steal? Or for a lustful person to commit adultery? After all, those are material circumstances."

"Well, that's the question. On what basis do we determine morality if material circumstances are all we have to go on? There's still the matter of the need to preserve order and justice in society, for the good and safety of all. But the best start we can make toward forming a truly just society is to throw out authoritarian dictates regarding moral principles, based on old and false notions of a divide between body and soul."

Tristan launched into a passionate defense of conscience and moral sentiment as functions of the soul and contended they ought to be the true basis of moral judgments.

I listened along with the others and thought about the points and questions the three of them raised. I stored up thoughts to talk over with Thérion, when he came that night. Harlequin sat next to me again, and once or twice his hand brushed against mine and he looked at me sidelong, surreptitiously, his long reddish lashes lowering and hooding his pale silver eyes. Was it his lips, his teeth, his tongue, that had left the marks on my neck under the ribbon? The thought aroused me and half-consciously, in my reverie, I stroked the tines of my fork. I glanced up at him again to see that his eyes were fixed on the movement of my fingers. He looked away quickly.

After supper, coffee and sweets were served in the music room, but I chose not to linger and left to go upstairs to my chamber. As I passed by Séléné's door, I heard a sound coming out of the keyhole again and couldn't resist bending down and glancing through it into the room to see if Donatien was with her. I made out a form huddled on her bed. She appeared to be alone, weeping as if her heart would break.

For a moment I wondered what to do. I tapped lightly on her door. She looked up, dabbed at her eyes with a handkerchief, and came to open the door. Her face fell a little when she saw it was me.

"Are you all right?" I asked. "I was passing by and I thought I heard a noise."

She sniffled. Her eyes were red, puffy, and swollen. "I'm fine. Just ... tired."

"Are you sure? Would you like to talk?"

"You can come in if you like." She drew me in and we sat on opposite ends of a sofa against the wall, facing each other.

"What happened?" I asked.

"Oh, I'm just an idiot. I made a mistake, trusting someone I shouldn't have trusted."

"Who?"

"Donatien. *Fils de pute.*" She punched the sofa cushion with enough force to shake the whole sofa. "But I guess he can't be blamed for abandoning me. I'm old and used up."

"What nonsense. What did he do to you? Did he hurt you?"

"It was all right at first. It was fun. He was different and it was rather exciting. What I didn't like was that he changed toward me from one day to the next, with no explanation. He made me think he cared about me. He spent a whole month writing me dear little notes, charming and flirting with me. He finally made his conquest, a couple of weeks ago, and we'd been meeting discreetly whenever we could. Then suddenly today, he was as cold to me as could be. He's chasing after Aurore, I think just because she has a reputation for being virtuous and incorruptible. He joked about what an accomplishment it would be if anyone seduced her, but I thought he was only teasing."

"It did seem he was paying attention to her and she seemed troubled by it."

"Well, I saw him go into her room just as I was coming up the stairs. So she can't have been as troubled as all that."

"Really? That surprises me. I hope she's all right." I thought for a long moment. "Do you think I ought to go and check on her? Suppose he's not a gentleman with her?"

Séléné snorted. "A gentleman. Right. I mean, I don't think he's so bad as to force himself on a woman. He prefers the thrill of the chase, and overpowering a woman by force wouldn't please his vanity so well as being able to talk her into it so she gives herself to him. He had me practically pursuing him in Paris."

I frowned. "I hope you're right and she'll be safe."

"Safe – that's another matter. He doesn't care what damage he does or whom he hurts."

"Oh, Séléné, I'm sorry. You don't deserve to be hurt like this."

"Perhaps I do."

"Why should you?"

"I'm a fool. I make terrible choices regarding men. I'm always getting my feelings hurt."

"But you seemed so confident. I thought perhaps, if you have had many love affairs, they might not mean much to you."

"You must have heard about my reputation. I can't say I haven't earned it. Yes, I've had many lovers. I'm not ashamed of that. I certainly take pleasure in the act itself, when the fellow's up to it and has some sense of what he's doing. And it was lovely with you the other night."

I stared down at my hands and felt sweat gathering along my brow and under my arms. This was exactly what I had hoped we wouldn't ever talk about. I swallowed and began to stammer, "I hadn't ever done anything like that before. I'm not normally ..."

"*Shhh*, don't worry about it," she said, laying a hand on my arm for a moment. "What I mean to say is, sometimes it is just fun. But having many encounters doesn't mean I have no feelings. I told you, didn't I, about my late husband?"

"A little. It sounded as if you had a terrible time with him."

"Well, after he died, I decided I'd never let anyone else determine what I did with my body ever again. I claimed my freedom. Do you know, one of my *chevaliers* wanted to marry me so badly he contrived to put a child in my belly, thinking that would persuade me. But I gave the child up to the foundling hospital. I wasn't going to let myself be bullied into marrying again, not after having a husband who used to beat me and force himself on me. You look horrified. I've shocked you, haven't I?"

"I ... never mind. Go on."

"The thing is, once you have the freedom to choose your own life, and to choose any lover who will have you, then you have the hope of finding something satisfying. It's hard to fail at it, again and again. If I couldn't hope to find true love, I shouldn't feel so miserable, perhaps, every time things fizzle."

"I think I understand what you mean. May I ask – what happened to the child?"

"The child? Oh, the foundling hospital you mean. It all turned out all right. The boy's father took charge of his upbringing and education, which was only right, given that I had no choice in the matter of giving him life."

"Ah."

"But tell me, you're a widow," she said. "Don't you find your freedom exhilarating? Or do you miss being married?"

"Goodness, no, I don't miss it." I didn't tell her I wasn't free, but a prisoner of the Castle of Enlightenment.

"What do you think you'd like in a lover? You know, ideally."

"Well ... someone kind, strong, intelligent, faithful ... I suppose I hadn't really thought about it in a long time. When I was married I read romances and dreamed of a knight who'd be chivalrous and devoted, who would rescue me and defend me. But in my dreams the details were always hazy. What about you?"

"I've thought about it a good deal," she said. "I long for a union of the mind as well as of the body. Perfect harmony. We might quarrel, but we do so lovingly, from a shared love of ideas, in the furtherance of our learning and knowledge together. Neither of us would ever be subordinate to the other. We'd be equals. We'd support each other in our intellectual efforts. He wouldn't mind my writing, or make fun of it, but would be proud of it, and I'd be proud of him too, whatever his field of endeavor."

"And you've never met anyone who seemed able to live up to that ideal?"

"There've been those who said they were in love with me. Those who wanted to take up all my time. Those who were good in character but unbearably dull. Men like Donatien who were exciting but vicious. Those who only cared to make love and never stimulated my mind or my imagination."

"I wonder – what do you think of Ulysse? I thought I heard the two of you talking together today in the garden."

"Ulysse? Ah, that's a long and complicated story. We've known each other for years and years. When we first met we fell straight into bed with each other. Then we quarreled and I broke it off with him, but we've stayed friends. He's more like me than any man I've ever known. Perhaps we're too alike to be lovers. Yet we always seem to be drawn back to each other."

"Do you think he means to make a protégée of Clio?"

"It's possible. If he doesn't I think I shall. She's a wonderful little person. Gifted, clever, charming and pretty. Someone certainly ought to help her."

I nodded. "If she wants help, that is."

Leaving Séléné distracted and comforted by new thoughts, I hoped, I settled into bed to wait for Thérion. When the lights at last went out and he arrived, he asked me whether I'd like to try with him some of the things I had seen Donatien and Séléné do. I was a little frightened, but I said yes.

"Whenever you want me to stop," he said, "if it gets to be too much, you only have to tell me and I'll stop." His voice went a note deeper. "Sit up and turn around, on your hands and knees. Yes, like that. Now put your hands here." He guided my hands and I let him tie them to the bedpost with soft cords. He ran his hands along my prone, bent body, from my breasts to my knees, and pressed his hard *sexe* against the back of my thighs with a low groan. He wove the outstretched fingers of one hand through my unpinned hair, closed his fist around it, and began my punishments.

In the nights that followed, our lovemaking grew increasingly rough and passionate. We talked less as time went on, for Thérion was always hungry for me, and I for him. He tested and pushed my boundaries, binding me, mastering me, teaching me, teasing me, even tormenting me, but the pleasure always outweighed the pain. Sometimes we switched places, and he gave me the upper hand, as much as my blindness with him allowed. I missed our conversations but was too caught up in our explorations of each other's bodies in the night to insist on pausing the language of touch for the sake of speech. There would be time enough for talking of books and philosophy after my new friends had gone home for the autumn, when years had passed, when we'd grown old together, when we'd long since learned every atom of each other's skin, when every time we made love no longer felt like the revelation of a new Eden, a new heaven and earth.

Sometimes I wondered dreamily during the days, as the others debated politics, metaphysics, science, and morals, whether I had only one lover, or two, or many. Was Thérion really every man at Boisaulne, coming to me in turn? I came to love each of them in their own way. Above all Harlequin, who excited me with his air of mingled reserve, attentiveness, and humor, always speaking little but listening keenly and watching with his silver-blue eyes, sleek and dangerous-looking in his dark, rich dress, with his high cheekbones, dress sword, and ebony earrings. Tristan with his idealism and guilelessness, his opinions always contrary and his manner sensitive, gentle, and melancholy. The Scotsman, who was always kind, sensible, and moderate, ugly and steady as a rock. Donatien with his elfin beauty, sensuality, and seductive charm. Ulysse with his roaring laugh, skewering every form of injustice and hypocrisy with his boundless energy and ruthless sarcasm.

Later that week, I saw Séléné lead Tristan into the garden toward the fountain of the spring after dinner. On the same evening, Aurore confessed to me that she had let Donatien take her.

"I don't know how to feel about it. I always believed in honoring my vows. I'm no Deist like the rest of you – I still hold to my faith in the truths of the Church. But then it didn't seem I'd harm my husband or anyone else by it, which makes it hard to feel too terrible about it. It's been so long since I felt wanted by a man or wanted one in return."

"And – how was it, being with him?" I asked her.

"It was … strange. He was very passionate. But I expected my pleasure to be more. I felt as though he was mainly interested in taking something from me, not in giving to me. I felt hollow afterward, and he wasn't very affectionate. I suppose I regret it. Though not as much as I probably ought to."

That was her initial confession to me, but her mood worsened and her regret seemed to increase as time passed and Donatien continued to toy with her – taking her up and dropping her, repeatedly and coldly, even as he pushed her to do things she'd never considered doing in the bedroom before. At last she broke with him, only to be met with harsh indifference. After this I noticed Donatien began to watch me all the time, much as Harlequin always had, in a hungry way. At the same time he began to pay more attention to Clio.

I was not immune to his charm and felt inclined to forgive him. It was hard to turn my eyes away from him when he was in the room. His clothes were always near works of art in their tailoring and trims, their gorgeous fabrics and colors, and he moved with the confident grace of a lynx. As long as I didn't succumb to his seductions, as long as I took wisdom from Séléné's and Aurore's suffering, I supposed there was no reason why I couldn't admire him from a safe distance, appreciating the good in him and evading the bad.

I consented to walk with him in the garden one day, for I was curious to hear his side of why things had gone the way they did with Aurore. I had never met a man so free of scruples where seduction was concerned, and I felt a kind of botanist's interest in studying and examining his character, trying to see into and understand the soul that underlay it.

"I know Aurore must have taken it badly," he told me as we walked through the shaded, sweet-smelling bower under a roof of trellised white roses. "The last thing I ever mean to do is hurt anyone." He heaved a sigh. "But I'm a strange man, I know, inwardly malformed and difficult to love."

"She was very distressed, I can tell you."

137

"It wasn't that I didn't love her, that's what you have to understand. She inspired me, and still does, with her sweetness and virtue."

"Which you wanted to corrupt."

"No! Well, not only." He laughed. "She made me wish to be a better sort of man, the kind she could love and admire. I sent thirty gold *louis* to a charitable organization she favors in Paris, a home for orphans, only in the hope of earning her regard. I thought she seemed lonely, confined as I know she's been in that sham of a marriage to an old invalid. I thought it might give her pleasure to be made love to. Only, I just – I'm restless. I'm no good at patiently following the conventions. And I can't trust my own heart to feel the same from day to day."

I nodded, considering whether perhaps all men felt like this, and the flaw that made him seem villainous to some was only his sincerity and honesty about it. We spoke of his family, of his father, an uncannily successful and shrewd investor whom Donatien had always admired greatly, but who had never paid much attention to his children in his passion for acquiring ever more wealth and influencing the men of the court. Much as Donatien's stories drew me in, I still tried to keep my distance in heart and mind.

"And whom do you intend to seduce next?" I asked boldly. "Clio? Or me, perhaps?"

He laughed and spread out his hands in a gesture of innocence.

"Me, seduce anyone? I don't know where you get these calumnious notions from."

I giggled, and he looked at me with unexpected tenderness.

"Would you like to sit down for a while?" he asked, pointing toward a bench. His eyes went to my waist and traveled back up to my face, full of longing. The pain in them affected me, and for a moment I imagined sitting with him as Aurore had done, letting him put his arm around my waist and lean his head in toward mine. Mightn't it be a pleasure to be with him as long as one had no expectations of a lasting liaison? Thérion had said it was for me

138

to choose with whom I made love. With a twinge of sadness I thought how sitting in the warm afternoon sun on a garden bench with a handsome admirer was something I could never do with Thérion, who would never walk with me in the daylight or allow me to look into his eyes when we made love. If Thérion denied me such simple pleasures, he shouldn't begrudge me taking them elsewhere.

As I stood wavering, my hand slipped down into the pocket of my skirt, where I had taken to keeping the medallion of Cernunnos that I had borrowed from the chest, as if it were a kind of protective talisman. My fingers closed around the metal, and I took in a deep breath and let it out. The solidity of the pendant in my grip, its grooves under my thumb, recalled me to myself.

I made a show of looking up to gauge the distance in hand lengths of the sun from the top of the garden wall. "I ought to be getting back," I said. "I wanted to write a letter before supper."

Donatien's face fell. We turned back to make our way through the labyrinth of hedges out to the path to the arch, but as we passed a shady corner, he took hold of my hand and pulled me back into the shade with him. Stepping behind me, he wrapped his arms around my waist and chest and held me tightly. His movement was so unexpected that I didn't struggle but relaxed into his embrace. He kissed the side of my neck and whispered how beautiful I was, how he thought of me all the time, how I was different from anyone he'd ever known. I felt hot from the warmth of his body pressing against me from behind and dizzy from the biting pressure of his kisses. He began to move his hands down, and then I did struggle to free myself. His grip was iron and didn't loosen.

"Come, what have you got to lose? Let me pleasure you," he whispered. "I need this. I know you long for it too. What's all this enlightenment for, if not so we're free to reach the height of bliss together? No one else need ever know. *Ma foi,* you've the body of a goddess. You were made for love."

"Let go." I wriggled to free myself again, but he laughed and held me tighter. He was too strong for me. "I want to," I said, "you're right, but just not now. I'm not ready yet." His grasp slackened then enough for me to break free. The momentum of pushing away from him carried me several steps forward, and I turned around to face him, breathless, my knees and elbows apart and slightly bent like a wrestler facing an opponent.

He realized then I hadn't mean what I'd said, and his face darkened. He kicked the ground in disgust. "I don't understand you. Can't you see it's cruel to make me want you this way? I'd never hurt you. People think I'm unfeeling but the truth is, I'm alone, and it hurts to be pushed away. I hoped I'd have something lasting with Aurore, but she couldn't love the real me. She only wanted the fantasy. And now you, too."

Had I really hurt him? "I apologize. Please forgive me."

"Is it Harlequin?" he asked softly. "I've seen you look at him."

I stiffened in embarrassment.

"But he'll hurt you, I promise you that," he said. "I've seen it before. He makes women fall in love with him, acting as though he's in love with them. He strings them along as long as he can, for the sake of his vanity, but he never gives them anything. I'm not like that. I'm not withholding. I may not be perfect, but at least with me you know what you have and where you stand."

"I need to go." I turned around and walked quickly, almost running, around the corner of the hedge toward the exit of the maze, away from him, my head spinning with confusion and doubt. He didn't follow.

Ashamed of how I had nearly succumbed to Donatien, and of the parcel of regret and uncertainty that had lodged itself in my soul ever since, I said nothing to Aurore or Thérion about the incident in the garden labyrinth. Mercifully or unmercifully, Donatien left me alone for the most part and we behaved as though it had never happened. Two or three times I caught him looking at me intently from across the library, his book unread in front of him, while I spent the morning at a writing desk working over a poem, but the emotion behind his gaze was unreadable. I wondered, still, if I had truly hurt or upset him with my refusal and if he genuinely had feelings for me.

On another of those mornings in the library, as I made notes to myself about a new poem and gazed idly at the sunlight streaming in through the window shade, the idea came to me of concentrating on the image of Donatien's face as if I were going to write a poem about it. I had often found that when I began a poem this way – when I sat perfectly still and shut out everything from my thoughts and senses but a single image – a kind of intuition drew new knowledge to the surface of my consciousness that I hadn't been aware was in me. But all I could gather from engaging in this sort of meditation on Donatien's expression was a strange sense of ... *nothingness* in him. There was simply a blankness. Was it an absence of esteem for me, perhaps? What my intuition seemed to tell me was that Donatien simply didn't care for me, however charming and outwardly gallant he might be.

When I turned the meditation inward to examine my own feelings, what rose to the surface wasn't so much hurt or annoyance, but a pity twined with tenderness. I felt sorry for him for being so empty, incapable of returning the warmth, affection, and curiosity I had felt for him all the times he had made me laugh or I had admired his beauty and elegance.

I put the discovery to the back of my mind. Aurore, for her part, comforted herself after her disappointment with Donatien by spending more time in the Scotsman's company. I thought surely she couldn't love such an ugly man, especially not after a liaison with such a beautiful one. But the Scotsman became her most faithful and favored reader during her morning sittings with Clio. He read tirelessly and with animation, and in the afternoons they walked together in the garden, *à deux,* or accompanied by others. A quiet mutual respect and admiration grew between them as they spoke of books, the Scotsman's historical research and philosophical writing, and her work in gathering and compiling tales.

One night after dinner she read one of her fairy tales aloud to the company. It concerned a Persian maiden deceived by an ugly, wicked sorcerer who had drunk a potion to give himself the form of a handsome prince. Cast out into a desert and disinherited by her family, she endured trials and misfortunes before finally encountering a wretched beast that was half tiger and half antelope. She showed it kindness by giving it water and drying its tears when it cried over its ugliness. The beast then revealed itself to be the handsome king of a nearby kingdom who had hitherto been under a spell, and he made her his queen.

After that night, the Scotsman began to look at her with the lost expression of a lover. Although he was unfailingly respectful and gentlemanly towards her, he lost no opportunity to take her hand on a rocky part of the path, to lift her over a muddy spot by putting his hands around her waist, or to touch her arm when pointing out a bird or an unusual stone in the garden.

As for Clio, none of her male admirers succeeded very well in charming her. She spent the better part of her days painting and sketching, and neither Donatien nor Ulysse had the patience to sit with her as she worked in silence. Instead they went out riding with Harlequin, or they wandered the galleries of Boisaulne, while Harlequin explained the provenance of the *objets d'art* on the walls and pedestals and in the curiosity cabinets. Otherwise, Ulysse seemed mainly to devote himself to arguments and flirting with Séléné, who matched him with spirited rejoinders and arch teasing. Now and then he looked regretfully at Clio, as though ruing his inability to take a proper interest in her. She was friendly and cordial to him and seemed not to mind his lack of ardor.

Tristan, on the other hand, took great pleasure in watching her work, and she seemed to mind him least of her admirers. She sparked off a loud discussion at dinner by saying how she liked the novel he had read aloud, about the two lovers with their spiritual union. Ulysse was vocally dumbfounded that such an otherwise bright young woman could have such terrible taste in literature. Clio held her ground, insisting the story was fine and moving, and Tristan looked at her in worshipful gratitude.

"But he wouldn't know how to flirt with a girl to save his life," she confided to Aurore and me, talking about Tristan in the morning room over her breakfast chocolate. "And he hardly has a *sou* to his name. He's a genius, but he lives with some stupid laundry woman who can't even read, in a small town outside Paris, in a falling-down rented house. So I suppose we can't ever be anything more than friends. What a bother. Doesn't he have fine eyes, though?" She sighed.

"I'm sure he likes you a good deal," I said.

"And I'm sure his intentions must be honorable, or he wouldn't have told you about the laundry woman or the falling-down house," Aurore pointed out. "Better to have a friend with a good character than a lover with a poor one."

Clio propped her elbow on the table and rested her chin on her wrist dejectedly. "I suppose so."

"But surely he could leave his laundry woman?" I said, arranging a happy ending for my friend in my mind. "Perhaps she doesn't mean so much to him, if he hasn't married her. Have they any children together?"

"He made her *enceinte* a few times, but he couldn't afford to keep a family, so the babies were all given up to the foundling hospital. He's very honest about it."

Aurore and I exchanged glances with raised eyebrows.

"But I like that he's honest," Clio insisted. "There's no harm in our having a friendship is there?"

"He's lucky to have a friend in you," Aurore said. "We all are."

Nearly a month had gone by since I had first met Aurore in the morning room, and I hardly felt myself a prisoner at Boisaulne, now that I was surrounded by such lively companions during my days. The romances and intrigues of my new friends provided me with better entertainment than any theater ever could. It wasn't always enough to distract me from missing Aimée and Valentin, but distraction enough that I felt guilty sometimes over how long I could go without aching for the sight of their faces. My only other twinges of unhappiness came in the form of wistfulness when I thought of Thérion. As I saw my new friends falling in and out of love with each other, I wished for the normalcy, even the banality, of such love affairs. To read together in the library, to walk in the garden together, to sit on a stone bench in the sun with our arms around each other – what delightful luxuries those must be. If only I could gaze on Thérion's face, just once, and caress him with my eyes too, not only with my hands. And suppose it wasn't the face I had dreamt of, suppose it wasn't Harlequin's – what of it? I would discover my true lover then. I was ready to face the truth.

Thérion was adamant, though, and deaf to my entreaties. Now he met them only with silence, as though I had not spoken, and made love to me all the more fiercely until I wept with pleasure, and tears continued to seep from my eyes.

I sought ways to keep a light in my room, hiding candles and lanterns, flints and tinder, but the darkness that accompanied Thérion seemed to be a part of the magic of Boisaulne. My flint wouldn't spark, candles guttered out, the fire died in the fireplace, and the lantern wicks were snuffed out by the mysterious invisible hands of Thérion's servants. The shutters of my window were silently shut and locked against any light of the moon or stars.

One morning I awoke to find a folded letter perched on top of my *Book of the Rose*, which I always kept next to me on my bedside table while I slept, with the medallion of Cernunnos tucked between its pages. The letter was from Edmée, who wrote that my father had fallen ill. She begged me to come home, and to forgive my father, who cried at the thought of the wrong he had done me in sending me off to Boisaulne. My silence had weighed heavily on him, and M. du Herle's assurances that I was well had not consoled him. Enclosed was a letter from Valentin, spattered with teardrops. I was delighted to see how greatly his handwriting had improved in the few months he'd been away at school, but he wrote that the other boys beat him, and the Jesuit fathers also doled out beatings as punishments. The food was meager and terrible, and he was always cold and starving. He wished to come home and study on his own, or perhaps to become a farmer like his uncles. Aimée wasn't getting along well with her cousins either, who were jealous she had a governess and didn't have to do chores. Both of them missed me terribly and wished I would come home.

XI

I HAD TO leave Boisaulne as soon as possible. What a selfish fool I had been, neglecting my children and father for the pleasures of this place. Hadn't I known, ever since Séléné showed me the way out through the door behind the fountain, that I could leave at any time, whether or not Thérion wished to permit it? In fact, the front door had also reappeared in the anteroom as soon as the guests arrived, yet I had never once tried to go out by it. At the very least, I could have written to the children, instead of letting my spite and bitterness toward Father and Hortense keep me cruelly silent. How long had Edmée's letter taken to reach me? There was no date on it, and even if there had been, I had long since lost track of the days and weeks. Father could be dead already. Valentin might have run away from school and come to grief.

And yet – how could I go without speaking to Thérion, or at least saying goodbye to him? Surely he couldn't be so cruel as to prevent me from going home under these circumstances. Would he have allowed me to see the letter otherwise, knowing it would make me desperate to leave?

There was also the matter that I didn't know the way home from Boisaulne, and Harlequin had warned me never to go alone outside the garden at night. I remembered the figure of the *roi des aulnes,* the Erl-King, and shuddered. I recalled the patch of blood on Harlequin's sleeve and his shame when I had pointed it out. Harlequin, M. du Herle ... Erl-King ... something itched just then in the back of my mind, but I let it be. I needed to decide what to do. I couldn't speak to Thérion until midnight, and time was of the essence. I resolved to speak to Harlequin at the midday meal, where I saw him most often, or earlier if I could find him in the maze of the manor's rooms and gardens.

As soon as I was dressed, I went to the library. Neither Harlequin nor anyone else was there. Curiosity drew me to the dictionary of demons, where I had first read about the *roi des aulnes.* It had never occurred to me before to look up *Harlequin,* who had his own entry since he too was a devilish figure.

I read about Harlequin's role in the Italian *commedia del'arte.* He was the trickster who aided and abetted his lovelorn master, the *inamorato,* in seeking to be together with his lady-love, the *inamorata.* This certainly seemed fitting for the handsome Harlequin I knew, who had procured me for his master, and whom Thérion had compared to an old lady matchmaker in the village. He had also kept an eye out for possible protégées and ingénues for his friend, Ulysse.

Then something in the last paragraphs caught my eye. The name Harlequin came from a legend of an old pagan king of England who was called Herla. Herla was later corrupted to Herrequin, Hellequin, or Harlequin, as the name made its way to the French-speaking territories and further into the Continent after the Norman conquest. It was said Herla spent three hundred years under the earth in the kingdom of the fairies, and it was from Herla's legend that the figure of the Elf-King emerged in Saxon lore. Herla was a leader of the wild hunt in the myths of the Celts – the *mesnée d'Hellequin* or *maisnie d'Herrequin* in old-fashioned French.

Maisnie-la-Forêt was the name of the village across the bridge ...

Thérion thought himself a descendant of the *roi des aulnes.* And Harlequin had chosen a nickname that referred to the same legend. They must be one and the same. They must be. I had unveiled my lover at last. If I told him I knew, would he let go of his pretenses and disguises? Could we be lovers in the daylight as well as in the night? Could we at last join body and soul, like the fragile meeting of sun and moon at twilight? I had to try. I had to speak to him.

But Harlequin didn't appear at the midday meal. All afternoon, all evening, I wrestled with myself in an anguish of indecision, whether to flee or wait. Darkness fell. When I understood Harlequin wasn't coming to the evening meal, I excused myself and went back up to my room, to wait for Thérion. If he didn't come that night, I would leave at first morning light, make my way to the village and Madame Jacquenod's house, and from there find my way back home, somehow or another. Perhaps someone would be traveling down the mountain and I could persuade them to let me walk or ride with them. Surely any terrors that lurked in the forest outside Boisaulne's walls at night would be quiet and harmless during the day.

I sat in the bed with the candelabra on the bedside table next to me and waited for the flames to gutter out at the stroke of midnight. The clock tolled twelve times, but the candles stayed lit. Terror engulfed me. In an effort to calm myself, I thought, *What a strange thing, to be more frightened of the light than of the dark, now that it warns me Thérion is gone.*

My door opened, and Donatien entered the room.

"Good evening, Violaine," he said. He came to sit down at the foot of my bed, where Thérion always sat.

For a moment I was too stunned to respond.

"What?" he said. "No words of greeting for your lover?"

A great surge of horror rose up in me. "You're not him."

"Aren't I?"

"Your voice isn't his." I pulled the coverlet up over my chest and clutched it tightly. "And how did you know my name was Violaine?"

He tugged off his embroidered satin coat and laid it down carefully over the foot of the bed behind him. He slipped off his shoes, stitched in delicately embroidered ice-blue fabric with gleaming silver buckles, first one, then the other. Before I could fully grasp what he intended, he had climbed into the bed on top of me and pressed me down so I couldn't get out from under him.

"What are you doing?" I gasped.

"You begged to see your Thérion's face in the light, and now I'm here. Don't you like what you see?"

His face looked enormous and distended, like that of a giant insect staring down at me, much too close.

"You listened at the keyhole." I turned my head to the side in disgust and tried to wrench myself free. "This isn't funny. Get off of me. Stop it. Help!"

"I want to see you in the light too. It's time you are exposed for what you really are."

This couldn't be happening. I imagined for a split second I heard a roar, a terrible roar from an enormous beast, my Beast, Thérion, come to rescue me from my attacker. And then I realized it was only the roar of my own blood in my ears, my heart pounding as Donatien and I struggled and he wrested the coverlet from me. He shoved it aside and pulled my chemise up to my waist, tearing the hem of the fabric. Thérion wasn't coming to rescue me. For all I know he truly was Donatien. But I knew with certainty I didn't want this and I needed to get away. Donatien pressed an arm against my shoulders and chest to restrain me and with his free hand began to unbutton his breeches, ignoring my forearms flailing and my fingernails trying to claw at him through the fabric of his shirt and waistcoat.

"I mean it," I cried, "please, stop it. Let go."

He laughed. "But this is what you were brought here for, wasn't it? To add to the castle's amusements."

My vision jerked between the gargoyle shadows dancing on the candlelit ceiling and walls, Donatien's grimacing face, the momentary darkness of my closed eyelids, and then the brilliance of the flickering candles next to me. The candelabra. I contorted my right arm painfully under his weight to reach out for it. It was almost too heavy for me to lift, and it took every last ounce of my strength to raise it up off the table, swing it through the air, and bring it down onto the back of Donatien's head.

He let go of me, shouting and cursing. I shoved him aside, wriggled the rest of the way out from under him, and fell out of the bed onto the floor, bruising my shoulder and hip. The coverlet had caught on fire from the candles, and he beat at it frantically with his coat to smother the flames. I pushed myself up and ran out of the room.

At first I didn't know where I was going. I was only running, barefoot in my thin chemise with its torn hem, down the hall to the staircase, and then down the stairs. The notion formed that I must get out of the château. I should have long since left for Father's house, and Boisaulne wasn't safe. At the bottom of the stairs, I yanked at the handle of the front door, but it didn't budge. Whatever dangers lay outside, I couldn't wait for daylight. Better to risk going out through the grotto and find a horse in the stable, better to leave now than stay another day and have to look the others in the eye, now that I had been shamed and humiliated like this.

I turned and hurried in the other direction, to run out the back of the anteroom along the length of the gallery, out the double glass-paned doors, and into the garden. I alternated running and jogging toward the far back wall of the inner garden, wishing I had brought a lantern. My lungs heaved and I stumbled and nearly fell several times in the dark. As I ran, I blamed myself. How could I ever have felt pity for Donatien? Why hadn't I heeded the warning of my intuition, which told me of the emptiness in him? It was no mere lack of esteem for me, but a hunger for cruelty.

Why hadn't I defended myself better? Why had I ever let such a creature put his hands on me?

There, finally, was the fountain and the bricked-in arch behind it. In the faint moonlight, I could just make out the stone mermaid figure on the side of the wall by the arch. I leapt up and pulled down on it with my whole weight, and the gate rumbled open an arm's width.

I hesitated before the opening. I was prepared for it to be pitch-black inside and for my eyes to be as blind within the grotto as in my room at night with Thérion. Instead, a faint glow in shifting colors shone from within. Time seemed to slow down, and the lights called to me, mesmerizing me. I moved forward through the opening, pushed the door shut behind me, and walked down the inner steps in a trance.

The gemstones, the crystalline formations, the channel in the rock of the spring above, and the walls of the grotto all glowed and glimmered and sparkled, giving off light of every color. There were two ways I could go: either forward and out to the forest, passing the fork in the tunnel that led off to join the old mines below the streets of Paris, or down through the low, narrow opening to the right that led underneath the channel of the spring, deeper into the earth. A faint tinkling of bells sounded from the glittering depths of the passage to the right under the spring. The longer I hesitated, the more it sounded like some lovely music just beyond my hearing, plaintive, woven of sorrow and joy, swirling in a seductive rhythm. I couldn't resist a longing to hear it more clearly, to know what it was about, to dance to it, to feel it resonate through my skin and flesh and bones. My feet carried me forward down into the passage, and I was just about to turn a corner when a new sound tore through the fabric of the air.

The lights and colors rippled before my eyes. Everything tilted, was disrupted.

It was the neighing of a horse. The concrete absurdity of this barnyard whinnying made everything around me, the lights, the jewels, the far-off music, seem unreal. It *was* unreal, I understood then, with the feeling of waking from a dream. The seductive tinkling music was just the clatter of rocks shaken in a bucket. The walls of the passage weren't crusted in iridescent shimmering jewels, they were stained and slimy with black algae. I was heading down into sulfurous, damp darkness. I stumbled backward, back up to the path that led out the other side into the forest. Now that I had seen what was real instead of the illusion, I understood that the inside of the grotto was faintly lit by a phosphorescent glow of some substance in or on the walls – some natural organism, moss or mineral, like the glow of fireflies, not magic. I panicked for a moment in the greenish darkness, as the rattling of stones continued in the passage below and I stumbled around, recoiling as my groping hands encountered more wet and slimy walls.

The horse neighed again. It was close by, and I went toward the sound, gradually leaving the phosphorescence behind as the ground sloped downward. There was a long stretch of emptiness on my left hand as I passed the broad tunnel that led down into the old mines, and then the path went upward and out to the open air and the standing stone in the starlight at the edge of the forest. Zéphyr, the white stallion who had first carried me to Boisaulne, stood waiting by the stone, his coat pale-gray against the darkness. He was saddled and tied to a tree branch, neighing as if to ask what had taken me so long.

"My friend, you saved me," I said, throwing my arms around Zéphyr's neck and burying my face in his mane. "What are you doing here?"

He snorted and tossed his head, and I let go of him.

"You must have known I'd need you. Someone must have. How long have you been waiting here for me? All day?"

Was it Thérion who had made sure Zéphyr would be waiting there for me? Donatien was lying – of course he was, he could never be Thérion. Yet my confidence of this morning that Harlequin had been my true lover all along was undermined now, and I no longer knew what to think or whom to trust. Someone had left me the letter from Edmée. Whoever had left the letter was my friend. And I could only think that the same friend had tied Zéphyr up to wait for me, expecting me to leave and guessing I would need his aid.

But there was no time to waste. In the dark I felt for the reins and untied Zéphyr from the tree branch. I climbed into the saddle and gave the horse a gentle kick in the flanks that started him walking.

"I don't suppose you know the way back to my father's house in the village?"

He whinnied and increased his speed to a trot, and then a canter, and finally we were galloping through the forest. We forded the stream in the dark and lurched up the other side of the bank. I gritted my teeth and focused all my concentration on keeping my seat, holding tight to the reins and ducking my head low to avoid being slashed or struck by branches. Soon after we had left the stream behind, he slowed his pace and kept to a trot the rest of the way.

Just as the rising sun began to paint the snow-capped peaks fuchsia and salmon, with fiery yellow tufts of clouds clustered at their edges, Zéphyr and I arrived at my father's house. I brought Zéphyr into the stable room and settled him in to rest with our old mare Claudette and the other animals.

Edmée came in as I was finishing up. She let out a cry of joy when she saw me and rushed to embrace me in a close hug, as if I were her own daughter – a thing she had never done before in all the years she had lived with us.

"Thank God, thank God, you're back," she said. "And so quickly. I didn't know if we'd hear back from you at all, let alone that you'd be here so soon. But Mary Mother of God, you're nearly naked! Why on earth have you come in only a nightgown?"

I looked down and folded my arms over my chest, trying to cover myself. "Forgive me," I stuttered, "I left in a great hurry and rode all night to get here. How's Father?"

"Mercy, you'll take sick yourself like that." She stared me up and down and shook her head. "Oh, he's much better since the doctor came. But quick, come on in by the fire."

"A doctor was here?"

My teeth had begun to chatter and I shivered convulsively as she put an arm around me and led me through the door from the stable into the main room of the house. Whether my shivering was from chill or exhaustion or both, I couldn't tell.

"Didn't you know?" she asked. "A doctor by the name of Guillon came from Thônes. He said the Marquis de Boisaulne had sent for him, so I assumed ... but here, let's get a blanket on you." She positioned me before the fire and draped a woolen coverlet around my shaking shoulders. "The delirium seems to have passed and the fever's broken. Thank God, thank God."

She left me there for several minutes and came back with a pair of shoes and a pile of my old clothes that she helped me put on. When I was dressed, she sent me into the front room to see Father.

He was sitting up in bed, drinking an herbal tisane. His face was gray and his hair and beard looked whiter than when I had left. He was thinner too and seemed barely able to muster the strength to raise the cup to his lips. I fell on him and embraced him and then sat down on a low three-legged stool next to the bed.

He pulled away from me to cough into a handkerchief. When the coughing fit subsided after long minutes, he wheezed, "Violaine. You came."

"*Shh*, don't talk anymore. Of course I came."

XII

I SAT WITH Father for an hour, long enough to assure myself he was truly no longer at death's door, and then I begged to be excused to sleep in my old bed in the back room for a few hours after my long night of riding.

As I slept with the shutters closed against the daylight, I dreamt I heard Donatien's voice in the dark.

"Violaine, Violaine, come on, let's go out to the standing stone. That was fun, wasn't it? Are you wearing your ring?"

"No, what ring? What are you talking about?"

"We're married. I'm your husband."

"You're insane. You tried to hurt me." I wanted to get away but couldn't move. He ran a finger down my arm from the crook of my elbow to my wrist. "Stop it. No."

I jerked awake with a little cry. Slowly my surroundings came into focus and my sense of horror receded. Donatien couldn't be Thérion. I recognized his voice in the dream, though it was dark. And Thérion would have stopped when I asked him to. Thérion was always kind; he would have listened to me. I pushed myself up and shook off my drowsiness.

It was early afternoon. I got up and went back to the main room to eat some bread, and then took up my post on the stool by Father's bedside again. Edmée sat knitting in a chair as Father slept. He looked better than he had that morning. His color had returned a little and he wasn't coughing, though there was still an audible wheeze in his breathing.

"Will the doctor come back?" I asked Edmée in a whisper.

"He's supposed to. Tomorrow morning, he said."

"Has there been any word from the Marquis?"

"Only what Doctor Guillon told us. He said Monsieur du Herle rode into Thônes to fetch him and give him directions to get here. He didn't tell us you were coming. Did you have a quarrel with the Marquis?"

"No – maybe. Perhaps a misunderstanding. I couldn't find the Marquis or Monsieur du Herle to ask permission to come after I received your letter. I waited all day and into the night, but neither of them came back to the manor. I was afraid if I kept waiting it might be too late, so I just left by myself in the middle of the night. I hope the Marquis won't be angry with me."

"Oh, dear. You shouldn't cross him. What a thing, to ride around the countryside in the middle of the night in only your chemise! What in heaven's name were you thinking?" She shook her head again. "I didn't know what to do but write you. Your sisters were here to watch by his bedside, but it was you he kept asking for."

"It was right you wrote to me," I said, looking at Father and not at her. "I needed to come home."

"But you'll go back? You haven't run away for good?"

"I – I don't know."

She sighed. "It's not a good time for there to be trouble between you and the Marquis. Your Father just signed a lease on a house in Annecy before he fell ill. He's getting too old to spend the winters up here, now that he can afford to move. I'm to go with him and we'll have room for Aimée and her governess, and perhaps Valentin, if you want to take him out of school. But if the

Marquis thinks you've betrayed him, running off like that ..." She broke off as Father stirred restlessly in his sleep. Then she turned back to catch my eye and look me in the face. "I hope you weren't thinking of coming back here to stay. That would be difficult, now there's been so much talk. People saw you riding off with a well-dressed gentleman, and rumors started going around. It was as we feared. We told everyone you'd gone into service in another town, but no one believed you'd humbled yourself enough to become a housemaid."

I nodded, feeling struck in the chest. I might have expected as much, but it was still a blow to learn I wasn't remembered with kindness or forgiveness in the village. At least there would be no more offers of marriage to contend with.

"Is that why you wanted to leave? Because there were rumors about me?" I asked.

She looked thin and worn out. Her braids of straw-blond hair were going gray under her coif and there were dark bags under her eyes.

"As long as father can still afford the house in Annecy, it doesn't matter. But if it falls through because you offended the Marquis ... it might be best if you did go into service. How we'd find a position for you, I don't know. But never mind, we can speak of it later, when he's better." She looked at Father intently, and seeing how easily he breathed, she closed her eyes for a moment in relief.

I tried to imagine what my mother would have said, if she were still alive and sitting here instead of Edmée. She might have asked whether I was happy with the Marquis and whether I was treated well at the manor. But Edmée didn't ask.

After some time had passed with the two of us sitting in silence, I asked, "Will you be all right here with him if I go to Hortense's to see Aimée?"

She smiled, "Yes, go and see them, and Françoise-Angélique too, otherwise they'll scold me for keeping you here so long when they didn't know you'd come. You've plenty enough daylight to get there on that horse of yours. I wonder what a stallion like him thinks of the society in our stable. It's like a prince bedding down with peasants," she said, chuckling a little.

In the barn, Zéphyr seemed to have gotten his rest also. He snorted and paced as though eager to get out of his stall. When I went to saddle him, I felt a weight in the saddle bag, a rectangular form I hadn't noticed in my haste in the dark the night before. My *Book of the Rose*. I opened it and found a letter from Thérion tucked into the cover.

"Dearest Violaine, by the time you read this, I'll be missing you terribly. Forgive me not writing more just now and, as I wrote before, for not sending Harlequin to accompany you. If you leave a letter here in the book's cover, it will make its way back to me at Boisaulne, and you'll also find my letters to you here. When you're ready to return to Boisaulne, Zéphyr will carry you back to me. Don't tarry too long, I beg you. Every night I don't hold you in my arms is a wound. Send word when you've arrived safely."

The medallion of Cernunnos was still between the book's pages, too. I slipped it into my pocket and carried the book into the house, into the back room. This was all very strange, even for my strange Thérion who concealed himself behind masks within masks within masks. I sat on my bed and reread the note several times. The words "as I wrote before" made me think I must have missed a letter from him, and the missing letter would explain some of the odd events of the day before – why Harlequin was absent, why Zéphyr was saddled and tied up by the standing stone, as though waiting for me. Of course I knew now the reason Harlequin was missing was that he'd gone to Annecy to fetch the doctor.

I tiptoed back into the front room.

"I thought you'd gone," whispered Edmée.

"The Marquis left me a letter," I whispered back. "I just found it. All's well, but I need to write back to him and let him know I arrived safely."

"God be praised." She set down her knitting, and helped me find a quill, ink, and paper amidst Father's untidy papers.

I hurriedly wrote to Thérion that I was safe there at Father's house. I explained my confusion and worry from the day before and asked whether I might have missed a letter from him.

"I'll write again soon," I scribbled, "but I must leave in a moment to be sure of getting to my sister's house before dark. Thank you a thousand times for sending the doctor. It was wisely done, and Father appears to be out of danger." I left it for the next day to tell him what had happened with Donatien. I tucked the letter into the book's cover and placed the book under the mattress of my bed so that Edmée wouldn't disturb it by mistake.

I rode Zéphyr to Hortense's house. I brought the stallion into the stable and found Pierre-Joseph sitting at a table in the corner mending a tool. He half-stood when he saw me, before sitting back down again and returning to his work, not looking me in the eye.

"Evening. How do you do?" he said gruffly. "You've come a long way, eh?"

With equal stiffness, I half curtseyed. "I came to see Father. He's much better. Are Hortense and Aimée inside?"

"Don't know. Go on in. I've got to finish this and clean up. I'll take care of the horse too, in a minute," he said, indicating Zéphyr and nodding me toward the door into the house. I supposed he was none too pleased to see me if I had drawn gossip around the family as Edmée had told me. But no matter. Thérion still cared for me and longed for my return to Boisaulne, so I was spared the reckoning of my lost honor for the time being.

Stepping into the kitchen, I heard music coming from the next room. For a moment I thought of the fairy music that had nearly drawn me down into the realm beneath the earth, then I shook my head, trying to clear my ears of the illusion. The sounds were still there. I opened the door into the next room and saw Aimée seated on a stool before the hearth with her hands on the strings of a harp taller than she was. She was plucking out a melody lovely enough to draw the fairies' envy.

She jumped up when she saw me and ran to me, crying, "Maman! Maman!" I lifted her up and hugged her to me, tears springing to my eyes. Her hair was braided smoothly and tied with satin ribbons in perfectly even bows, as I had never managed to do it myself. She introduced me to her governess, Madame Grasset, who had been sitting on the bench by the wall looking on. She was a pleasant, middle-aged woman with a *lyonnais* accent. When I had paid my regards to her and learned Hortense had gone out to the pasture to call my nephews home for supper, Aimée and I went outside to walk and look for them.

I told Aimée what her brother had written to me in his teardrop-spattered letter.

"But it's true," she said. "Cousin Ronald and Jacquot have been jealous and mean to me ever since Madame Grasset came to stay. Tante Hortense says Madame Grasset takes up too much room with her harp and turns her nose up at the suppers Tante Hortense makes. It's always 'In Lyon we do this and in Lyon we do that,' and it gives Uncle ideas of trying new things Tante Hortense doesn't want to do, so then they quarrel and everyone's cross."

"Do you want to go with Grandfather and Edmée and stay in the new house in Annecy? Edmée says there'll be enough room for you there."

"Only if Madame Grasset can come too."

"Of course she'll come. I'm sure she'd be more comfortable in a town house than up here on the mountain, where she doesn't even understand what anyone says in *patouè*."

"And Valentin? Maman, I miss him. He wrote me some letters too, and Madame Grasset helped me read them. You should see how well I can read now, almost as good as you already. But Valentin sounds so sad. He shouldn't be with those fathers, the Jesuits. He ought to be learning music with Madame Grasset like me."

"I don't know, sweetheart. He does sound unhappy, but your Papa would have liked him to become an educated man. I think your Papa would say it was better for him to stay, and the

discipline will toughen him, and it's the ordinary price of learning."
Imagining what the Pastor would have wanted for Valentin,
however, was already in itself a sign that it wasn't what *I* wished
for my son.

"But they don't feed him properly," Aimée insisted. "He could
get sick from the bad food. And it's not fair, he's beaten worse than
the other boys. They punish him for being a bad Catholic because
he doesn't always know how to recite all their prayers. One day
perhaps they'll guess he's no Catholic at all. He'd be happy with
Madame Grasset, I know he would. She's always nice and doesn't
scold except when I'm really bad. And the harp is the best thing on
earth. Do you know she has a fiddle too? He could learn the fiddle
with her and we could play duets."

"Well, perhaps we can talk about it with Madame Grasset
later and see what she thinks."

"I've missed you too, Maman, so much. Aren't you ever
coming back to stay?"

The question twisted my heart painfully. "I don't know,
darling. The agreement was that I would stay with Monsieur le
marquis as long as it pleased him to keep me."

"I wish you'd never leave again and would stay here with us
forever."

Could I do it, I wondered? Boisaulne felt long ago and far
away, as if it had never been never anything more than a
wonderful dream. If I hadn't had the reassuring weight of the
silver medallion in my pocket, I might have doubted I was ever
there. But I couldn't truthfully tell her I didn't wish to go back.
Thérion's love had become as necessary to me as bread, as water,
as breathing. I had lived in the world formed by his imagining, a
place that was the expression of his soul. It was wrenching to think
of ever leaving all that behind me, yet this beautiful dream stood
in opposition to my own children's hunger for love and happiness
and my duty to them. But even if it were possible to break the
agreement my father had signed with Thérion, even if my heart
didn't cry out in anguish at the thought of never being with my

love again, Edmée had already made it clear it might cause no end of trouble if I didn't return to Boisaulne.

"I can't come back forever, darling," I told her. "But once the Marquis sees he can trust me to visit here and return, when he sees how faithful I am to him, I hope he'll permit me to visit more often."

"Do you love him more than you love us?"

"Of course not. But the love between grown-up men and women is a different kind of love than that between parents and children. It would break my heart if I could never be with my Marquis again, but it also breaks my heart not to see you. If I could, I'd bring you and Valentin and Madame Grasset all to live with us in the manor, or at least I'd visit you in Annecy every month. When I go back I'll speak with the Marquis. God willing, he'll no longer deny me the wish of my heart to see my own children more often."

Aimée nodded, but still looked anxious, so I added, "Anyway, as soon as your Grandpapa's well again, I'll do my best to see whether you and Valentin can go and live with them, and Madame Grasset too. And then when I visit I can see you all at once."

With so many mouths to feed at dinner, Hortense was busy and distracted, and there was little chance of speaking with her until the last of the pots had been scraped clean and Aimée had gone to bed. Then she and I walked together with a lantern to the house of our younger sister, Françoise-Angélique. I hadn't spoken with her since before Father had come back from his trip at the beginning of June. Françoise's twin girls had been born in April, just as the midwife predicted. Now as the three of us sat whispering around the table before the fire, she alternately nursed each baby to drowsy contentment, while Hortense or I held the other twin who slept.

"Never mind about us, everything's gone on just the same here," Hortense said, when I asked them for the news of the villages. "We want to hear all about your life at the manor. Was I right to tell you to go?"

"Well, it's done now," I said. "I do wish I'd been here to take care of Father when he got sick, and I missed the children terribly."

"Of course you did," Françoise said. She gave the baby on her breast a kiss on top of her fuzzy head. "But have you been happy, apart from that? Do they treat you well there?"

Much as I hated to give Hortense reasons to feel pleased with herself for how she had treated me in June, I couldn't refrain from describing Boisaulne in rapturous terms. They listened in astonishment. I didn't tell them about the invisible spirits who served Thérion and his guests, for they would have thought I'd gone mad, and there was no way anyone who hadn't been to Boisaulne could believe the things I had seen. Hortense asked whether the servants were well-trained, whether I had my own maid, and whether it fell to me to manage them and give them their orders. I answered in the same phrases Harlequin had used when he had first brought me to the manor, that the Marquis had trained all his servants to be exceedingly discreet, well-nigh invisible. I had little need to speak with them and there was no duty on my part to manage them, though I received some assistance with dressing and arranging my hair.

"And does the Marquis give you gifts?" Françoise asked. "Do you have jewels and pretty clothes?"

"He has the most marvelous library you could possibly imagine. It's filled from floor to ceiling with books. Every wall is covered with shelves and shelves of them, and I can read any of them I like, whenever I want, any time of day or night."

"Ah," Françoise said. "That must be nice for you. But, how about clothes? Do you have brocades or satin things?"

"The clothes," I shrugged, "well, they're not always the most comfortable, and at first I was constantly afraid of getting them dirty. But everything's always so clean and smells nice there, that's what I love, even more than the rich fabrics."

"What are the dresses made of, velvet? Or silk?"

"Yes, and there are brocades also. I have a wardrobe stuffed full of them. There's a fresh chemise laid out for me every time I go into my chamber. The bedclothes are wonderfully soft, too, and the mattresses are all of feathers. I don't think I've seen a single bug or mouse inside any of the rooms since I got there. Oh, and there's a garden, and a park with paths, almost as big as a village. I can walk for hours in it, and there are always flowers in bloom. For the first month and a half, I was lonely, and the only friends I had were in the garden, birds and deer, squirrels and rabbits, lizards, frogs, insects and spiders."

Françoise drew her brows together. "It's too bad you were so lonely. I wish you'd written."

I took a deep breath. I didn't know when I would have another chance to apologize. "I'm sorry I kept silent," I forced myself to say. "It was cruel of me, and foolish. Forgive me."

"You really should have written," Hortense said, "if only for the children's sake. I could understand you being angry at me and at Father. But Aimée cried herself to sleep every night for the whole first month."

I felt lower than the lowliest worm. Tears prickled at the corners of my eyes.

Françoise frowned at Hortense. "Hush, you don't have to make her feel worse." To me she said, "Of course you were grieving and angry. Anyone would be in your shoes. Only it makes me sad to think of you so alone."

"But I wasn't lonely for long. That was the best gift of all I've gotten, charming company, men and women of learning and brilliance who've come from Paris and Scotland and all over." I tried to describe my new friends and the conversations we had, though I didn't tell my sisters about Donatien or his visit to my room the night before and what he had tried to do to me.

"But it's strange," Hortense said, "I'd have expected you to come back looking like a duchess, but you're dressed just the same. We'd have liked to see you in your new finery. Why didn't you bring some of your clothes back from the manor to show us?"

"And couldn't you have brought something back for us, too?" Françoise asked, her eyes wistful as she patted one of the twins on the back, trying to get her to burp.

I stammered, "I didn't think of it. Forgive me. I wish I had. Next time I'll try."

Both of them squinted at me and cast glances at each other.

"I don't know what's the good of a rich gentleman and a fine manor," Hortense grumbled, "and leaving your children and losing your good name for his sake, if you can't even bring away any good clothes or jewels."

I thought of showing them the silver medallion in my pocket, but to them it wouldn't look like anything but a shabby old trinket, more fitting for a forest witch than a nobleman's mistress.

At last they came to the subject of the Marquis himself.

"Is he handsome?" Françoise asked. "Is he young? What does he look like?"

I thought, if I cannot share at least this secret with my own sisters, with whom else could I ever share it? So I confessed to them what I hadn't told any of my new friends in the Castle of Enlightenment, that I had never seen my lover's face. That he only came to me in the dark. We talked in the dark, made love in the dark. I couldn't say whether he was handsome, only that his tenderness and roughness and passion fed my soul.

"But surely you can come up with some way to light a candle or a lantern once he's gone to sleep and see his face that way?" said Hortense.

No, I explained, I had tried many times, and it appeared to be all but impossible.

"But how can you make love to a man you've never seen?" Françoise asked incredulously. "Suppose he's some monster? Or a wanted criminal, a highwayman who's taken on the Marquis's identity and hidden himself away in the woods? Suppose he's a Jew, or a Moor, even?"

These thoughts hadn't occurred to me. Françoise might even be right. I was prepared to find out my lover might be a cripple or deformed, but not that he might be in hiding from the law, or a member of some outcast group, or a dark-skinned foreigner. I supposed I would still love him even if he were ugly – but could I still love him if he turned out to be an African or an Arab or a Chinaman?

I hoped I would. I thought of Shakespeare's *Othello*. Hadn't Desdemona loved her Moorish husband truly? Thérion's mind and soul were beautiful, and he was masterful in bringing my body to a state of ecstasy, making every inch of my skin tingle and feel alive. If he were a villain I could not bear it, but the color of his skin could make no true difference to me. And if I discovered he was of another faith than I, what of it? My God was Nature now. Yes, I hoped I would still love him.

"But I'm almost certain I know who he is, in any case," I said.

"Who then?" asked Hortense.

"I don't like to say, in case I'm wrong."

"Then you can't be all that certain."

"But I nearly am. Only I'd be much embarrassed if I said it and it proved false."

They look at each other again and shook their heads.

"An honest man isn't mysterious," Françoise said. "Honest men don't hide."

Perhaps not in their world.

In the morning I rode back to Father's house. The doctor had already come and gone. To my joy, Father was able to get out of bed to take his midday meal with Edmée and me before going back to his room to rest. In my *Book of the Rose* I found a new letter from Thérion.

"I'm grieved to learn you didn't receive my note along with the letters I left out for you from home. I don't know how it went missing. I'd left instructions for you to take Zéphyr and go to your father's house at once. I'd already sent Harlequin to Thônes for the doctor and told him to go on from there to Annecy to see to your father's affairs in town. I had to leave the manor myself to take care of a few matters, but foolishly I had no fear for your safety, thinking you'd be traveling in the day with Zéphyr. I only hope you can forgive me and thank God you arrived safely in spite of the mix-up. I'm much relieved, too, to hear your father is recovering. How soon can you return? I'm sick already with missing you."

I spent a long time composing my reply, trying to explain what had happened with Donatien. But suppose I wasn't believed? I could hardly have believed it myself if it hadn't happened to me. My hand trembled and I felt sick to my stomach as I wrote. I spilled a streak of ink across the paper and had to waste the entire sheet and start over again. I tried to explain, too, how much it meant to me to see the children again, and why I needed to stay at least a week, or maybe two – to help Father and Edmée with the move to Annecy, once Father was well enough, and to see Valentin and take him out of the Jesuit school. As I wrote, it pained me to remember that my new friends at Boisaulne were only there through to the end of the summer, and if I stayed too long they might leave before I got back. Then I scolded myself for thinking of my own selfish wishes instead of my duty.

When I was finished, instead of tucking the letter under the cover of the *Book of the Rose*, I folded it up and put it in my pocket. I wanted to mull it over, reread it again later, and be sure of my words before letting Thérion read them.

By day's end, much had been accomplished. Father continued to regain his strength, and Edmée and I made arrangements to send a few wagonloads of furnishings down the mountain to the new house in Annecy, where it was agreed the children and Madame Grasset would go to live as well. Before I went to sleep, I took the letter out of my pocket, read it again, and tore it up and threw it in the fire. I had expressed myself too clumsily, and it would worry Thérion too much. I would write a better letter the next day and wait till I returned to Boisaulne to tell him in person what had happened with Donatien. To ward off any more nightmares of Donatien, I went to sleep with the medallion of Cernunnos around my neck, as if it really were a protective talisman. I wished Thérion were there to wrap his arms around me, but at least the medallion reminded me of him.

In the morning I found another letter from Thérion. "I miss you more than I can express in words," he wrote. "But I can well understand you must be busy caring for your father and children. Only think of me and know that without you, there's a darkness in me even deeper than the night I always carry around me. Please return as soon as you can bear to."

I tried to comfort him by writing a cheerful letter, giving him the news of my family, assuring him I missed him too and was grateful to him for making it possible for me to come. I avoided any mention of returning to Boisaulne.

That day I helped Madame Grasset pack up her harp into a crate, and we brought it along with the first wagonload of furnishings to the new house in Annecy – Aimée and the governess riding in the wagon and I on Zéphyr. After we had unloaded the wagon, we went to Valentin's school together.

One of the cassocked fathers brought Valentin down the narrow stone stairwell to us, where we waited in the entry hall. The priest excused himself and went back upstairs. For a long moment Valentin simply stared at the three of us sitting there across the room from him, with the saucer-eyed, dazzled gratitude of a prisoner granted a pardon on the brink of the scaffold. Then he propelled himself into my arms. Aimée piled on with an embrace on top of ours, sobbing. When we had dried our eyes, he showed us the bruises on his back and shoulders, and on his shins under his stockings, from the beatings at the hands of his masters and schoolmates.

He and Madame Grasset sized each other up. She had brought her violin with her in a handsome hard leather case, and she took the instrument out to show him how to hold it with one end tucked under his chin and the bow in the other hand. He almost dropped it when she instructed him on how to draw the bow along the strings and it sang out a quavering note. Oh yes, he said, he'd like to learn to play, and he'd be good, gooder than any boy had ever been in the whole history of the world. He'd learn all of his lessons and never talk back, if only he could come home with us. So I went up the stairs to find the priest and settled up his school fees, and we took him home.

In the morning I rode back alone along the lakeshore, through the valley, and up into the mountains back to Father's house. At home, I found a new letter from Thérion tucked into the *Book of the Rose* under my mattress. He told me once again, with even more urgency than before, how he missed me and longed for my return as soon as possible. My absence was like an illness, and with little exaggeration, he said, he might well die of it if I were to stay away too long.

"But there's something else I wish to ask you," he wrote. "I hope it won't cause you any offense, but Harlequin tells me there's been some trouble among his guests. The young painter, Clio, has made accusations against his friend Donatien and he doesn't know how to judge the truth of them. The girl claims Donatien accosted her in a way that frightened and hurt her. But Harlequin and Ulysse have known him many years and wanted to avoid rushing to judgment with no proof of his guilt. Donatien says he's the victim of a malicious falsehood and the girl is merely angry at him for toying with her affections. So I ask you – with regret, since I don't wish to distract you from your visit home – have you ever witnessed Donatien behaving as this girl described?"

Ice crept through my veins as I read the letter. God in Heaven, what had I done, keeping silent about Donatien? Now Clio, too, had been drawn into the nightmare, and it was all my fault. I sat down at once to write my response, explaining in as much detail as I could bear to my own experience with Donatien and urging Thérion to believe Clio's story. I couldn't help but wonder as I wrote – if I had told him sooner, if Clio had never said anything, would I have been believed, given that she was doubted and questioned? Would Thérion believe me now? Would he think I had brought it on myself, as I had accused myself of doing in my own mind?

I asked his permission to stay through the rest of the week, to finish helping Father and Edmée with the move to Annecy. Before I went to sleep, I left the letter inside the cover of the *Book of the Rose* and put the book back under the mattress. In the morning, my letter was gone, but there was no answer from Thérion. I took Zéphyr and rode alongside the hired wagon driver again to Annecy to bring the second load of furnishings and see the children in the new house. I stayed overnight in Annecy and set out again in the morning to return.

In the last hour before I reached the village, the clouds turned dark purple-green, and then charcoal. A jagged line of lighting speared a tall pine on the ridge above me, so close I could smell smoke as the branches exploded into sparks and flames. Zéphyr reared up and almost threw me. He wheeled around in a circle three times, snorting and shaking his head while I clung to the reins and we veered at right angles. When I urged him back onto the lane, pulling back on the reins to slow him, he ducked his head so low I almost tumbled forward onto the ground. We righted ourselves at last and fell back into the rhythm of a walk, both of us jittery and shaking. Thunder drowned out the clopping of Zéphyr's hooves and rain began to pour down in such thick sheets I could barely see the path in front of us. By the time we cantered up to Father's house, Zéphyr and I were both as drenched as if we'd swum through the lake.

It took me a long time to get changed out of my sopping, muddy clothes, and to wring out my hair and dry it by the fire. I warmed myself with the hot verbena tisane and a swallow of *génépi* that Edmée served me. Outside, the deluge showed no sign of letting up. I went into the back room, my heart pounding in anticipation of an answer from Thérion. But when I pulled the book out from under my mattress, there was still no letter under the front cover. I flipped through all the pages to be sure I hadn't missed anything, but couldn't find a scrap of paper with any note from him.

Something was wrong. Did my last letter upset him too much to respond? What if he was sick, or hurt?

I sat down to pen a new note to him, telling him how his silence made me anxious. "But Father's well enough to travel at last," I wrote. "So I should be able to take Zéphyr back to Boisaulne tomorrow, or as soon as the rain lets up. Father and Edmée finished packing today, and Pierre-Joseph and his sons came and brought our cows and goats back to their farm. Father's plan before the storm came was that they'd lock up the house tomorrow morning and drive down to Annecy in the buggy. I only hope they won't get stuck in the mud, and the rain doesn't go on too long. But I promise, I'll come to you just as soon as I've seen them off, even if we have to wait another day or two for the roads to dry."

I fell asleep to torrents of rain and wind pummeling the roof and rattling the shutters. In the dark before dawn, when the storm had finally exhausted its fury and subsided to a light drizzle, the quiet was so abrupt it woke me up. I reached for the book under the mattress, but my groping hands found only scraps of loose hay.

The *Book of the Rose* was gone.

XIII

"*I* HAVEN'T SEEN it, I swear," said Edmée. Like me, she was woken by the sudden silence outside, and sat at the table now, her face half-illuminated in the glow of a lantern. "I didn't even know you had a book like that."

Father hadn't seen it either. While the last of the rain tapered off, I began a search of the house, looking into every corner from the hayloft to the cellar. The sky lightened outside through the white clouds and mist clinging to the chain of peaks across the valley. Father and Edmée decided it was best to travel right away before the deluge started up again, and Father went out to hitch up Claudette to the buggy.

"I can't find it," I called to him as he stalked back into the main room from the stable. I wrung my apron in my hands. "It's as if it's vanished into air."

"Your horse is gone too," he said, grim-faced.

"What?"

"The stallion. He's run away. The storm must have spooked him, I don't know." He gave a shrug of despair. "I can't believe it was a thief, out in that weather. The door was unlatched from the inside, so he had to have done it himself, the bugger. Too smart, that horse. You still can't find the book either?"

"No, it's nowhere."

He shook his head, staring away from me at the dead ashes in the fireplace.

"How could it be a thief?" he said. "How could anyone have known you had it under your mattress, or gotten in to take it without us hearing? It's impossible."

I let go of my apron to press the fist of my right hand into the palm of my left. "Something's wrong. I've got to go back to Boisaulne at once."

"How will you get there, with no horse? The Marquis isn't going to like it when he finds out the stallion's been lost. That saddle of his was worth a journeyman's wages for half a year, at least."

"I'll go on foot. I remember the way. The sun's not even over the mountains yet. If I leave at once I can reach the village nearest the manor by sunset. I'll stay overnight in the tavern and then go the rest of the way in the morning."

"But Violaine," said Edmée, rising from her chair at the table, "it's a harebrained ... no."

Father agreed with Edmée. "Go back you must, but alone? Walking through the woods? Suppose you meet with bandits, or worse?"

"There's nothing along that path but chamois and marmots," I said. "No one lives in those woods."

"What if you meet wild beasts?"

"I'm not afraid of *marmots*." I drew out the last word sarcastically, but my bravado didn't fool Father.

"What if you lose your way? What if you're caught in the storm? I don't like it. If I had all my strength back I'd go with you, but I can't trust myself to walk so far and back again."

"Why don't you both ride there together on Claudette?" Edmée said. "I'll wait here."

"No, it would tire Father too much," I said, "and there's no need to put off your trip. You don't want to lose the dry weather. I'll take a lantern and a knife and a cloak, just in case. The trail wasn't hard to follow. I won't stray from it."

Father bit his lip and drew his brows together. I was a bad liar and he could tell I was exaggerating how easily I could find my way. But from his desperate glances at the shuttered windows, I knew he was loathe to put off leaving for Annecy while the weather was right, when another rainstorm sweeping in could churn the roads into still deeper bogs and delay the trip for days. Nor could he tell me to come along with them to town, since his finances were still entwined with the Marquis's interests and we both knew everything could be at risk if I didn't go back to Boisaulne.

"It was always the plan for me to go back alone," I said. "The only difference is that I was going to ride on Zéphyr. But we hardly went more than walking pace most of the way the first time, so it won't take much longer on foot. The Marquis trusted me to come back safely. And I will."

Father sighed. "We'll at least drive you as far as Hortense's in the buggy. You can sit on top of the luggage in back. We'll let you off at the lane and you can go on from there."

I waved goodbye to Father and Edmée from the lane just beyond Hortense's farm. As I started out along the road, my satchel with the lantern and knife and round of bread felt light, but I stumbled under the weight of my fears. It had been a terrible mistake to delay writing to Thérion and to have stayed away so long. Now something awful must have happened, I knew it. Perhaps he was angry with me for what I had said about Donatien, or for not writing sooner, so that Clio, too, had been put at risk. Perhaps he hadn't even received my letters and thought I meant to stay away for good. He wrote that he was sick and low with missing me. What if he had really fallen ill or met with some accident?

I supposed I hadn't taken it seriously, that he could really miss me so very much. He had never once said he loved me, after all. As a child I was taught to examine my faults every day, to avoid the sin of pride. When I began to read, I often thought of the words of a lady author I admired, Madame Pringy, who wrote, "To know much, one must love oneself little." I wished to know much, so I tried to love myself little. Those habits of mind had made it easy to convince myself that when Thérion called me beautiful, intelligent, and good, he was only saying it to be kind and flatter me. I hadn't minded loving him more than he loved me; I had only thought myself lucky to receive his attentions. But suppose all along his feelings were as deep as mine, or deeper, and now I had truly hurt him?

The thought of losing him was like a hole torn in my chest, a gaping wound the size and shape of my book. The ache came in waves, swelling until it almost overwhelmed me, then receding, like the labor pains I'd had when my children were born. Above me the clouds thickened and grew feathery at the edges, and it began to mist and sprinkle. Following the lane, I passed beyond the cleared lands around the village houses as the path wound into the woods. By the time the misting rain had cleared and the sun burst through the clouds in blinding streaks of light an hour or two later, I realized I had gone too far and had missed the trail that led off into the woods. I turned around and retraced my steps, keeping my eyes fixed on the side of the lane for some familiar mark or sign.

Was it here that Harlequin and I had left the path when he came to fetch me, this cathedral-like arch between two alder trees? It felt right and looked like the game trail I remembered. I squeezed the medallion in my pocket for good luck. But as I left the lane and began to walk along the muddy trail, it seemed my fear had drained the world of color, and what had been a wood of richly-shimmering sunlit green leaves when I passed through in June now looked gray, barren, and rocky. My limbs felt leaden, as though I were pushing forward through a waist-high snowbank or leaning into the headwind of a gale.

At midday I sat on a boulder and rested for an hour to eat my bread. It tasted of nothing and I had to force myself to chew through mouthfuls, nauseated with anxiety. Nothing had looked familiar since shortly after I had left the lane, and I believed I was lost. If only I saw any animals, like the galloping chamois I remembered from before, I could at least follow them to a stream, because they would have to drink eventually. And if I found the stream again, I could follow it to the village. But the woods were silent and empty, without so much as a birdsong chirruping through the branches. What were the animals afraid of that had driven them into hiding in their holes and nests?

When night began to drape itself around the treetops like thick smoke, I knew with certainty I was lost. The tinder in my satchel was damp and smoked when I held it over the sparks from the flint. By the time I managed to get the wick in the lantern lit, the stars were winking into view in the blackness above me. At least there were stars. Relief washed over me as I recognized a constellation of them, three close together, three more spread out beyond them in a perpendicular line. A sword extending from a hilt. It reminded me of the silver sword Harlequin wore at his side and it pointed east, in the direction of Boisaulne.

I stepped forward with new determination, now that I had the stars to lead me. I would find Thérion, and if he was ill, I would nurse him back to health. If he was in despair, I would comfort him. If he was angry with me, I would plead for forgiveness. If he was in danger, I would do all I could to rescue him. But suppose he was simply tired of me and had fallen in love with someone else? Suppose all along he had been visiting others besides me at night in the Castle of Enlightenment? But if that was so, it was better that I should know it instead of being tormented by fears of unknown disasters.

I began to stumble over roots and brambles in the darkness as the undergrowth thickened, and my confidence faltered. Owls hooted back and forth to each other in the branches above my head. Signs of life in the night forest at last; but then what else might come alive in the dark? My chest seized up with terror at the thought. The wind rose and the pines and elms and alders swayed against the stars, bowing to me, or perhaps menacing me like bullies drawing back fists to strike. Something rustled in the bushes around me, and little feet pattered quickly over the ground. It could be squirrels, mice, chipmunks, marmots, rabbits ... then there were heavier footfalls and louder rustling that could be deer or chamois. Or something worse.

I found myself whispering desperate prayers, though I had long ago decided the only God I could believe in was one who comprised all being and nature, and not a God to whom it made any sense to pray.

"Please, please, don't let me be eaten by a bear this night. Please don't let that noise be a lynx or a boar. I've always been kind to your animals. The birds of Boisaulne could tell you how I've fed them and sung to them. I even helped your beetles when they fell over onto their backs and couldn't get up again. I complimented your spiders on their beautiful webs and never broke a single one if I could help it."

But perhaps it wasn't the clockwork God of the Deists I was praying to. Perhaps it was the old pagans' Cernunnos, the stag-god whose image was stamped on my medallion. The alder-king, whose power was strongest in the heart of his sacred alder wood.

The hours passed, and I pressed on through the terrors of the looming trees and stones. I was cold and shivering under my cloak, my feet were blistered and aching, and my throat was dry. At last I heard the sound of rushing water and hurried toward it. The stream! I must be close now.

I stopped at the muddy bank and held my lantern out. The water spread black and opaque below it like polished obsidian. The stream hadn't been nearly as deep either time I had crossed it before with Zéphyr, but the heavy rains had swollen it to a flood. If I tried to cross it here I would be swept away, and I didn't know how to swim.

I tried to piece together my fragmented memories of the stream and the village and the forest. With Harlequin, we had forded the water and gone uphill alongside the stream to reach Maisnie-la-Forêt, but then further uphill we'd had to cross back over the bridge to reach the château. When I escaped with Zéphyr, the night Donatien attacked me, it seemed we had forded the stream in the other direction. If Boisaulne was a real place, and not just some imaginary fairy palace I had dreamt up for myself, it had to lie between two branches of the river that joined downstream before the village. I could follow the water upstream for a ways and if I came to a place where the waters divided, at least I would know I had gone in the right direction and was nearer to Boisaulne.

I followed the stream, but my lantern cast too little light to see across to the other side, and I couldn't tell if I had gone too far or passed a divide. I came to a place where a fallen tree made a natural bridge over the water. I kicked hard at the log with the toe of my shoe. It didn't budge. Stable enough – and who knew when I'd find a better spot to cross?

I had taken only a few steps forward over the water, holding my lantern out to one side and my satchel of provisions to the other for balance, when I realized I hadn't counted on the log being so smooth, wet, and slippery. My old shoes with their worn soles gave way, and I plunged into icy black water, scraping my hip, bruising my elbow, and pulling a muscle in my shoulder as I let go of my lantern and satchel and frantically tried to grab the slippery log, to no avail. My heart nearly stopped from the shock of the cold, and the wall of the current pushed me backward, downstream, away from Boisaulne.

For a split second in the freezing watery chaos that enveloped me, time seemed to stand still, and I thought to myself, curiously serene, *So this is how I die. I drown. This is my end.*

Then in a burst of energy I struck out with both legs and both arms at once, kicking and paddling furiously, spitting out water, feeling warmer air on my face. I sucked in a great gasp of breath.

Something slammed hard into my hip and arm, so hard I thought my bones had broken. I had hit a rock. I reached out with my fingers, and something reed-like, slimy, and hard sliced into them. Despite the pain, I tightened my grasp. I must be holding on to thin tree branches or roots that trailed into the river. Between the rock and the roots, I resisted the pull of the current long enough to be able to scramble up onto the bank through a layer of mud and pebbles that scraped up my cut fingers still further.

I curled up on my side in a pile of damp pine needles, panting and shivering. My lantern and satchel were gone. I was soaking wet, coated in mud, bleeding, and in pain. I didn't know anymore which side of the river I was on or how far downstream it had carried me. I couldn't find the sword of stars anymore in the sky, though the moon had risen and shone faintly through the clouds. My shivering turned to shaking. I lurched dizzily onto my feet. If I didn't keep moving, the cold would be the end of me.

I didn't know if I had broken any bones, but my bruised hip hurt with every step. I limped forward, trying to think through the daze of my pain, shock, and cold. Uphill. Boisaulne and its grounds would lie uphill, set into a broad flat terrace on the mountainside. I must go where the ground sloped upward. I held my scraped-up hands out to feel my way forward. Trees, spider webs, more trees, more webs. Forgive me, friends, I didn't mean to harm your webs.

In the distance, the howling of wolves. The sound I had been dreading. My heart nearly beat its way out of my sore, bruised chest. Surely there must be better prey for them than me on this mountain. I stumbled faster, still blindly, from tree to tree. Was I going uphill? Would I live to see the morning? More howling. Closer.

"Please, oh please," I breathed aloud through my chattering teeth. I pushed my hand into my wet pocket and found the silver medallion was still there. I wrapped my bleeding fingers around it. "Cernunnos, alder-king, help me. I need to stay alive. I need to find Thérion again. They say he's your descendant, your grandson's grandson. Your power runs through his veins. I love him. Help me find him, please. Help me find Boisaulne."

I was nearly delirious now, dreaming on my feet. The wolves had caught my scent and were approaching. I couldn't see them in the darkness, but I could sense their presence, the amber eyes, foul breath, snarling lips, cruel teeth, flecks of saliva glinting in the moonlight. In my mind's eye, I saw one of them crouch to spring on me and bring me down, to unleash the depravity of his hunger on me as I struggled under his inexorable weight and he tore into me with his teeth and claws.

I tripped over a tree root and fell to the ground, gasping in pain and terror. When I opened my eyes again and looked up from where I lay with my hands and face in the dirt, something glimmered faintly through the trees. It shone like the ghostly white of birch branches, only smaller, thinner, a thicket of curved and vertical upstretched claws, like the lacy stonework on the cathedral of Annecy. Antlers, a swaying, gothic chandelier of them balanced gracefully on either side of a white stag skull, glowing palely in the night and moving through the branches.

It was the *roi des aulnes,* come to fetch me to his kingdom of death. As he stalked closer, the tall, gaunt man's figure dark beneath the bleached stag skull mask, the wolves bent their necks down toward the ground and began to edge backward, whimpering and slinking away, gradually disappearing into the depths of the woods. I watched the ogre stride toward me and was paralyzed, entranced, appalled. I squeezed my eyes tightly shut, waiting to be torn to pieces. Then I felt a gentle, moist nudge against my forehead. I opened my eyes again and saw a giant stag with a towering rack of antlers kneeling before me, nudging me with his round black muzzle, in place of the horrible vision of the *roi des aulnes*. The gleaming silver iris of his eye, blinking a hand's breadth away from mine, reflected the moonlight like a silver coin. Warm puffs of breath from his nostrils stirred the loose hairs on my forehead. They smelled of lilies of the valley.

183

He wished me to mount onto his back, I understood somehow, as though he had sent the image into my mind. I found I was able to stand up without my bruised side and shoulders hurting too much, and I climbed onto his back, my wet skirt and petticoat bunched between my legs.

He lurched up off the ground and I leaned down and hugged tightly around his neck to keep from falling off. Then we were leaping through the moonlit forest with a grace and speed glorious and terrifying. We went uphill, up and up, the trees flying past us, I didn't know for how long, until suddenly at last a familiar outline took shape before me. It was the standing stone outside the entrance to the grotto.

The forest king who had carried me there brought our mad ride to a halt next to the stone. I reached my arms around the stone, hugged it, and slid off the stag's back, until my feet came to rest on the ground. In a flick of moon-silvered hooves pounding over the ground, he was gone. For a long time I clung to the stone, fearing I would lose my balance again and fall if I let go. Dim light came from inside the grotto, and now the strains of fairy music reached my ears, as before.

I let go of the standing stone, plugged both my ears with my fingers, and tottered forward over the uneven ground, down into the entrance. One elbow brushed against the cold smooth side of the tunnel wall as I went, and I squeezed my eyes tightly shut against the vision of glowing jewels, letting the wall guide me. I moved carefully and slowly, feeling the way forward with my shoes still squelching out water from the stream. After what seemed an eternity, I felt the steps under my feet that led up to the door of the arch. I shoved against the door with my shoulder, keeping my ears plugged, until it opened wide enough to let me through. Quickly I tumbled out through the opening and felt along the wall next to the fountain to find the lever of the mermaid statuette. I pushed it upward to close the door again before the music could draw me back in.

For a moment, my ears rang from the sudden silencing of the music, as if the closing of the gate had deafened me, and I swayed on my feet in the dark foredawn. The stars and moon were completely hidden by clouds now. The fountain of the spring splashed merrily, and the birds began to chirp and chitter to each other about dawn being on its way.

"I'm here," I whispered hoarsely. "I've come back to Boisaulne." I tried to take another step forward, but I shivered too violently in the morning breeze. My knees crumpled under me, and I lost consciousness.

XIV

"Violaine, Violaine," Thérion said in the darkness. His lips pressed against my forehead, my cheeks, my lips. I moaned and my body convulsed with shivers. A warm coat was wrapped around me. "Thank God you're alive."

"Thérion," I murmured. "Is it really you?" I placed my trembling hand against his cheek to feel the familiar outline of his jaw.

"*Shhh*," he said, and I was lifted off the ground and wrapped in his warm arms, carried like a child. "My God, you hardly weigh anything."

My eyelids fluttered open. The day had dawned under a clouded sky, and in its light, for the first time, I saw my lover's face.

"Harlequin. I knew it was you all along. Thérion, my Beast. I love you."

"*Shhh*. You must never tell anyone. I love you, too. More than I've ever loved anyone or anything. But for your own safety and that of your children, you must pretend you don't know me. I'll say … good God, what will I say? That you're a village girl … you were lost in the forest and wandered in here … I don't know."

"But why? What's happened?"

"We've been found out." He was carrying me through the garden now. "It was Donatien. He got his vengeance on me by telling my wife how to reach Boisaulne. She never knew it existed."

"Your wife?" I said through my chattering teeth. "Then you believed me about Donatien."

"Of course I believed you. I'd already decided before I got your reply, that Clio had to be telling the truth and it was wrong of us to doubt her."

"If only I'd written sooner, she might have been spared."

"She wasn't harmed, thank God. And it happened before he attacked you."

"It did?"

"That was what made me doubt her story at first. If it really happened, why wouldn't she have told someone at once? But she's so young. It took her a while to get up the courage. And when you left she was worried for you and felt she ought to say something, in case Donatien had attacked you too and that was why you left."

"But thank God she wasn't hurt. Your letter made me think ..."

"She had a little set of tools she carried on the end of a chatelaine, for trimming her brushes and scraping paint. She was alone with him in her rooms after supper and apparently he wanted to take things further than she did. She had to threaten him with a pair of scissors to get him to leave."

"Would that she'd stabbed him!"

"After I got your letter that night, I searched his rooms. He'd spied on us and taken the letter of instructions I'd left you and hidden it, to be sure of finding you alone while I was away in Annecy. I escorted him back to Paris myself and told him he was no longer welcome at Boisaulne and none of our friends would receive him in Paris anymore."

"Why didn't you write back to me? I was so worried."

"Léonore was in Paris, by a stroke of bad luck. She insisted I stay for a day and a night. And she's here now."

"Léonore?"

"Catherine-Éléonore, my wife. She's been wanting to end our estrangement. Ordinarily she spends six weeks with a friend in Chambord while I go to Boisaulne, but she'd cut her visit short because her friend had fallen ill."

"I can scarcely take it all in. I'm so tired and cold. You must explain it to me later."

"You don't understand. There may never be another chance for us to speak privately. This is what I was afraid of, the reason I was so careful all along. It's why I hid myself, even from you. She also now knows it was I who drew all the cartoons for the gazette under the name of Harlequin. Donatien told her. If I cross her there'll be a *lettre de cachet* against me and I'll be imprisoned in the Château de Vincennes. There's no refuge for me even in Savoy, because her father is a friend of the governor, and I could just as easily be sent to the Château de Miolans. I'm utterly at her mercy."

"But what wife would be so cruel? Who would send her own husband to prison?"

"You don't know Léonore. She found your *Book of the Rose* and threw it in the fire. It's gone now, forever, and all your poems with it."

"What?" I struggled to sit up in his arms and then lay back again, too weak.

"Thank God, I managed to burn all your letters before she found them. But she found your poems in the book, signed with your name. Donatien told her I had a mistress here, and she knew at once the poems were yours."

"But the book was there with me in my father's house. I kept it hidden under the mattress so it would be safe."

"When you fell asleep at night, it would come to me at Boisaulne. I don't know how. I've never understood how my own powers work. Only that I see in the dark, that I can bring darkness around me, and this place formed its beauty in accordance with my wishes. And your book came to me in place of you, when I wanted more than anything to have you here in my arms. I'd find it on a table in my study with your letter inside, and I'd leave my letter for you in it. Then while I slept it would travel back to you. Perhaps it wasn't my power at all. Perhaps the book had its own magic. But when Léonore arrived, she sensed at once it was something precious to me. And destroyed it."

"I th-thought the book was lost or s-stolen. Zéphyr was gone too, when we woke."

"I called Zéphyr back to Boisaulne. I hoped it would delay you leaving long enough for me to get word to you that it wasn't safe to come back anymore. If only I could have made you forget I ever existed so you'd believe the whole thing was only a dream."

"Was it real after all, then, and no dream?"

"Oh, Violaine. But I can't call you that anymore. She knows that was the name of the woman I loved. Donatien guessed everything and told her all of it. We need a new *surnom* for you. I'll call you Psyché. She also had a lover who came to her only in the dark. We'll say ... you're a cousin of Aurore's from Grenoble ... Aurore will protect you, I know she will. They all will, if I ask it of them. But what will I tell them? No one can ever know what we've been to each other. You'll never be safe from Léonore. The sooner you can leave here and stay away for good, the better."

We reached the house, but instead of going through the glass-paned doors, we turned off to the side and went through a small door around a corner that I had never noticed before. It led down into a cellar, dimly lit by daylight coming in through a grating on one side of the ceiling. We came up out of the cellar into an unfamiliar narrow stairwell, up several flights of stairs that seemed to mount endlessly. At last we came to the top of the stairs, to a locked door. It must be the garret. Thérion was staggering and struggling under my weight now, however light he had claimed I was at first.

"Can you stand?" he whispered.

"I think so." I seemed to have only bruises, no broken bones as I had feared.

He set me down onto my feet with a grunt, tugged the coat more snugly around me with both hands, and then reached into the coat's pocket and drew out a heavy ring of keys. He unlocked the door and beckoned me in. It was a small, cramped servant's room, furnished with only a narrow iron bed and thin mattress, a table and chair, and a chest.

"We need to get you out of your wet clothes," he said. "How on earth did you get here without Zéphyr, anyway?" He slipped the coat off my shoulders, and I let him tug off my dress and stays, and my chemise underneath.

"I walked through the forest. I tried to cross the stream, but I fell in. I made it to the other side, but then there were wolves."

"Wolves!"

I was naked now, and he pulled me close, caressing me and trying to warm me with his arms through his shirt-sleeves.

"My God, your skin is ice-cold. Here." He went to the trunk next to the wall and pulled out blankets and a soft new chemise. He drew the garment over my head, then made me lie down on the bed and covered me in the blankets. They were as warm as though someone had placed a hot brick between them. "We need some hot tea," he said.

When I looked over at the table, a steaming pot of tea and a cup were on it, and he poured tea into the cup and handed it to me. I propped myself up and blew on it to cool it. He frowned and shook his head.

"Wolves. I can't believe you went into the woods alone at night. That was incredibly dangerous and foolish. It's a miracle you weren't lost. You must have come in by way of the grotto, too. You could have been drawn down into that tunnel ... That was why I wanted you to promise never to go that way alone at night."

"What is that tunnel? I heard music and saw lights coming from it, but then it seemed they weren't real. If Zéphyr hadn't been there, neighing, I'm sure I would have gone down into it."

He peered at me, as if trying to gauge whether I was prepared to believe him. "Do they tell tales in your village of the *demoiselles,* the forest fairies in white dresses, who live in caves and govern the springs?"

I shook my head. "Not often. We were forbidden to speak of them – *demousélas,* they're called in our patois."

"My nurse from Maisnie would tell me stories of them when I stayed at the manor as a boy. She meant to warn me away from the spring in the grotto, of course. One was never supposed to go there alone after dark. I'm only grateful no worse harm befell you, if there really were wolves."

"I dreamt I saw the *roi des aulnes* again. I dreamt he rescued me from the wolves."

"Good God. Violaine – Psyché – I have to get used to calling you that. Why did you take such risks?" He sat next to me on the bed and stroked my cheek.

"I love you. Can't you believe me when I say that? I was afraid you were sick, or hurt, or in danger. I wanted to help you or rescue you if I could."

"No one can save me now. It's too late. I made a terrible mistake ten years ago, and it's my curse to live with it until Death has mercy and takes one or both of us."

He stood up, put on his coat, and moved to the door. He hesitated, his hand on the doorknob.

"Rest and be well."

He left me.

I slept soundly and dreamlessly. When I woke, it was because Aurore was sitting next to me on the room's solitary wooden chair, smoothing back the hair from my forehead.

"Darling, are you awake?" she said. "You've been sleeping all day. It's almost supper time."

"Oh, I'm so glad to see you." I sat up, and she leaned over to embrace me and kiss me on the cheek.

"We thought perhaps you'd gone back to your village to stay. Clio was worried it was because of something Donatien did to you.

She knew he'd been hanging around you, and he'd done things to frighten her, too."

Haltingly, I told her of Donatien's attack and how I left with Zéphyr in the middle of the night. Her usual pleasant smile slid from her face, and her expression was dead-eyed.

"I can believe it all too well."

"I hadn't thought him capable of it," I said. "Séléné thought his vanity would forbid it, if nothing else. I trusted him."

She shook her head. "I could have told Séléné, and you too. He didn't force himself on me. In the end, I let him. But I'm not sure he'd have listened if I'd said no."

"But what's happened since I left? Harlequin told me he took Donatien back to Paris and forbade him to come back ever again. And he said his wife came back with him, and she's here now at Boisaulne."

"I couldn't believe it. It turns out Harlequin was the Marquis de Boisaulne himself, all this time. Had you any idea?"

"I did suspect," I admitted. "But the others had joked about being the Marquis, too."

"Well, he had me fooled. He fooled everyone, even his own wife. She never knew he had a second *marquisat,* any more than the rest of us did. But his secret's out now."

"What's she like, his wife?"

"She was ... rather chilly toward me. I went to chapel with her this morning. She brought a friend, an *abbé* who seems to be a sort of counselor or advisor to her. She only got here the night before last, and we met her for the first time at dinner last night. It's bizarre to imagine her and Harlequin as husband and wife. They're so unlike each other."

"You hadn't met her before in Paris?"

"Not really. I knew *of* her. I knew they were married, of course, but she never came to my or Séléné's *salons*. I didn't really even associate them with each other in my mind since Harlequin didn't use his title amongst his friends. The Marquise du Herle, on the other hand, had friends at court and moved in the highest circles. You'd hear sometimes of her entertainments, but I'd never been introduced to her before yesterday."

"Harlequin seems terrified of her."

"He told me Donatien had convinced her you and Harlequin had been lovers. That was Donatien's defense for his appalling actions, apparently. That you were a low courtesan with social ambitions, and you'd seduced first Harlequin and then Donatien. He claimed Harlequin only sent him away out of jealousy. What an awful, sordid business."

"Harlequin told me she'd threatened him with prison if he crossed her. And he was afraid for my safety if she found out I was here."

"I don't know. I suppose she always had a reputation as a – how should I say – a forceful personality? People said she took offense easily and could be vindictive, and liked to throw her influence around. If you weren't invited to her balls, you were shut out from court circles altogether. Her father's someone powerful in the government. But I thought Harlequin must love her on some level. He never spoke much of her, but I never heard of him having an affair or anything but the most harmless of flirtations."

"Is it any wonder he wanted to keep Boisaulne a secret from her, though, if she's really threatening him with prison?"

"I don't know what to think of it all. Ordinarily I'd say husbands and wives shouldn't keep secrets from each other. But I always fibbed and told my own husband I was going to visit my sister in Grenoble when I wanted to come to Boisaulne. And anyway, I can certainly keep it a secret that you're the one who accused Donatien."

"Oh, thank you. That's the saving grace, I suppose – the Marquise doesn't know what I look like, unless Donatien thought to describe me to her."

"Right. We'll all call you Psyché from now on instead of Belle-Âme. Belle-Âme's gone away for good, as far as any of us know. The story is, you're an impoverished niece of mine from Grenoble. I've written to my sister and asked whether you could come take up a position in my house in Paris as a companion, which is something I've felt the need of since my poor husband's been ailing. And you just arrived from Grenoble today."

"I'm sorry to put you to so much trouble."

"It's not the least bit of trouble. It's not even a lie about wanting a companion in Paris. You could come with me when we all go back at the end of the week. You could even send for your children, and they could stay with us too. I miss having little ones around."

My mouth fell open. I hadn't thought of anything like this. What would it be like in Paris? Could I bear to be so far from my father and sisters? Could I bear to live in such a great city, so far from my mountains with their constantly shifting canvas of green meadows, gray rocks, pine forests, snows, sunrays, and shadows? Would I ever see Thérion or Boisaulne again?

"Well," she said, "you needn't decide at once. We have till the end of the week. If you're well enough to come down, why don't we get dressed for dinner? We'll share my rooms, if you don't mind. Harlequin's arranging for another bed to be brought in. The Marquise took your rooms, because they were the nicest in the château, apparently."

I stretched and sat up with my feet on the floor.

"I wonder what happened to my old wet clothes," I said. "I suppose they've disappeared, the way things do here. I'll have to sneak downstairs behind you in my chemise. Keep a lookout ahead and warn me if anyone's there."

"But what's this?" Aurore asked, looking down at the bare little table.

A circle of silver glinted on it. I breathed out a sigh of relief. "My medallion. I thought I'd lost it."

"What is it?"

"Oh, nothing. An old good luck charm." I stood up and put it round my neck.

❀

195

Aurore took pains to make sure I was dressed for dinner in a convincingly provincial fashion; she tied a lace kerchief around my neck to cover my bosom. We were the last to arrive at the supper table.

Léonore, the Marquise du Herle, sat at the head of the table, with Thérion at her right hand, and a gentleman I didn't recognize at her left. She was proportioned like a giantess, taller than anyone else at the table, her face puffy and heavy-jowled, her bosom large enough that she had to tuck a napkin round her neck to avoid spilling soup into her décolletage. She wore a lofty, elaborately curled and powdered wig. There was no telling what her natural hair color was, for she had painted her eyebrows black, and the rest of her face was heavily powdered and made up. For all that, it wasn't an ugly face, and her coloring and features seemed pretty enough beneath the paint.

Aurore presented me to the company, and everyone else pretended, absurdly, to be meeting me for the first time. It was all any of us could do not to burst out laughing – all except for Thérion, whose face was expressionless, as if he had never known me and didn't care to.

The Marquise narrowed her eyes at me suspiciously.

The gentleman on her other side was introduced simply as the Abbé. He wore the little collar and short mantle of those Catholic scholars who were neither priests nor monks, but who benefitted from a churchly association without being subject to any requirement of ascetic rigor in their manner of living. He was nearly the opposite of the Marquise in all respects: short where she was tall, rail-thin where she was fleshy, beak-nosed, wearing a short unpowdered wig of the kind ordinary to his profession. While the Marquise flashed a brilliant smile around the room that was belied by the instants when her eyes narrowed like those of a hawk about to strike, or her brightly painted mouth twisted in a bitter, subtle display of contempt, the Abbé had a dreamy, gentle gaze.

196

"So you've just come from Grenoble, have you?" the Marquise said to me. "I can only imagine how vile and provincial it will seem to you once you've moved on to Paris."

Without waiting for a response from me or Aurore, she launched into a long monologue about all the pains she had taken to eradicate every last bit of country style from her house and wardrobe in Paris, including the costs of various articles of furniture and linens. As she went on, the others grew distracted and began to fidget and whisper amongst themselves.

At last she paused for a breath, and the Scotsman said in his mild, genial way, "But you must admit, the climate is much more pleasant here in the summer than in your capital."

"No. The only thing that ever makes the countryside bearable is the chance to go hunting."

"Ah, you're keen on the sport, are you? In my country it's become quite the fashion for those of noble birth to hunt the fox with hounds. But I must say, I'm fond of the game meat we've been eating all summer here. If one's going to hunt it seems more sensible to me to do it for food."

"But that's not at all the point," the Marquise said. "You've never seen magnificence till you've been along on a royal hunting expedition. It's not about meat, it's about power, opulence, blood, the thrill of the chase, those of us who are noble establishing our mastery over nature. Why, I've had the privilege of seeing dozens of deer and boars rounded up and shot – what a thing, to see these prideful beasts brought low! I'm not a bad markswoman myself with a musket, you know. Some might say it's not ladylike to hunt, but I find it invigorating, and plenty of ladies at court enjoy the spectacle and thrill of it."

Most of the rest of the dinner was spent with the Marquise droning on about the sport of the hunt.

I whispered to Aurore, "I can see why she's considered so dangerous. There's a good risk she'll bore us all to death."

Aurore giggled, earning us a dagger-edged glare from the Marquise. I half wanted to laugh out loud, just to spite her, but then I remembered what Thérion had told me about the Marquise throwing the *Book of the Rose* into the fire. Tears sprang to my eyes at the thought of my lost book and poems, and my lost love, and I had to dab at them with my napkin. Thérion wouldn't look in my direction at all.

As if she had guessed my thoughts, the Marquise directed a small self-satisfied smile my way.

"But perhaps Madame la marquise could indulge her love of hunting here at Boisaulne," said Séléné, with what I recognized as a poisonous sweetness. "Harlequin, you must have a few muskets about. The château's always so well-provisioned with everything one could want." Her tone was so arch, I seemed to hear a double meaning in every word. I made a mental note to ask her about her late husband's hunting accident, as I remembered how much joy the memory of it had seemed to bring her.

"It's a curious thing," the Marquise said. "My dear husband claims the woods here make for poor hunting. Yet when the Abbé and I spoke to the curé in the village, we heard an entirely different story. It was astonishing. We were told the villagers have free rein to hunt on Boisaulne's lands as long as they don't cross the river. Moreover, a considerable amount of meat and skins from this side of the stream goes to the villagers in exchange for a paltry amount of foodstuff, hardly any more than Boisaulne's guests need to eat."

Thérion looked pale. "Most of Savoy has been in a state of famine the past few years. Every autumn you see a heartbreaking exodus of boys from the villages setting out to make their way on foot to Paris to become chimney sweeps and servants. Those who don't find work in the city, far from their parents, become beggars in the slums, or they simply starve. But Maisnie-la-Forêt has kept its children. The famine hasn't touched here. I've simply tried to do the right thing by the villagers." He had been drinking steadily throughout the meal, and his speech had begun to slur.

The Abbé cleared his throat. "I hardly see how making poachers of the people can truly benefit them in the long run.

When their hands are chopped off for thievery, will they thank you?"

"Indeed," the Marquise said, "one has to think of the welfare of the soul and not just the body. There'll be no more of this, letting these worthless poachers take advantage of us. It enrages me, just to think of it. It's lucky I'm finally here to take a hand in things. To imagine, all this time, a mountain hunting manor being neglected and run to ruin as you let people cheat and rob us. And I certainly intend to get a count of the game population in the forest on both sides of the river. The Abbé's something of an authority on animals. He can help us with it."

The Abbé chuckled. "Madame la marquise, you flatter me. Of course, I did help the Duc de Montvalère to gather together the animals for his game park. But I think of myself more as a man of science, a naturalist. I've been collecting a few samples to study and had meant to collect more live ones when the weather clears up. This could lend itself to survey of game species at the same time, but I must warn that it's an inexact procedure."

"Might I accompany you?" the Scotsman asked. "I'd love to see how you do it. I had noticed, too, that there were a great number of species in the region unfamiliar to me. Perhaps I could even be of some assistance to you."

"Quite. It would be my pleasure. Speaking of a survey, do you know, I was looking at some maps of the area in the Marquis's study. It appears the domain of Boisaulne borders on several villages of heretics – Vaudois, as they call themselves. Degenerates worse than Huguenots, so wicked even the Calvinists would hardly acknowledge them as among their own. These depraved dregs of humanity ought to have been wiped out with the rest of their kind a century ago. But quite extraordinarily, they've been treated with indulgence and particularly protected by the lords of Boisaulne. Apparently there's a history of the domain being infected with this terrible disease, the idea of so-called religious toleration, which has become such a scourge to the stability of the governments of Europe in our times."

The Scotsman coughed delicately. "Perhaps you don't recall, sir, that my own countrymen are Presbyterians for the most part? We're but a hair's breadth from being Calvinists ourselves."

The Abbé smiled his gentle, peaceable smile. "My dear friend, I don't mean to cause any offense, but I'm firmly of the belief that Protestantism is the greatest calamity that ever befell Europe."

The Scotsman smiled too. There was admittedly something amusing in hearing such a declaration made in in such a gentle, friendly tone.

"Worse than the Black Plague?" he asked. "Worse than the earthquake of Lisbon?"

"Protestantism has been responsible for the bloodiest of wars and civil conflicts. And that's not even the half of it. It threatens to destroy our future. It threatens the stability of every government, even those of countries such as your own where it's embraced as the state religion."

The Scotsman raised his eyebrows and awaited further elaboration.

"The State and the Christian faith are two sisters," the Abbé said. "They've sometimes quarreled, but they cannot do without each other. The one sustains the other. Legal codes take their precepts from the faith, and the state protects the faith. The faith in turn upholds the state and the monarch's authority. These twin pillars of order used to rest on a foundation of majestic infallibility, which led by way of blind trust in authority, and renunciation of individual reason, to a set of universal beliefs."

The Scotsman nodded. "With this I can't disagree."

"Then innovators weakened this foundation by undermining it, seeking to dig deeper. How did they do this? They replaced obedience with discussion. They set the arrogance of individual reason and judgment against Catholic judgment and the authority of long tradition."

The Scotsman looked ready to burst out laughing. But I was still trembling at the mention of the Vaudois villages. I saw how slit-eyed the Marquise was as she listened and how Thérion grew paler still and gulped down another goblet of wine far too quickly and filled it again. Now his eyes looked glazed over and his stare was vacant.

One by one, while the Scotsman and the Abbé had been speaking, Séléné, Ulysse, Clio, and Tristan had each slipped out of the room.

"Excuse me," I said, folding my napkin in front of me on the table, "but the journey from Grenoble was tiring today. I think I'll go upstairs now. It's been such a pleasure becoming acquainted." Aurore and the Scotsman excused themselves too. The Marquise, her face now a rictus of the friendliest goodwill, wished us a good evening and we went out, leaving Thérion alone with her and the Abbé.

*A*URORE AND I undressed and got ready for bed, but before we could blow out the candles, there was a quiet knock on the door.

"It's Clio. May I come in?"

Hurriedly we put on dressing gowns, and I opened the door. Clio came in and sat down at the foot of my narrow bed. Just as she opened her mouth to speak, there was another knock. This time Aurore rose to answer it. It was the Scotsman.

"Ladies, good evening. I'm so terribly sorry to bother you. I hate to intrude on your privacy, but I wanted to have a word ..."

There was another knock at the door.

"*Ach*," said the Scotsman. "This is rather embarrassing."

Aurore shook her head. "No matter. Would you be so kind as to see who it is?"

He opened the door and let in Séléné and Ulysse, who looked around the room and laughed.

"I see we're not the only ones who thought it was time to have a talk about things," said Séléné.

"We're only missing Tristan," said Ulysse. "Shall I go and fetch him? Our would-be knight might think it's unchivalrous to go knocking on ladies' doors at night."

"Would you mind?" said Aurore gently. Ulysse disappeared and came back a few minutes later with Tristan.

Despite the somber nature of our gathering, it had the air of children's party or a costume fête, with all of us in our dressing gowns. One by one, our visitors found seats on the sofa or the armchairs or one of the beds.

Ulysse tipped his tasseled, Oriental-style embroidered nightcap to us in salute and said, "I suppose we're all thinking along similar lines. This is a crisis situation, is it not?"

"These people are horrible," Clio said. "They're going to ruin Boisaulne for everyone if we don't do something."

Séléné folded her arms across her chest. "Not only that, but Harlequin's a dear friend, and this woman's going to kill him. He's done nothing but drink since she got here. Who can blame him? She'd make me want to drink myself to death too."

"And this priest makes me want to set something on fire," Ulysse said. "Like maybe that hideous wig and collar of his."

"The priest – I mean, the Abbé – is Donatien's uncle," Clio said. Her round freckled cheeks were pink with anger.

"What?" My mouth gaped open in shock.

"So he told me, yesterday. He blames me, and you, for seducing Donatien and tempting him. Of course he doesn't know you're you, Belle-Âme, since we switched to calling you Psyché. This afternoon when they got back from going to church with Aurore, he pulled me aside and said he wanted to talk to me about it. He led me into a corner of the library and sat down too close to me on the sofa – like this –" She scooted over next to me to show us how uncomfortable the distance was, and then moved back. "He took both my hands in his. He said I ought to seek forgiveness from the Lord, and beg Donatien's forgiveness too."

I shook my head. "But that's disgusting."

"Oh, it got worse. He said his nephew was so generous and forgiving, he wanted to become my patron, and I ought to accept the offer and 'submit' to him and let him guide my career." She shook her head. "What a repulsive piece of ..."

"That's an astonishing hypocrisy. What did you say?"

"Well, I pulled my hands away as if I'd touched a manure pile. I ought to have told him to ... to go and fuck himself. But I was too stunned to say anything. I just jumped up walked away without a word."

Tristan looked grave and pale with fury on Clio's behalf.

"And the Marquise," I asked, "how is he connected with her?"

The Scotsman said, "It appears the Abbé's been her spiritual advisor for some time. Harlequin must have known him, but I don't think anyone realized he was a relative of Donatien's."

"I'd practically forgotten what Harlequin's wife even looked like," said Séléné. "They move in such different circles. I'd seen her once or twice at Madame Dufaud's *salon*, long ago. But she's no great intellect, obviously, so I can only imagine *salons* would bore her. I tried asking what she'd read, and she looked at me like she'd bitten a lemon. I can only think she must be a vulgar, ignorant creature, devoid of culture."

Ulysse snorted. "No better way to fit in at court. La Pompadour's the only one with any polish there."

"But it isn't any wonder now," Aurore said, "why Harlequin was always so silent on the subject of his marriage."

"Perhaps," Tristan observed, "that was the real reason all along for the rule of not talking about families at Boisaulne. I admired Harlequin's attempts to take philosophical stances in favor of Enlightenment, but that rule always struck me as strange. After all, every philosopher through the ages has discussed the family at some point."

"I think you're right," the Scotsman said.

"Do you know though," said Ulysse, "going back to the subject of Donatien, I'd heard some rumors about him, now that I think about it."

"What rumors?" Clio asked.

"Something about him getting into trouble with the law over mistreating some prostitutes. Everyone wrote it off as nothing or laughed at it. Now I wish I'd said something. But he'd always been a friend of my family's – his father knew mine. And the rumors sounded silly, something about giving the women pastilles with Spanish Fly that made them sick, flogging them, and making them piss on a crucifix. Of course I wasn't bothered about the crucifix – '*Écrasez l'infâme*,' and all."

"It's rather ironic then," the Scotsman said, "that he's got such a Catholic uncle."

"No, it isn't," I said. "They're two sides of the same coin." Given the cruel persecutions of my Vaudois forbears, this was a subject on which I felt entitled to speak with authority.

"How so?" the Scotsman asked.

"It's a wish to dominate, in both cases," I explained. "Didn't you get the sense the Abbé's interest in Christianity was more for the sake of its political uses than any love of Christian principles for their own sake?"

"You've put your finger right on it. Bright girl," Ulysse said.

"Anyway," Clio said, turning to me, "now you're back, and you see how things are. Boisaulne is ruined. Should we all just leave and go home early? Or is there anything we can do?"

"I think we need to rescue Harlequin," Séléné said. "We need to come up with a plan."

"There's something I should tell you all," I said. Suddenly, all eyes were on me and the room went quiet. Quickly I got up out of bed and went to the door, opened it, and peered out into the hall, just to make sure no one was listening. The corridor was empty. To make sure we weren't overheard, I took a handkerchief from Aurore's vanity table and stuffed it into the keyhole. I got back into bed, under the covers, and then I said, "Harlequin and I were lovers."

Ulysse looked both amused and pleased. Tristan's eyes widened. Aurore nodded thoughtfully, and Séléné's mouth rounded into a silent *Oh*. The Scotsman cocked his head, Clio frowned and looked struck. From her reaction, I was seized by a sudden fear.

"Am I the only one?" I asked, my voice choking up a little.

The others all looked inquiringly at each other. I met Clio's eyes, and there was a tense moment of silence. "Clio?" I asked. I ought to be brave. I ought to be willing to face the truth. "Did you sleep with him, too?"

She drooped and looked down at her hands in her lap. "No. I – well, I wanted to. I kissed him once, on the lips." Her cheeks were flushed, and I was so relieved, I found it charming. "He pushed me away. He wasn't unkind, but he said he was much too old for me, and besides, he was a married man."

I looked around at the rest of their faces. "Am I the only one, then?"

There were a few nods, and Aurore said gently, "I told you, I'd never heard of him doing anything of the kind. He always had a great reputation for fidelity."

"I figured he must be one of those odd people who don't care for lovemaking at all," Séléné said. "He has no children. I thought perhaps he was simply a cold fish, as they say. Or perhaps he liked gentlemen, though I'd never heard of him indulging in that preference, either. I certainly tried with him a time or two. But no."

"So the Marquise was right to be jealous of you," Aurore said. There was only the slightest hint of a reproach in her tone.

I swallowed. "She was. I was his mistress. He didn't want anyone to know, not even his friends, because he was afraid of the Marquise finding out. For a long time he kept his true identity a secret even from me."

I didn't have the heart to try to defend myself any further, to tell them my father had sold me to Thérion to pay his debts, or that I couldn't help falling in love with my master and jailer when he came to me in the dark; or how the Marquise had always seemed so far away, more dreamlike and unreal than any of the magical things at Boisaulne. I had never imagined I would have to meet her face to face, that she would intrude on our joys, sever our bond, and destroy my book and our peace. I had all but forgotten that in the eyes of the rest of the world, the man I loved was an adulterer, and I was the fallen woman he had sinned with. It had seemed to me love justified us and bound us together in a way no marriage ever could, by a law as ancient as the *roi des aulnes's* woods.

"My dear girl," said Ulysse, "I don't think any one of us is really in a position to cast the first stone. I, for one, love Séléné, and she'd sooner skewer me in a duel than marry me."

Séléné looked up at him from her seat on the sofa, blinking. He was perched on the arm of the sofa next to her, half standing. Were there tears in her eyes? There were. She wiped them away with the heel of her hand and smiled. "But darling, you never even asked."

"You'd have said no, wouldn't you?"

"True. Still, it's sweet of you to think of it. I'd shack up with you, if you liked."

"I'd like that very much."

The two of them looked tenderly at each other. He placed a hand on her cheek and stroked it, and she rested her head against his hand.

Tristan said, "Can we return to the subject at hand? Ulysse and I rarely agree on anything, but he's right that we can't cast stones. And this woman is no less horrid for being his lawfully-wedded wife."

"But it's not as though there's anything we can do about it," the Scotsman said. "There's no legal divorce in your Catholic lands, even for kings."

"Oh, shove it in our faces, why don't you," grumbled Ulysse.

"He could convert and flee to Genève," said Tristan. "The lady who took me in when I came to Annecy did it the reverse way. She emigrated to Savoy and became a Catholic so her marriage could be annulled. It might work in both directions."

"Shouldn't that be for him to decide?" said Aurore. "Anyway, I think it'd be quite difficult to throw away everything you have and leave your home and friends forever. He'd be penniless there, and a fugitive from the law if he ever came back. Her father's a *fermier général*. All that's needed is a *lettre de cachet* against him, and she and her father will control all his goods, in essence."

"And it's just what she's threatened," I said. "She can expose him for the cartoons he's published. He's not safe even in Savoy because her father knows the governor and could have him sent to Miolans. My own husband was locked up there, in the dungeon of Miolans, and they only let him out to come home to die when he got sick."

Clio put her hands on her cheeks. "The poor man. It's monstrous."

"What we really need," said Séléné, "is a good hunting accident."

Everyone stared at her. She looked around at our shocked faces and laughed. "Oh, but come now, I didn't mean it like that. I'm no murderess. My late husband's gun misfired, fair and square. He was thrown from his horse, broke his neck, and then was trampled on by the horses, too. Dead as you like, with no one guilty but himself for being an arsehole who enjoyed killing defenseless creatures by the cruelest methods."

"The Marquise certainly seems keen on hunting," the Scotsman conceded. "But for one thing, death by hunting accident seems rather a harsh sentence for a woman we all merely dislike intensely. For another thing, plenty of bloodthirsty numbskulls go hunting all the time and live to tell the tale. We can't count on being so lucky, if you call it that. Good Lord, I can't believe we're even having this conversation."

"Suppose we simply made it very disagreeable for her here," said Clio. "If it's very dull, or if she thought there were ghosts, or if we played pranks on her. Perhaps we could drive her away."

"I think she'd be more likely to expel us all," Aurore said. "After all, she's the lady of the manor. It's her château. We're merely her guests."

"Much as I hate to say it," I said, "I think we'd probably do best by trying to stay on her good side. At least then we can be there for Harlequin. If he's this despairing and driven to drink with us here, imagine if we abandon him."

"We don't have much longer here anyway," Aurore reminded me. "Normally we all go back home at the end of August."

I shrugged. "Who knows what will happen to him then? But for now, at least we still have some chance of helping."

"Oh, but it sounds like there's no hope," said Clio. "What can any of us do?"

"If only I could talk more with him," I said. "Alone, without arousing the Marquise's suspicions."

The Scotsman shook his head. "I don't think she or the Abbé have left him alone for more than five minutes at a time since they got here. Not that I've seen."

"But he rescued me," I said. "When I came back through the woods and the back gate. I'd fainted by the fountain of the spring. He carried me back inside and spoke to me a little."

"This morning?"

"I suppose it was. It all seems so long ago already." I suppressed a yawn, beginning to feel drowsy again.

"That was when they went to chapel with Aurore in the village," the Scotsman said.

Ulysse chuckled. "I think our dear Marquise and her Abbé were rather irked that the rest of us stayed home. I shouldn't have liked to draw down lightning bolts on that picturesque little chapel, which I'd surely have done by setting foot in it."

"Perhaps if they go to chapel again before the end of the week," Aurore said. "You could speak to him then."

"But there's no telling whether they'll do that," I said in dismay.

"No," said Clio, "but I've a brilliant idea. We'll convince her to let me paint her portrait. If she's vain enough to agree to it – and it seems she is."

Séléné nodded vigorously. "That could work. Ulysse, you're charming. Convince her. If anyone here has the gift of persuading ladies, it's you."

Ulysse waved a hand to deny it, but his eyes had lit up.

I clapped my hands together. "Oh, thank you, both of you. It's worth a try, isn't it? But −" I knitted my brows together − "what about the Abbé? How do we keep him occupied?"

"Nothing could be simpler," the Scotsman said. "We've already made plans to gather botanical samples and fauna specimens in the forest tomorrow."

"It's perfect," Séléné said. "It'll work."

The Scotsman and Tristan left with the Abbé before sunrise on their expedition to gather specimens in the forest. At breakfast in the morning room, Thérion was absent.

"My dear husband is still sleeping," the Marquise said in a sugary tone that betrayed her annoyance.

Ulysse, coming into the room behind her and overhearing, mimicked drinking from a bottle, to imply Harlequin was hung over. Séléné tittered, and the Marquise whipped around to see the cause of the merriment. Ulysse bowed to her with a flourish and winked.

"We must endeavor to amuse you this morning," he said, "since your husband's been so remiss as to leave you alone." He slid into the seat next to her.

The Marquise looked Ulysse up and down, seeming mollified. She nearly simpered as she asked, "What shall we do? Perhaps a game of cards?"

"Er, by your leave," said Clio, "I have an idea. I thought perhaps you might indulge me by allowing me to sketch you. You have such fine fair skin and pretty features."

"Why, that's a capital idea," Ulysse said. "Indeed, you absolutely must sketch the Marquise."

The Marquise demurred coyly, shrugging with her double chin tucked into her shoulder. "Oh, I hardly think so."

"No, but really. She could paint you as Diana, goddess of the hunt. It would be so attractive, imagine it. You could be dressed in Grecian robes, wearing a laurel crown, with a bow and a quiver of arrows."

Clio clapped her hands together. "Oh yes, that's brilliant. What could be more perfect? Won't you?"

The Marquise pursed her lips and tapped her chin, pretending to consider it, though it was already clear she meant to accept. "Would I need to sit quite still for a very long time though?"

"I could do a preliminary sketch for a larger painting in just an hour or two," Clio said. "And perhaps someone would be kind enough to read a story aloud to keep you entertained while I do it. Ulysse is a wonderful reader."

"Say no more," Ulysse said. "I'd be delighted. Have you a favorite author?"

The Marquise frowned and thought for a long time. "I don't mind Madame Riccoboni's novels. They're usually decent."

The color drained from Ulysse's face, even as his smile widened so that his dark pink lips strained over his teeth. Only the week before last, he'd spent a couple of hours one afternoon telling us all the reasons why Madame Riccoboni's novels were dreadful, worthless treacle. Aurore and I glanced at each other and barely suppressed our giggles, while Séléné raised her eyebrows in mute sympathy.

"Wonderful," he said, rubbing his hands together. "I quite adore her novels myself. You have *such* good taste, my lady."

When breakfast was finished, Ulysse, Clio, and the Marquise left for the library to find the novel the Marquise wished to hear read. Aurore, Séléné, and I followed them, and we stayed behind in the library after they had left for Clio's studio upstairs with the book.

I had hoped to find Thérion there, as he sometimes spent mornings writing letters or sketching caricatures at one of the writing desks.

"I suppose he must be still asleep," I said. "Perhaps our cleverness will all be for naught."

"Oh, don't be silly," Séléné said. "Go and wake him."

"I don't even know where he sleeps. He always came to me in my room at night. But wait, I think I have an idea." I went out into the gallery, and Aurore and Séléné trailed after me to watch. I remembered the day he'd had blood on his sleeve, the day we had looked into the chest of antiquities and I had taken the Cernunnos medallion from it. Afterward he had walked down the hall ... he had pulled aside a tapestry, opened a door ...

I moved forward, letting memory guide me, almost to the end of the hall. Was this the tapestry? I pulled it aside and groped for the concealed handle. Something pushed inward with a click, and the door opened. I waved to Aurore and Séléné and went in.

Inside, I wrinkled my nose at the close, sweaty smell of the room, which had clearly been too seldom aired. Little light entered from the large window, which was covered by heavy black velvet drapes and shuttered where the drapes narrowly parted. The room was dimly lit by candles on a large writing desk and a fire flickering in the grate of a curious octagonal iron stove that gave off generous heat. It was part study, part bedchamber, with a wide bed on a platform draped in black velvet like the window. Next to the writing desk was a cabinet of drawers, and on the other side a set of shelves filled with books.

A rustling came from the bed as Thérion emerged from behind the bed curtains. He stood barefoot in his long, wrinkled shirt, unshaven, looking at me.

"Violaine?"

"Psyché," I reminded him.

He looked down, as though ashamed of his appearance, and then back up at me. His eyes were wide, anguished, pleading.

I couldn't help myself and began to cry.

"Oh, Thérion." I wiped my eyes with the back of my hand.

"We'll be in terrible trouble if she finds us here." He stood stock-still, and his voice was soft and strangled with fear.

"But it's safe. We came up with a stratagem. Clio convinced her to sit for a picture. And the Abbé will be gone till dusk."

He breathed out and his rigid posture relaxed. He stepped forward and I came to meet him, and our arms twined round each other, but his embrace was weak and restrained. He let go of me quickly and stepped back.

"If she catches you here, she'll realize you're the Violaine of the poems, and she'll find a way to exact retribution on you and your family. She was already suspicious when you arrived yesterday. Your children may be in danger. Your villages already are."

"I'm not afraid of her. We're not in France. Savoy has laws and courts, and she's a foreigner."

"All she'd have to do is send a letter to the governor and mention her father's name. It would be nothing to her to buy off the police, and she can well afford it. Your father could find himself accused of fraud, arrested, and sent to the galleys. Your children – she'd find a way to see they're taken from you. She could have you placed in an insane asylum. It's the sort of thing she'd do."

I put my hands on my hips. "But even if she really meant to do us so much harm, how would she find them out?"

"I have account books I keep here, and now she has access to all of them. She already noticed the transfers of funds to your father and questioned them. I told her he was a business associate, but I don't know if she was really convinced. Thank God I managed to burn the contract we signed in the stove before she found it."

If the contract that bound me to Thérion had been burnt, did that mean I was free? But I no longer wished to be free. I wanted nothing so badly as to remain a prisoner of the Castle of Enlightenment forever.

"But what makes you think she'd do such things?" I asked. "Has she destroyed others in the past?"

He turned his face away from me as though I had landed a fist on his cheek. Slowly, stumbling, he backed away and sat down on the end of the bed between the curtains.

"My child. She destroyed my child." He didn't look at me. His eyes gazed forward as if into darkness, unseeing.

I sat down next to him an arm's length apart. I had never felt further away from him. "You had a child with her?"

He shook his head. "She had some sort of herb or drug the Abbé gave her that she used to avoid becoming *enceinte* with any child of mine. In private she used to say how much she despised children. But I wanted to have one with her, very badly. When we first married, if you can believe it, I was attracted to Léonore, and hoped to convince her. Perhaps I was even in love with her. I didn't mind that she wasn't well-read, or that she had a temper, or that she was taller than I was. I admired her strength and confidence. And I was touched that she fell in love with me and wanted to marry me, even though I had nothing.

"I don't know at what point exactly I fell out of love with her. She lied about things, twisted the truth. The more distant I became, the more bitter and spiteful she was. Then I fell in love with someone else. Renée. She was only a barmaid, but she was beautiful, and kind, and one of the most intelligent people I'd ever met, though she had little education. We had a daughter together ..."

He broke down weeping, but managed to choke out, "Charlotte. She was only a few weeks old when Léonore found out. Renée had recovered so well from the birth, and Charlotte was the healthiest, prettiest baby. She would have lived. But Léonore had her sent away to a wet-nurse and ensured she was neglected. A week later ... I had to bury her. I wanted an inquest. I wanted the nurse put in prison. So Léonore admitted it was on her orders, and I'd be wasting my time, because the police wouldn't care."

My stomach felt as if it had dropped to the floor. So many mysteries began to make terrible sense now. "That's why you forbade talk of children at Boisaulne."

He nodded, tears streaming down his cheeks, his eyes fixed on the ground. He said softly, "In another life, I'd have liked to have your children here, to be a father to them. I couldn't bear it if any harm came to them. It was dangerous and selfish enough of me to bring you here, the only place I could hide from Léonore. So long as she lives, I'll never have a child around me, or let one come within a hundred paces of her, if I can help it. A child's no safer here than in the lair of the ogre-king of the forest."

I wanted to weep for him, but my horror was too deep for tears, and my eyes were dry now.

When his sobs subsided, I asked, "How did you manage to keep Boisaulne hidden from her?"

"I told you how I was sent off very young to school in Paris, after my parents passed away. My school friends thought all Savoyards were filthy chimney sweeps, and no one knew my family, so I pretended to be French and never told anyone I was born in Savoy. Everything here was boarded up and falling into dust, anyway, and I couldn't have afforded to keep it up. When I married Léonore I never mentioned it. All she and her father cared about was my title and estate in Picardy, even though it was little more than a ruin with some woods and pastures attached. My grandfather bought them and named the place Le Herle when he first made his fortune on the stock market, in the days of the Duc d'Orléans's regency."

"And then you started coming here after ... after this all happened. Through the tunnel of the grotto?"

"No, I only found the tunnel later. When I came at first, it was through a drawing." Seeing my questioning look, he explained further, "When I was at a low point, I started to draw sketches from my childhood memories of summers at Boisaulne. One day I had a strange feeling as I drew. It's hard to describe it. My longing was so intense to be here, to be away from the dullness and constant irritations and the underlying horror and misery of my life with Léonore. It was like the drawing felt alive under my hands. I was sketching the fountain at the end of the garden. I looked at it for a long time, feeling that strange sense of aliveness, and then it was as though I was looking *into* it. It *was* alive. It was real, not merely a drawing. And then I was there, by the fountain. I found I could travel back and forth to and from Boisaulne that way in an instant, by looking at the drawing and making the wish to be there. To return to my study in Paris, I only had to look into the fountain and make the wish to return.

"So I spent as much time away from Léonore as I could get away with, either at Boisaulne, or with my friends and at their *salon* gatherings. It was always understood that if I ever betrayed Léonore again, if I even carried on so much as a flirtation, she'd find the cruelest way of punishing her rival, and I'd bring down disaster on whomever I loved. Léonore had informants, and I knew word would get back to her no matter how careful I was. It's clear now that Donatien was meant to be spying on me all along."

The memory came back to me of Donatien in the garden, trying to get me to admit I loved Harlequin. He must have begun watching us after that, if not before. And he'd had no fear of punishment for attacking me, since he knew he'd be able to accuse me to Harlequin's wife afterward. A flame of anger spurted up in my chest.

"And you brought me here, knowing I'd be in danger."

He covered his face with his hands. "I was so alone. I was so ashamed of what I'd done. You're the first person I've ever told. It doesn't justify what I did to you. Nothing can. When I first had your book and your poems, I used to dream of you, imagine a life together with you. I thought sometimes of committing suicide, but I lived for those daydreams of you."

He set his hands back in his lap, and I reached out to take one of them in mine and held it tightly. I was in tears again. "But you made me happier than I ever imagined I could be. Perhaps I shouldn't forgive you, but I do. I love you. You opened up worlds to me. Even if she finds me out and punishes me, perhaps it was worth it. If only I could keep the children and my father safe. What happened to … to the barmaid you loved? To Renée?"

He heaved a great sigh. "Losing Charlotte was too much for her to bear. She disappeared and I never heard from her again."

"You don't know whether Léonore did anything to persecute her further?"

"I don't know. I hoped to God there was nothing of the kind. I imagined every manner of catastrophe."

"But listen, the others and I, your friends, we want to help you, in any way we can. We met as a council last night. A kind of war council."

He took his hand out of mine and set it back in his lap. "I told you, there's nothing to be done. All I can do is endure it, and stay as far away from you as possible, so as not to bring down ruin on you and your family. If you love me, you'll leave Boisaulne with the others at the end of the week. That would be the best way to help me, to let me see you safely away from here."

"But you can't. I can't. You shouldn't have to live the rest of your life like this. The others were quite inventive trying to think what could be done. Séléné seemed to be hinting she wanted to arrange for a hunting accident."

He made a dry sound, nearly a laugh. "Wasn't the creature talking about going hunting last night? There's a lot I don't remember."

"Yes. Your wife went on about it for quite some time. She seemed passionately keen on the notion of shooting something with a musket."

"Somehow I've got to talk her out of it. Perhaps that's one way you could help. Ask the others to help me persuade her to give up the idea or distract her from it."

"Why? Are you afraid of a real accident?"

He shook his head. "Just the old tradition. No one hunts this side of the river. The forest here belongs to the *roi des aulnes*."

"Do you believe in him?"

He nodded. "I still wonder sometimes whether I become him. I dream of him often, of hunting and darkness and blood."

"Have you ever seen him?"

"No. But you have, haven't you? Didn't you tell me you'd had a vision of him?"

"Twice now. Or maybe I was half-mad. Delirious from my fall into the stream."

"Perhaps he only shows himself to the pure in heart," he said with a wry smile.

"But what do you think would happen if someone hunted in the alder-king's woods?"

"I don't want to find out. Perhaps Boisaulne would be cursed then and lose its magic. Perhaps the village would lose its protections and cease to prosper."

"Maybe you could poison her," I said, only half joking.

He shook his head and answered seriously. "I'm not a god. I'm not a master over life and death as they say the alder-king is. If I can't bear to take the life of a stag, do you think I could kill a woman?"

"Even a woman who's a murderer herself?"

"Even such a woman as that. Besides, the Abbé would know if she was poisoned. He's an expert when it comes to every kind of herb. I'd have to flee the law. We all would."

I nodded.

He lowered his head and wiped tears from his eyes with the sleeve of his shirt. "I must seem so weak to you. Not being able to find my way out of this. I must disgust you."

"Don't speak that way." He raised his eyes, and I found and held his gaze. "You're not weak. You've survived terrible things and you've kept your kind heart and your noble mind. Only a strong person could do that. There's hope ..."

A sharp knock sounded on the door to the study, and we both jumped.

"She's come back," he said, his eyes wide with terror.

XVI

"No, SHHH, DON'T worry," I said. "It has to be Aurore. She saw where I went in. She's warning us."

"She's on her way here, then. Hide. Quickly."

"Where?" I looked around the room desperately.

"Under the desk? No, here behind the bed."

The back of the bed was hung with more velvet drapery, and there was just enough space for me to fit between the curtain and the wood paneling of the wall, if I crushed my bustle and skirts and squeezed in my stomach.

I heard the door open, and footsteps.

"Just getting up?" the Marquise said. "Still in your nightshirt? It was repulsive how much you drank last night. You're not permitted to drink anymore."

"Good day to you too," Thérion said.

"I mean it. It's an insult to me to have you so obviously stinking drunk in front of everyone. How can you think it's acceptable?"

"Forgive me. I thought my being drunk would shame you less than my blood spattered on the floor from shooting myself."

"Don't bore me with your melodramatic nonsense. You took a vow before God to be a husband to me. I'm owed the honors of a wife."

"Why do you care what my friends think? They're not your set, are they? I shouldn't think they'd be grand enough."

"You do have a great love of trash. That Monsieur Ulysse has refined manners at least, but those women. Everyone knows the one is a gutter whore, and the other one, the blond bumpkin, is – what? – the wife of some near-dead old army officer? A nobody. Then there's her little relative with the long face who was so cowed she hardly said a word. Not to mention the so-called painter, who's clearly a gold-digging slut. I know her type. She wants to ruin some honorable marriage by entrapping a man to support her. And she's after you. She pretended to want to paint me, but her sketch showed a complete lack of talent. Do you know what I think? She meant to make me look ugly, to get away with insulting me without saying what she thought to my face."

"I'm sure she only meant to do you a kindness."

"Are you defending her now? I expect they're plotting against me. They think I'm stupid and can't tell what they're up to. But I do love it when people underestimate me. It makes it so much sweeter when I catch them out and expose them."

"No one's plotting against you. You're always your own worst enemy."

"Tell your friends to leave. I'm putting my foot down. We'll invite some people of quality to have a grand hunting expedition."

"No."

"No? What do you mean, no? Finally you might bring something to this marriage, after years of being a worthless, drunken, cheating parasite. And you'd have the gall to try to deny me a perfect opportunity, at last, to reciprocate for the hunting party expeditions I've been invited on?"

"It's just – it's not that. There's a long tradition that we don't ..."

"Tradition? You scorn the teachings of the Church, but you raise tradition as an objection? You're just uncomfortable around my friends, around good society, because it reflects to you your own unworthiness. Oh, I know you better than you know yourself. You just want to flirt and leer at these ugly whorehouse *salopes*."

"They're all going home at the end of the week, anyway. It will cause talk if you send the whole party away early. Ulysse admires you, and he's an influential man. He's even corresponded with Madame de Pompadour, and she's spoken favorably of his books. No need to ruffle any feathers when it's only a matter of waiting a few days."

"*Hmph*. Good riddance to bad rubbish. But I do plan to organize a hunting party before we go back."

"I was trying to tell you, it's not a good idea." He paused. "The woods here aren't safe. Believe it or not, I care about you and don't want to see you hurt."

Her voice softened. "Of course. But you needn't worry. We'll be properly equipped, I'll make sure of it."

He took a deep breath. "You're a good Christian. Perhaps you can understand – I believe there are unholy things in those woods. You can't protect yourself from them with mere muskets."

"Oh, *pish*. The Abbé's a man of God, with the power of the Cross behind him. We'll go in broad daylight, when any ghosts or evil spirits wouldn't dare to show themselves."

"You'll risk bringing down a curse on us."

"Enough. I don't wish to discuss it anymore. Speaking of the Abbé, he tells me your book collection is worth rather a lot."

"He's welcome to borrow whatever he likes."

"I think it'd be a better use of it to garner some favor for me at court."

"What do you mean? Inviting your friends here to read in the library?"

"I mean to give the books away, as gifts. Surely you don't need so many."

He sputtered, dumbfounded. "You can't give away my books. They belong to me."

"I'm your wife," she said sweetly. "And I'm the one who understands the proper value of things. And you owe me everything, so they belong to me, and I'll dispose of them as I see fit."

"I'll sue for a separation. Have me sent to the Bastille if you like, or Miolans. I don't care."

"Oh, I hope it will never come to that. You won't be able to take any books with you to prison, I promise you that. So it would rather defeat your purpose."

He made a sound that was half a growl and half a wail of despair.

"And another thing," the Marquise said. "All these sketches of yours. I want you to stop wasting your time on drawing. You're a grown man, not a child. Apart from the danger of soiling my name by publishing this political rubbish, it's a boorish hobby. And I'm sorry to be the one to have to tell you this, but I do it out of love – you have no talent."

He made no reply.

"Now, clean yourself up," she said. "You're filthy and you stink. It's time for luncheon. I want us to go in together and show these so-called friends of yours we're a happy couple, and it's useless for any of these greedy trollops to try to lure you into their beds. Go on. I'm waiting."

There followed an interminable half hour in which my arms ached and ached from pressing back my skirts and bustle behind the velvet drapery, and I focused all the rest of my energy on trying to breathe silently, while Thérion washed, shaved, and dressed, and the Marquise continued to throw the occasional cruel jibe at him. I heard her tapping her feet, pacing, pawing through the papers and ledgers on his desk. She tore up two of his sketches. He ceased to speak or respond to her in anything but monosyllables.

At last he was ready and she said to him, now in a warmer, kinder tone, "There, see how handsome you are. If only you'd be this way all the time. I want you to come to me in my room tonight and make love to me. The way you used to, when we were first married. I love you more than anyone in the world, you know. All you need is me steering you in the right direction."

At long last, both their footsteps went out. I waited another five minutes, just to be sure, and emerged from behind the bed curtain.

Just as I put my hand to the doorknob to go out, footsteps tapped toward the room from the hall, and then the doorknob turned under my palm. There was nowhere for me to hide, but as the door opened, I backed away silently and squeezed myself as tightly as I could into the corner behind it. The Marquise entered, her back to me. She moved forward with a vigilant air, advanced on the bed, and pulled aside the front curtains, and then the back ones where I had stood hidden earlier. She patted down the pillows and bedclothes and looked underneath the bed. She had left the door ajar, and I pressed myself into the wall and hid in the shadows as she came back towards me. She went out and closed the door behind her. I waited another ten minutes before I crept out into the hall at last, dusty and breathing hard.

Before dusk, the Abbé, the Scotsman, and Tristan returned and showed us the specimens they'd collected in the forest. The Abbé had set up a small, dungeon-like laboratory space, lit by lamps, in a storeroom next to the cellar, the same one by way of which Thérion had carried me into the house the morning before. We all gathered there to watch. The Abbé shook mushrooms from a bag onto the table and laid out an array of them on a handkerchief for us to admire, organized by shape and color. He left them to dry and did the same with bags of leaves, twigs, berries, and wildflowers. He set out a row of small glass bottles containing foul-smelling fluid, in which he had embalmed beetles, dragonflies, and spiders. He pinned dead butterflies and moths to a board.

In a corner of the room on another table, he set down two crudely constructed cages of woven branches fastened with thin leather cords. In the smaller cage was a small purple-feathered bird, a kind I'd never seen before, twittering and shuffling and rifling its wings anxiously. In the larger cage a dun-colored rabbit blinked and trembled. A circle of dark brown dried blood ringed one of the rabbit's legs like a bracelet, where it had been caught in the Abbé's snare.

Thérion's eyes widened when he caught sight of the cages.

"What is this?"

"Oh, I'm not much of woodsman," the Abbé said genially. "But I have some rudimentary skills at improvising instruments of captivity for live specimens."

"Is that alder wood?" Thérion's tone betrayed his horror. The Abbé didn't seem to notice.

"Ah, yes. Your noble estate's namesake. Alder wood cuttings make for good, flexible material."

"Which tree did you cut it from?"

"Oh, goodness, I hardly thought to remark which tree."

The Scotsman said, "It was one right next to the standing stone at the edge of the forest proper. Is something wrong?"

Thérion looked pale. "Oh, nothing. There are a few traditions, local ones, about the alders of those woods. Some were thought to be sacred."

The Abbé shrugged. "No matter. God gave man dominion over the earth. Surely his holy word holds more power in it than old traditions of witchcraft and devil-worship."

The Abbé prepared a kind of surgical theater, with three sharp knives – small, medium, and large – a saw, shears, sponges, a basin of water, an empty bowl to hold blood, and a carving board with grooved edges to channel fluids.

"Does he mean to kill and dissect the poor thing?" Clio whispered to me.

"It doesn't look good for our friend in the cage," I whispered back.

"Now," the Abbé said, "I must ask our gentle ladies to leave the room."

"Why?" asked Séléné. "What do you mean to do?"

"A scientifically important procedure, which the delicate nature of females renders inadvisable for you to observe."

"I'll stay," the Marquise said. "I've seen you do it before. I'm not squeamish."

The Abbé nodded to her. "Of course, Madame la marquise. I meant for the others who'd likely be unfamiliar with modern scientific practices."

"Modern scientific practices," said Séléné. "Is this to be a dissection of a live specimen?"

The Abbé raised his eyebrows and nodded more deeply. "There are unique insights to be gained from the examination of internal anatomy and organs while there's still a pulse of life in a beast."

A low hiss of disapproval came from Tristan. "If I'd known this was your purpose, I'd never have gone with you. If science is to be advanced through cruelty and torture, then it ought not to be advanced." He turned on his heel and left the room. Clio watched him go out, and then followed behind him. Séléné left too. Ulysse bowed.

"Gentlemen, Madame la marquise, if you'll excuse me, I have some correspondence to attend to before dinner." He went out, and Aurore and I did too, leaving only Thérion, the Marquise, and the Scotsman with the Abbé. We gathered outside the door.

Ulysse quoted in a low voice, "'Natures that are bloodthirsty toward animals give proof of a natural propensity toward cruelty.'"

"Montaigne," explained Séléné, and the rest of us nodded to each other.

Clio shook her head and whispered, "That man is a horror. He's worse than Donatien, if it were possible."

An unearthly squealing came from the room.

227

"Oh, please, let's go," I said, and we hurriedly filed up the narrow stairwell. I could still hear the rabbit screaming a long way up.

At dinner, the Scotsman defended the practice of the vivisection of animals to Tristan.

"I can't argue with you about there being a regrettable element of cruelty to it. Animals feel pain and the desire to preserve their lives, just as we men do."

"Precisely," Tristan said. "Why should they not therefore have a claim on our compassion, just as our fellow men have?"

"But there are higher moral purposes that justify stifling our natural compassion at times, in the case of both animals and men. For example, we take the lives of animals to feed ourselves. There are ways of minimizing the pain of the beasts in doing so. In fact, several religions contain edicts that govern the slaughter of beasts, to make it as humane as possible; Mohammedanism and the Hebraic religion for example. It's said the good Indians of the New World say a prayer to their gods when they take the life of a deer in hunting, because they consider the animal's blood to be sacred."

"But what purpose could there possibly be in vivisection, that couldn't be served as well by killing the animal humanely first and then dissecting it?"

"The purpose is the advancement of natural science. To observe the functioning of the machine of the body in action, and not merely its component parts. Just as, for a clockmaker, there's value in watching how the pieces of a clock function while operating together with one another, not merely in seeing all the parts of a disassembled mechanism."

"Ah, but there's more to it than that," said the Abbé. "Why, vivisection and so-called cruelty to animals are justified by the whole structure of the natural world."

"How so?" asked the Scotsman.

"Nature is a constant war of all against all. The lowliest worms are eaten by your gentle-seeming birds, who are eaten by foxes, who are food for wolves, whom men destroy with bullets or arrows. All is blood and storm and violence, strength against strength, strength against weakness, weakness against strength through cunning and trickery, weakness against weakness with its own feminine forms of warfare. Power over animals is a man's birthright, and cruelty is in our natures, ordained in us by God. It's only right that we exercise it, for our very blood and that of the beasts calls for it."

The Scotsman's mouth fell agape and when he met our eyes, there was shame in them for having sided with the Abbé earlier.

"You're a man of such great insight, my dear Abbé," the Marquise said. "You've also summed up some of the many reasons why hunting is not only a privilege of the nobility, but also such a great pleasure in itself."

"Ah, yes, and when does your ladyship have in mind that we'll have a hunting party here?" the Abbé asked.

"What was your estimation from your survey of the woods? Is there game enough to make it worthwhile?"

"Oh, very much so. There's a healthy population of red deer. We saw signs of them all over. But they'll likely go further down the mountain to warmer feeding grounds as the weather turns colder."

"Marvelous. It would be best to take advantage of the last days of the season. If only we had hounds and a few muskets. I wonder if anyone in the village ..."

"No need," the Abbé said, "we're in luck. I already had a letter from Donatien before dinner. He's on his way via Dijon. He'll bring his own trained hounds and the dog boys from his estate. It'll be his pleasure, he said, and he was glad for the chance to make amends for any past misunderstandings."

I shook my head. Could I have misheard? Donatien was coming *here*? I almost forgot myself and spoke the question aloud. Clio met my eye, warning and silencing me. She opened her mouth as if to speak, but then reconsidered and instead turned to Tristan next to her and whispered in his ear. Thérion stared down at his plate and looked as if he was about to cry. Ulysse and Séléné had been carrying on their own conversation in low voices at the other end of the table, but Tristan touched Séléné's arm next to him and whispered in her ear. She murmured to Ulysse across from her, and Ulysse spoke.

"I beg your pardon, Madame la marquise, did you say Donatien's coming back?" His tone was jocular. "I thought that miscreant had been banned from Boisaulne for being a little too charming with the ladies." He winked at her.

The Marquise smiled and dismissed this with a wave of her hand, her many jeweled rings flashing in the candlelight. "Nonsense. I know the boy's a bit of a flirt, but he means no harm. He's quite beloved among my friends at court, and he has a kind heart. He donated thirty gold *louis* to my favorite charity, just last month."

Ulysse gave an exaggerated nod. "And when is our charming friend expected to arrive, did you say?"

The Abbé answered, "He left Paris straight away after talking to us last Thursday. I knew he meant to visit his estate, so I directed a letter to him there. He's written back that he hopes he might be here already by tomorrow, but I'd say he's being overly optimistic. It must be nearly twenty leagues from Dijon, and traveling with hounds will necessarily slow him down. But it's truly admirable that he's taking so much trouble to bring them, just for a few days, and then to go back again, purely to please Madame la marquise."

The Marquise lifted her chins and ran her jeweled fingers down her neck, preening. "Isn't it? Let's cross our fingers we'll see him tomorrow then, or the day after at the latest."

I felt cold and exchanged glances with Aurore. This was the end. I had to leave first thing in the morning, with or without Aurore, whether for Paris to become Aurore's companion, or to

Annecy to rejoin my father's household and perhaps find employment as a housemaid. If I was still here when Donatien arrived, he'd identify me to the Marquise, and God knew what disasters would befall us then, Thérion and me. Time had run out for me to help my love. Unless some miracle occurred, he would remain in the hands of this wretched woman and her execrable abbé. They'd make Boisaulne into a true hunters' retreat, and my love and I would never meet again.

XVII

WE ALL FILED out of the hall after supper, and the others headed up the stairs to the library. Aurore had finished a new tale and had promised to provide the evening's entertainment by reading it aloud to us. I lingered behind and walked alone down the hall of the gallery to use the privy. I also wanted a moment by myself to think, to grieve, to plan and ready myself for all I needed to do now. When I had finished, I went upstairs to join the others. On the landing, I nearly ran into Thérion coming down.

My heart thrilled as he took me in his arms, kissed me, and held me tightly for a long minute, so tightly he nearly squeezed the breath out of me.

"I must leave at dawn," I said in his ear. "Goodbye, goodbye. My heart is with you forever."

"You gave me the greatest and only happiness I've had in the past seven years. I'd have been lost if it weren't for you. I love you with all my being. So long as there's life in me, I'll love you."

"Be careful, someone might see," I whispered. "I'll go in. I love you. If there's ever a way I can help you or come back to you, send word and I'll come, no matter what."

"No, it's no good to think that way. Think of me as someone you once loved who lies now in the grave. Go and be happy in a new life far away from me. You've already done more for me than you could ever know."

We broke apart, and I composed myself quickly, dried my eyes, and went into the library, while he went down the stairs.

"Did I miss anything?" I asked brightly, as I took my seat on an ottoman beside Aurore. I didn't look at the Marquise, but I could feel her stare boring into me.

"Not yet," Aurore said. "Once everyone's ready and Harlequin's back, we'll begin. Madame la marquise, Abbé, are you familiar with fairy tales? The others are used to me reading them to the company sometimes of an evening, but mine are rather different from nursemaids' tales."

"Peasants' tales," the Marquise said, "I suppose one catches the servants telling them sometimes. The common people dream of making their fortunes, of becoming rich by magic without working for it. They'd think my father's life was a fairy tale, since he began with nothing and ended by becoming as rich as a prince, but he had no fairy's help. He worked for it. They'd think my life was a fairy tale too, since I married a marquis. But they have no idea how much hard work that is, either."

Aurore smiled kindly. "Running a household can certainly be a great deal of work. I'm sure all married women would agree."

"Particularly when one's husband needs a good deal of managing," the Marquise said.

Clio sighed aloud. "If only one could avoid ever being married. If I could do nothing but paint, and make my own living from painting portraits, as my father did from painting fans. I'd be as pleased as if a fairy had granted me a fortune."

"Perhaps your wish will yet be granted by an admiring patron," said Séléné. "But do you know, I think in some more enlightened age in the future, no woman will need to be married, unless she should desire it for love. Women will be the equals of men and will be able to engage in any trade they like, and manage their own properties and investments. Women will be able to choose their own husbands and divorce them too, if they wish, or simply take lovers without getting married at all."

The Abbé had gone red in the face. "You paint a vision of hell. Would you abolish the whole of the Christian religion then?"

"God gave us the capacity to love," Séléné said. "Marriage is indeed a Christian institution, but perhaps savages in the New World, who live together at will and part ways at will, give more honor to love."

"Love," the Abbé said, "is a cruel, ferocious animal, capable of the most horrible excesses if it isn't tamed by civilization. These noble savages you speak of are the very ones who practice cannibalism in their wars against one another. Here in Europe, one need only look at the history of those kings who wished for the freedom to divorce, and thereby to throw off the yoke of the Holy Church. Their excesses led to the Wars of Religion that bathed the whole Continent in blood. Love must be chained, if one does not wish to see it devour all. It can only be chained by terror, by the awe and absolute authority of the Church and its rulers and institutions."

Séléné burst into peals of laughter. "Marriage – a chain of terror to bind love. You're really not helping your case, my dear Abbé."

The Marquise's eyes were flashing with fury, and she opened her mouth to speak just as Thérion came back into the room. Her anger turned to a smug smile and instead of blustering at Séléné, she merely raised an eyebrow, as if to say that in her case, terror had won.

"Ah, Harlequin, there you are," Aurore said with relief. "I'll begin then."

> Once upon a time (Aurore said, taking up her manuscript and reading from it) there was an ogre who lived in the forest. He was an ancient, ageless creature, not ugly at all, but tall and fair of

235

face, with long black hair that streamed down his back like a cape of raven's feathers. But no one ever saw how beautiful his face was, for he often used his magic to take the form of a stag with silver eyes – a forest king mightier, more graceful, and fleeter of foot than any other beast of the woods, crowned by a diadem of antlers. The rest of the time, when he took the form of a beautiful man, he wore over his face a mask made from the white skull of an enormous antlered stag's head. The villagers at the forest's edge called him the *roi des aulnes,* the alder-king, for it was said that certain alder trees were sacred to him. His bow and arrows were of alder wood, and when he rested he sat on a throne of woven alder branches in the deepest heart of the forest.

The alder-king was a hunter by night, when he took on a man's form, for this powerful being was lord of both life and death in his domain. When he hunted, he blew on a horn of carved bone that made no sound the human ear could detect. His silent horn called to wolves, who served him as his hunting hounds and aided him in bringing down whatever prey he chose. These were no ordinary wolves, mind you. They were hounds of hell, great and shaggy and black, nearly as large as horses. Their eyes glowed orange with hellfire and their teeth were sharp as knives.

No creature fell in the forest, night or day, without the knowledge and blessing of the ancient ogre, the alder-king. Like Nature itself, he was as benevolent as he was bloodthirsty. It was said his antlers carried healing powers, and he could give life as well as take it. His life-giving power made the plants and creatures of the forest grow and thrive, and brought prosperity and peace to the inhabitants of the villages roundabout.

Then, one day, a nobleman who lived near the forest and who had, unknowingly, prospered for many years on account of the alder-king's magic, was visited by a wicked fairy who came to his hall in the form of an old, bent, fat woman, begging for a crust of bread. Although the beggar woman was ugly and looked like nothing as much as a warty old toad, the nobleman was kind-hearted and invited her in to have a hearty meal of stew, fresh soft bread, and a pitcher of good strong ale.

"Warm yourself by my fire, Grandmother," he said, "and you may sleep on a feather mattress in front of it, with a coverlet of the softest lamb's wool, so that your old bones may be comfortable."

"Ah, you're most kind," the fairy said, and she entered the nobleman's hall, ate of his food and drank of his ale, and warmed herself by his fire. When the nobleman's servants had brought out the feather mattress and the nobleman had come himself to lay the blanket over her like a dutiful son, she said to him, "Because you've been so kind, I'll tell you the truth. In fact, I'm a rather powerful fairy, and I'd like to grant you a wish. Is there anything you lack, my lord?"

The man laughed to himself, for he could only think the old woman was senile. But since he was kind, he humored her.

"A powerful fairy! I'm all the more honored to have you as a guest under my roof. In fact, there is something I lack. I wish to find a good husband for my eldest daughter. But I'm not a very rich man, and can't afford much of a dowry for her, so I've had a hard time arranging a suitable match."

"Why, it's the simplest thing in the world to solve your quandary," the old fairy said. "In the deepest heart of the forest is a throne of woven alder branches. You must chop it up with an ax and you can use the branches for firewood, if you like. Underneath the throne lies buried in the earth a great chest of gold, which, if you dig it up, you may use it for a dowry. As for a husband, you'll see a stag, a swift, strong, and beautiful creature with silver eyes. Slay the stag, and he'll be transformed into a handsome king who will gladly bring your daughter to his palace and marry her, for he'll be grateful you've freed him from the enchantment he was under, that made him take the form of a beast."

The fairy said all this because she wished to do an ill turn to the alder-king. For she had loved him when she was younger, and he had scorned her, saying he was not fooled by the illusion of her beauty and found her very ugly, and loved her not.

The kind nobleman, listening to the old beggar woman as he tucked her in for the night, pretended to believe her, but he laughed in his heart at her advice.

"Thank you, Grandmother, I'll certainly do all you say," he said, and kissed her on the forehead. The old woman closed her eyes, and the nobleman sat up a while by the fire alone, drinking his ale and watching over her rest. To his astonishment, when the clock struck midnight, the crone transformed before his eyes into a beautiful young maiden, fair with long silver hair, pointed ears, and a pair of iridescent wings on her back like a dragonfly. Only she still snored, loud as you please, just as an old woman would do.

The nobleman decided then that she truly must be a fairy and her advice must be true as well. He went to sleep, and when he woke in the morning, the woman was gone, though no one had seen her go out.

The next day he assembled a hunting party, with his servants carrying axes and picks and shovels. His eldest daughter went with him, for he thought it best she should see her husband-to-be before she was betrothed to him. Deeper and deeper, into the heart of the forest the hunting party went. It grew darker and darker around them as the trees and branches grew so thickly together they blotted out the light of the sun. At last the nobleman caught sight of the alder-wood throne, and his men dismounted and began to chop at the roots with their axes.

They had only been at it a moment, when the nobleman's daughter cried out, "Stay!" The men with their axes all froze in place and looked up to see where she pointed. What she had seen, they all now saw. It was the great stag with silver eyes and his kingly crown of antlers, leaping through the trees toward them. The good nobleman raised his bow and arrow to take aim and kill the beast, but his daughter said, "Wait, Father, please. Let me first meet him as the beast he is."

To the astonishment of the whole assembly, the stag came straight to them, brave as a lion. His silver eyes flashed with fury when he saw what the men had begun. The axes fell from the men's hands, and the mighty animal stamped on them with his hooves, and the tools sank into the ground like water and disappeared.

"Father, we've done wrong in following that fairy's advice," said the daughter. "You see how angry we've made my husband-to-be. If I'm to be his bride, we must take care not to displease him anymore."

The daughter moved forward toward the stag. All of the men, and her father most of all, trembled with fear that she should be trampled on as their tools had been. But the daughter curtsied and bowed her head deeply before him.

"O king of the forest, how handsome you are," she said. "Are you really under an enchantment, as the fairy told my father?" She reached out a hand, and the stag allowed her to stroke his muzzle, and rubbed his nose against her cheek. Quick and nimble as a doe, the girl leapt up onto the stag's back.

"I like my new husband well, Father. I'm going away to live with him. We'll make a home together in the forest."

With that, the stag leapt away, carrying the nobleman's daughter with him. The hunting party was much astonished, and the nobleman's heart was torn with fear that some harm would come to the girl. In the end, however, there was little they could do but turn toward home, with their tools vanished into the ground. By the time they reached the nobleman's hall, night was falling, and they could hear wolves howling behind them with terrible cries. Through the trees, they saw eyes that glowed orange, and they hurried inside to make themselves safe within the stone walls.

The nobleman mourned his daughter as one dead after that, for everyone thought she must have been eaten by wolves. Nevertheless, after nearly a year had passed, his daughter came at dusk to the gate of the keep. The servants might have turned her away but for the fact that they knew their master was wont to show kindness to beggars, for the girl was hardly to be recognized. She was barefoot and her dress was in tatters. Her hair was matted like sheep's wool, full of twigs and bird-droppings, and her skin and rags were filthy and crusted with dirt. Most alarming of all, her belly was large and swollen. For all that, her dirty cheeks were rosy, her limbs seemed strong, and she glowed with happiness.

She greeted the servants and her father affectionately, as though she had only been gone on a short journey.

"But what villain has done this to you? Who made you with child?" her father asked.

"Why, my own husband, of course," she answered. "The one you so wisely gave me. I've been happy with him, and only left because my labor pains were coming upon me, and I was afraid to give birth in the forest." With that, she gave a cry and stopped speaking, for her time was already close at hand. One of the serving women who had some skill as a midwife did her best to make the girl comfortable and to help her. Near midnight, she brought forth a healthy baby boy. Alas, when the girl had pushed out the afterbirth, she did not stop bleeding. She fell into a swoon and did not live to see the morning.

The nobleman took care of her child as his grandson and made him his heir, and had the babe christened with his own name. The boy grew up into a fine man, and in time he married and had children of his own. He and his son and his son's son, and so on down the line, all had gray-blue eyes like the silver eyes of the stag who had carried away his mother, and they all had the gift of being able to see unusually well in the dark.

Aurore put down her manuscript and looked around the room.

"That's the end. What did you think?"

Thérion looked thunderstruck. "But it's very much like the story my old nurse used to tell me when I was a boy, about my own ancestor. I'd forgotten a lot of it. Your telling is more detailed and has a good deal more art to it, of course. But where on earth did you get the idea for it?"

"When I went to chapel with the Abbé and the Marquise on Sunday, I met a very old woman from the village at the service. She must have been four-score years old, if she was a day. We got to talking, and I mentioned I was a collector of tales. She ended up telling me several stories she knew from her girlhood. I liked the one about the *roi des aulnes*, so I thought I'd write it up and embellish and expand on it a little. The other ones I made notes on and perhaps I'll write them up too, when I get a chance. Is it possible the woman might have been your old nurse?"

"I suppose she could have been. I never knew what became of her after I was sent away to school."

"I enjoyed the tale," the Scotsman said. "Only I'd have liked to know more about what happened to the daughter after she ran away to the woods."

"It's true," said Clio. "We hear a lot about the *roi des aulnes* in the beginning, so it would be nice to hear more about what he does in the middle of the story too."

"Very well," said Aurore. "I'll think about putting more detail into the middle."

From outside came a clamor of several dogs barking. Then, as if in answer, an unnerving howl pierced the air, a cross between the call of a wolf and a bear's roar, ending in a snarl that echoed through the woods. My hairs stood on end and I traded nervous glances with the others. It was just like something out of Aurore's story.

The Marquise ignored it and said, "It's obvious someone made up the story about the ogre long ago to frighten people out of going into the woods. There's an old story, too, about the Grand Veneur of the forest of Fontainebleau. He's supposed to be a devilish, ghostly figure who rides through the forest at night, hunting with his hell-hounds. It's all so much superstition and rubbish. I've been on several hunts in that forest, and no one I've met with has ever seen the Grand Veneur with his own eyes."

As she spoke, there were steps outside the room in the gallery, and my heart leapt into my throat. The dogs barking ...

Donatien walked in. For a moment I was too shocked to do anything but stare.

He flashed an easy smile at us. "Your gate was locked, and no one came when I called, so I had the dog boys help me up over the wall and let myself in at the back. I hope you don't mind. Good evening, Madame la marquise, Abbé, *mesdames et messieurs*. Harlequin, it seems our little misunderstanding's been resolved, eh? No hard feelings."

The Marquise rose to her feet and went to him, holding out her hands, which he took in his. "Donatien, what a pleasure to see you so soon after all. We thought we might not see you for another day or two."

He bowed his head to kiss her right hand, and then let her hands go. "The pleasure's all mine. You'll be happy to know the hounds took to the journey quite well. We'll get them settled into their kennels and the dog boys can sleep in the stable with them. Then we can have you out on a hunt as soon as you like. I've even brought a little present for you, a musket engraved with flowers, just right for a lady such as yourself."

243

The Marquise clapped her hands. "Oh, but how gallant. You're wonderful."

Donatien looked past her and caught my eye. I had half risen from my ottoman. My instinct screamed within me to fly from the room and hide. But it was too late. He cocked his head.

"Belle-Âme, you're still here? *Ma foi,* the Marquise is remarkably forgiving. You're looking very well. Perhaps we can have a tête-à-tête later on and pick up where we left off."

The Marquise looked up sharply to stare at me, her features contorting with hatred and rage. I willed myself not to faint, though all the blood seemed to rush from my head to fill my heart nearly to bursting. Then I was too weak to stand after all and fell back down onto my seat from my half-crouching position.

"That's her? This is the girl?" she asked.

"What, didn't you know? Yes, of course, that's Belle-Âme, the one who was the cause of it all."

The Marquise raised her eyes to the ceiling for a moment, as though seeking divine aid. Then she strode forward, bearing down on me, and slapped me across the cheek with a blow that knocked me off my seat onto the floor. For a second I saw stars before my eyes and my ears rang. I got up onto my hands and knees, shaking my head as if to clear it. I was dimly aware that some of the others had risen from their seats and were standing around us.

"Slut," the Marquise bellowed. "Sow. I knew it. It had to be you, you pox-ridden piece of filth. How dare you?"

Before I could stumble to my feet, before anyone could restrain her, the Marquise kicked me in the side with a force that sent me sprawling. The pain stole my breath away. The others gasped and cried out in shock. In a sweep of skirts Aurore rushed to my side and put her arms around me. I looked up to see a tussle, as Clio and Tristan both laid hands on the Marquise to pull her back. She shrugged and twisted her broad shoulders, struggling to shake them off, while the Abbé tried to drag Tristan away to free her. Thérion, my love, closed his eyes. His face was as though a hand had passed over it, wiping all the expression from his features, as if he had fallen asleep. He crumpled like a dropped handkerchief, hitting his head on the floor with a terrible thump.

For a moment there was silence, but for the sounds of labored breathing. The Marquise stood still before me and the others let go of her and each other. I caught my breath and drew in great gulps of air.

"Get out," the Marquise said. "Out of my house this instant. Now, or I'll set those hounds on you. Do you think I'm joking?"

Aurore helped me to my feet. The Marquise took a step toward me, her eyes blazing. I broke free of Aurore's arm around me and darted forward, around the Marquise, and ran out of the room. Outside the door, I paused only for a moment to catch my breath, and then I ran again, down the gallery toward the stairs, and down the stairs to the ground floor. I tugged at the front door, but it was locked, and I didn't know how to unlock it from the inside.

Where could I hide? I couldn't survive another night in the forest, with the howling of the wolves around me, without a lantern or a cloak, without food or water, save from the stream where I had nearly drowned before. I would have to stay out in the garden till dawn, protected within its walls, and then make my way safely out through the grotto and into the village in the morning.

I ran the length of the gallery to the glass doors at the end and went out into the sharp cold air of the mountain night. If I had to, I would walk the garden paths all night to stay warm. If only I could have brought more with me. I felt in my pockets. Besides my medallion, which had done me so little good as a luck charm in the forest, I had only a handkerchief, a couple of hairpins, and a folded-up scrap of paper on which I had scribbled a few lines of a poem. Donatien's hounds barked and howled from the other side of the garden wall, and again, an eerie answering howl-roar from the woods quieted them to whimpering and snarling.

I had hardly been walking in the garden for five minutes when I heard voices. I froze, conscious of the noise of my shoes on the gravel. There was the clunk of a large key turning in the side gate's lock and the scream of rusty hinges as the great iron door opened. The dogs' barking erupted again, louder and closer.

"Do you see her?" said the Marquise over their din.

"I can't see a thing," Donatien shouted. "It's the way she would have gone though. He keeps the front door locked from the inside."

"Go on then, let them loose."

"Are you sure you really want to do this? They'll tear out her throat, unless she can get up a tree first. It's how they've been trained. It'll make a bloody mess."

"I'm sure. It'll teach them all a lesson. Her blood will be on my husband's hands."

There was a pause. "I suppose," Donatien yelled doubtfully over the barking.

"She's nothing but a stupid village girl. The Comte de Charolais used to hunt peasants for sport and no one ever bothered him about it."

"Funny you mention the Comte de Charolais. He was my hero, growing up, but more for what he did with the peasant girls."

"You're joking, I know. The Comte de Charolais was depraved. I mean he never got in trouble, even though he was evil. But I'm doing it for my husband's good, to save him from himself."

"Oh, but of course, I meant it – tongue in cheek. Well then, if you're sure. Belle-Âme," he yelled louder, "if you're out there, you'd better run now. Cerbère, Charon, go kill! Good boys, good boys. Get her!"

The sounds of his last commands were indistinct, drowned out by the noise of the gravel under my feet as I set off sprinting for the fountain at the back of the garden with every last ounce of my strength, faster than I ever thought I could run. My eyes had grown used to the dark, enough to stay within the path's borders, but by the time I reached the fountain and flung myself onto the stone mermaid figure, the dogs were already at my feet. One tried to bite my leg through my skirts and tore the fabric, just as the brick gate rumbled open. Faint green luminescence shone from the opening. The other dog leapt up on me and snapped at my arm, but I pulled away too quickly for his jaws to close on my flesh. I squeezed myself through the opening and went down into the grotto.

My ears, unblocked, took in the entrancing music from the bejeweled tunnel as before, and my eyes were momentarily dazzled by the glamour of the lights and sparkling stones. Then the dogs leapt in through the opening after me before I could push it shut, and all I heard was their growling and snarling, as I backed up in terror against the threshold of the illuminated tunnel. They had cornered me and crouched to strike. In the shifting colors of the gem-lights their eyes and the saliva around their jaws gleamed.

Desperately I looked behind me into the tunnel where the music played, its lilting melody promising peace and safety. One of the dogs leapt at my throat and I jumped backward and tumbled head over heels down through the opening. Down, down, down I fell, through black nothingness, and the noise of their snarling faded.

XVIII

I CAME TO a halt on dry ground, painlessly, upright on my feet, as though I had floated down like a leaf on a gentle wind from the opening in the grotto. I opened my eyes, which had been clenched tightly shut, and blinked at the brilliance before me. I was in a grand chamber, the walls paneled in silver, white silk, and mirrors, the floor of polished parquet. In front of me was a low platform with a tall-backed silver throne, upholstered in lilac velvet padding and cushions. On the throne sat a delicate, diminutive blonde woman in a white dress. To one side of her a sumptuous banquet was laid on a long table. To the other side a group of musicians played music, and beyond them a small crowd of men and women in courtly dress milled around, talking as if at a royal reception.

I might have thought I was looking at a painting of one of the royal courts of Europe were it not for the fact that all the people, including the *demoiselle* on her throne, had iridescent wings protruding from their backs, like beautiful insects. The wings flickered and fluttered from time to time as they conversed with one another, like ladies' fans. The *demoiselle*-queen had a youthful, heart-shaped face framed by long pale hair, atop which she wore a silver diadem encrusted with diamonds and amethysts. She leaned forward in her seat and peered intently at me as though trying to ascertain what manner of creature I was. Her musicians, courtiers, and ladies all wore coats and gowns of lustrous satin or velvet in pastel shades, with gleaming trims of silver braid, embroidered flowers, pearl buttons, and jewels. The queen caught one of the musicians' eye and gave a nod so the players fell silent. The other guests gradually noticed and stopped speaking, until the room was quiet and all eyes were upon me.

"Welcome," the queen said to me. "It's a long time since we had a guest from up there."

I tried to speak but found my throat had closed up from terror and astonishment. I wished to say, "Thank you," but the only sound I could get out was a kind of terrible croaking, punctuated by coughs, like a strangled frog.

"Poor dear," said the queen. "Someone get her a drink, quickly."

A goblet was placed in my hand by an unseen helper. I coughed again and pretended to take a drink from it. It looked and smelled like water, but I remembered all the stories warning against accepting food or drink from fairies, so I didn't allow any of the liquid to pass my lips. When I had pretended to drink a long draught, the goblet was taken from me. I took deep breaths, trying to calm myself, then cleared my throat.

"Thank you, your Majesty," I croaked. "Excuse me, it's as though I had a frog in my throat."

She looked taken aback, as though I had insulted her, and I sensed a wave of surprise and disapprobation wash over the assembly. Whatever I had said to offend her, after a moment the queen shrugged it off.

"But tell us, how did you come here? We do love hearing human tales. Some of us write them down in books, and we tell them to our young to put them to sleep at night."

"Well, I ..."

"Start from the beginning and leave out no detail."

I almost laughed at the absurdity of it. I tried to think where to begin. If they liked hearing "human tales" as much we enjoyed our fairy tales, I had to take care in how I told it. It couldn't be too short or too long, and I had to leave out what might bore them and build to an exciting end. So I started with my father telling me I had to go to live with the Marquis de Boisaulne, and I ended with his wife setting the dogs on me. The queen seemed pleased with my tale.

"My goodness, chased by dogs like a hind! But never fear, you can stay down here with us as long as you like. And you really met the *roi des aulnes*? Fascinating."

"But truthfully, I might only have dreamt of meeting him. I was ill, delirious and half-frozen from falling into the stream." The mention of the *roi des aulnes* reminded me of the Cernunnos medallion in my pocket, and without thinking I slid my hand into the pocket to rub the silver metal with my thumb and reassure myself it was still there. The moment I touched the medallion, everything changed before my eyes, and I stumbled backward.

It all appeared before me now in double vision. The scene and ensemble of figures was just the same as before, but I saw another, entirely different scene superimposed over it. It was as if I had two sets of eyes and two separate minds to see it with, while having yet a single soul receiving both impressions. It was such a strange sensation that I feared I might go mad, so I took my hand off the medallion, and once again saw only the gleaming fairy court. But I knew what I had seen. Underneath the exquisite facade, there was no white-and-silver mirrored throne room, but a murky cave with black slime on the walls and a mud floor. There was no throne with a radiant fairy queen seated on it, but only an enormously fat, wart-covered toad crouching in the black-green muck in a coating of her own mucus, regarding me with protruding eyes and croaking with a noise like deep belches. What I had taken to be the assembly of the fairy court was a pulsing mass of common frogs in a patchwork blanket of dull dark grays and greens covering the rocks, flicking their long tongues in and out and puffing out their sides with croaks. What had appeared to be the banquet table laid with shining silver and porcelain, bearing heaps of mouth-watering roasts and mounds of perfectly ripe sweet fruit, was in fact a wide slippery sinkhole, a lightless abyss I couldn't see to the bottom of.

"But if you saw him as a stag, even if he only revealed himself to you in a dream, you must be highly favored of him," the fairy queen said.

I remembered now that the fairy in Aurore's tale had a grudge against the *roi des aulnes*. "But nay, Queen, the tales I hear of him describe him as a cruel, bloody-handed ogre. I only hope never to see the monster again."

The queen nodded thoughtfully, as though only partially satisfied by my answer. "Come then, my dear, you must be tired and hungry. Sit down at my banquet table and refresh yourself." She swept an imperious hand toward the table.

I touched the medallion for an instant again. The yawning void of the sinkhole was still visible where she had gestured that I ought to sit down. Involuntarily I took a step back. "Thank you for the kind offer, your Highness, but I already ate a large supper tonight."

The queen's eyes narrowed. "You have something in your hand. Something precious. Show me."

Panic flooded me. "N-no, your Majesty, it's nothing, just an old token I found. It soothes me to touch it, like a smooth pebble."

"You have the second sight. You see things as they are. Give me the token." Her voice turned to wheedling like a little girl. "I just want to see it. I don't even want to keep it. The second sight will drive you mad if you use it too much. I just want to see myself as I truly am. Then I'll give it back to you, I promise. We never break our promises, you know. We can't. It's against our laws."

I took another step back. "No."

"I'll give you something in return. I can help you. You're in desperate straits. Help me, and I'll help you. That's the law of the humans, isn't it? Tell me, what do you desire?"

"I just want to go back, to my own world up above. Safely."

"Is that all?"

"If there's more I could ask for, it's that ... I wish for my beloved to be safe, and for both of us to be together."

"Hmm, it's not a small thing you're asking for. Even we fairies have our limits. But I'll see what I can do. Only let me hold the token."

I could see no better alternative, and no other means of escaping this cave, so I slowly stepped forward and approached the queen. I reached into my pocket, grasped the ribbon, and drew the medallion out by it without touching the metal to my skin. I placed it around my neck so that it hung down over the fabric of the stomacher that covered my stays in front, and leaned forward so the queen could put her hand to it without it leaving my possession. The queen eyed it eagerly, reached out her slim white hand, and wrapped her long fingers around the horned figure of Cernunnos.

She screamed. It was a long, high-pitched cry of anguish, fear, and rage. She let go, and I fell back as though she had pushed me. For a long moment she stared at me, her breath heaving in and out, her eyes alight with fury.

"How dare you? You knew what I would see. How could you have let me look? Cruel human." She spat. "But a promise is a promise. Go away from here." She waved her hand.

A dizzying, whirling sensation came over me, as though I were falling from a great height in a dream, and the pit of my stomach sank out from under me. I blinked as the feeling subsided, and gradually I became aware of my new surroundings.

I was in darkness, a strange darkness like nothing I had encountered before. I blinked, trying to discern what was different about it. Slowly, as I blinked more and moved my head from side to side, the realization came over me that it was the way I saw things that was new. I wasn't blind in this darkness, though there was no moon or lantern for me to see by. My eyes had changed, and I had become like my Thérion, who could see in the nighttime. The outlines of objects were visible to me, though colorless, like one of the pen-and-ink sketches that he signed Harlequin.

I stood next to the sentry stone, above the ground outside the entrance to the grotto at the edge of the forest. I could feel the weight of the medallion around my neck on the ribbon, as before, but it seemed I must be naked, for my clothes all lay in a neat pile on the ground next to me. Reflexively, absently and without looking down, I tried to feel myself to see if I truly was bare-skinned there in the forest in the middle of the night, but my hands were gone.

My hands were gone.

I turned my neck, which felt longer than before, to get a view of my body below and to each side. Hooves at the end of slender, velvet-coated legs stamped up and down on the ground as I tried to move my arms. My chest, too, and belly were fur-covered. So were my flanks. Craning my neck, I could see the tip of a lighter-colored tuft of fur at the end of my spine.

The fairy queen had transformed me into a deer. It was I who was the beast now. Never again could I return to my children, my father, and Edmée. Even if I could find them, I'd have no power to protect them or speak to them, to warn them of the danger they were in from the Marquise. No refuge awaited me at Madame Jacquenod's tavern in the village. For all the days that remained to me, I would be forced to live in this forest, fleeing creatures who would kill and eat me, foraging for what food I could find, mating in season, giving birth in the spring. The fairy queen had kept her end of the bargain, but had betrayed me utterly.

XIX

My senses were heightened. A thousand scents swirled on the air, like the words of a long poem, asking me to interpret them, to sound out their meter, to dance to their rising and falling. I reared up on my hind legs and felt the strength in my haunches as my forelegs pawed the air. I leapt forward and darted in a circle around the nearest tree, and it was like flying. How swift I was now, how light and full of grace!

I let the scents guide me between food and not-food. I tasted the bright sweet flavors of grasses and leaves. The constant low cacophony in my ears began to resolve itself into distinct sounds that wove a landscape of creatures, objects, and their movements, spreading out into the distance. Standing still and listening, I learned that the dogs who had pursued me were safely away behind the walls of the stable, whimpering now and then as they dreamt in their kennels with their dog-boys curled up next to them on piles of hay. Mice, squirrels, and rabbits scrabbled through the bushes around me and scampered among the trees. Crickets chirped and beetles clicked away, pattering over bark and rocks.

My own kind were there too in the woods. Their musks charmed and intrigued me from afar. Beyond sight, touch, smell, taste, and hearing, a sixth sense in me was moved and informed by their camaraderie that reached like a fisherman's net undulating through water. It was a knowledge of belonging, of my place among them. I was not merely I, but also we. As a star in their constellation upon the earth I was a point in the picture they formed. I was sister, companion, daughter, mother. I was one of the herd.

I bounded forward to join them and as I ran, a tremulous awareness blossomed in me that *he* was with them, too. My lord and master, the king who commanded life and death. Half-fainting with anxiety and excitement, I leapt faster around trees and over bushes. My newly enlarged and quick-beating heart was eased as I caught sight at last of two sisters and their calves. They smelled me and knew of my belonging.

We slowed our pace and milled about, feeding on leaves and becoming acquainted with one another. The tread of mighty hooves announced the king's approach, and my heart beat fast again. At long last, his antlers shone through the branches, coming closer, closer. When he stood before me, his beauty was overwhelming, the beauty of a god, fatal and nurturing, the deadly life-giving force of a lightning bolt through a storm.

I bowed my head in deep obeisance to him, every part of my new body atremble with love and terror. My eyes were closed, but I felt him come close to me and raise me up, nuzzling his cheek against mine, filling my nostrils with the perfume of lily of the valley. Upright again, I opened my eyes and gazed into his, their irises silver-gray like rain, like the eyes of Thérion, his descendant. Then the king lowered his antlered head before me, so that for a moment I wondered whether he was bowing to me. Instead, he nudged with his nose the medallion I wore around my neck, acknowledging who I was and whence I had come.

We were alike, he and I, both of us dual-natured, half deer, half human. And yet not alike, for he was ancient and immensely powerful, beyond any notion of good or evil, immensely dangerous. He was love, he was death. And I was his.

I was his favorite now, his companion, his devotee. We walked side by side in his forest. We danced and leapt and played together. We raced, rested, fed, and slept. All the night we explored his domain. He showed me all that he commanded and at every moment I was suffused with awe at the beauty he had wrought through his powers. No painter, no sculptor had traced lines more delicate and intricate, no composer had orchestrated more brilliantly structured layers of harmonies. Through all the lovely tableaux were woven darker notes of fury, violence, blood, and death that made the light glow brighter, with its achingly fragile rush through the hours toward its changing and fading.

Among the dark notes were the scents and cries of the wolves. So long as I was by the king's side, I didn't fear them, but I shuddered at the thought of their teeth, the odor of blood and rotting flesh in their throats, and their mournful, pitiless hunting songs. My king could transform into a hunter to marshal them, could become the gaunt ogre of the bloodstained hunting gloves, but he kept himself beautiful and gentle for me.

The sun rose, igniting swaths of smells and colors that dazzled my new sight. Forgetful of the dangers to my human family, I laughed now at the fairy queen, and at the Marquise who had harried me and driven me down into the fairy queen's domain, both of them thinking to punish me and take from me my human life on this earth. Instead they had given me the joy of a new existence, new powers, senses, and strength, and the wondrous love of my king.

For the rest of the day we ran and rested together, the king and I, and then we shared another night, the sky cloudless and clear, illuminated by a crescent of waxing moon above us.

Then, in the ashen hour before dawn, the intruders came.

Horses' hooves beat over the earth. The steeds neighed and snorted. The dogs barked, their boys running after them, and the men and women called back and forth to each other in the tongue my own mouth had known before my changing. It was the Marquise's hunting party. In a flash of joy, I thought, *My love comes to me!* Thérion would be riding with them. The dogs with their clever noses would have shown them my discarded clothes on the ground by the standing stone. My love would fear for me but would know I had made it alive out of the garden and into the woods.

As they approached, I sensed more clearly who was with them. Besides the Marquise, Donatien, the Abbé, and Thérion, the Scotsman and Aurore were there. My joy turned to icy fear that squeezed my heart as my animal mind remembered the muskets. Bullets flew more swiftly than arrows. Even my king could be harmed by them. He had lived through millennia, never aging, and his powers were great. But surely the jealous fairy of Aurore's tale had counseled the nobleman to kill him in stag form, because she thought in that form he was vulnerable, so she would have attained her vengeance had it not been for the daughter's plea for mercy.

The riders came into sight. My brothers and sisters and I bolted, and the stag-king ran with us. The Marquise blew her hunting horn. The dog-boys let the hounds free from their leashes, and they barked and raced after us more swiftly than we could flee, over hillocks and bushes, over the warrens and burrows of our cousins who made their homes in the earth, through thick copses and clearings sweet with wildflowers. I had to warn the king about what we faced, but I had no words, no language in which to cry out to him, only my vague bleating of fear. He didn't know what muskets and bullets were. In his day, men had come with stones and spears and knives, bows and arrows, clubs and cudgels, hooded falcons, and hounds bred for scent, speed, or killing. His forest had been protected for so long, he had never faced these weapons that boomed like thunder and ignited with sparks and smoke, that struck with the force of a hundred spears and punched through flesh with the precision of an awl.

The dogs circled around us. We scattered before their snapping jaws and they began to drive us back toward the horses and hunters. I darted this way and that, trying to evade them, but always was met with those snapping jaws and the acrid odor of their malice. The stag-king tossed his mighty antlered head as though laughing as he loped alongside me. To him it was a game, and he had no fear of losing.

The king and I and two more of our kind were now separated from the rest of the herd, and the riders and horses joined the chase, leaving behind the dog-boys on foot. We began to tire, except for the stag-king who ran alongside me unwearyingly. He wouldn't abandon me to my danger, but I knew he was the one they would see as the prize, not me. What care did they have for a mere hind with no antlers? Through the woods we ran in an ever-narrowing circuit, the strength draining out of us.

Then in a clearing we were caught and surrounded. The stag-king stood at my right shoulder. The other two deer, a male and a female, cowered behind him, stamping and pawing at the earth in terror. The dogs growled, slavered, snarled, and slowly advanced over the ground toward us.

The riders had reined in their horses. I could make out their faces now in the gray foredawn, Aurore and the Marquise in riding habits. The Marquise sat tall and broad-shouldered in her seat astride, with a musket slung over her back. Donatien, likewise armed, was elegant as always in his riding clothes, while the Abbé seemed absurdly shriveled, diminutive, and bloodless seated on his great horse. The Scotsman looked rumpled and ill at ease. And my love, all in black on his black horse Hadès, looked sad and exhausted.

For a moment I forgot the muskets and tried to catch his eyes, which were are swollen and red-rimmed from weeping. He had to recognize me, even in my new form. Surely the eyes of love must see through disguises, especially his silver-gray eyes that could see in the dark, as mine did now. But it was the stag-king he stared at, whose eyes he met first, and whom he recognized. His lips parted in shock and a look of horror came over his face, for he saw that the stag-king's eyes were the same color as his, and that he stood before an ancestor and a god.

I tossed my head and reared up on my hind legs for a moment, trying to draw his attention. My effort succeeded, for now his gaze fell on the medallion around my neck, and his eyes widened still more.

The Marquise and Donatien had unslung their muskets and raised them to their shoulders to take aim.

"I say we both shoot at once," the Marquise said to Donatien, "or else the others will bolt. I'll take the big one. See if you can get a fix on the male behind him. You'll still have a five-pointer to take home."

"I'd have an easier shot at the hind in front. Better her than nothing."

"Up to you. I wouldn't bother. Say when you're ready. Fire on the count of three."

"Wait," said Thérion. "Don't do it."

The Marquise and Donatien ignored him and took aim, each tightening a finger against the musket trigger. Donatien followed the Marquise's advice and aimed at the male behind the forest-king, instead of at me.

"Stop!" Thérion shouted. He slackened his reins and allowed Hadès to carry him forward a few paces.

"What is it?" the Marquise said in an irritated tone.

"Don't kill them. For the love of God. You don't know what you're doing."

The Marquise puffed out her breath derisively.

"Ready," said Donatien.

"One. Two. Three," the Marquise said. "Fire."

I leapt to save my liege, the stag-king, to save Thérion's ancestor. I bounded up in front of him as two shots boomed through the air.

A great force struck my chest and knocked me backward, as though I had been punched. One leg went out from under me, and I crumpled to the ground.

❁

I blinked, dazed, and looked up. The Marquise swore.

"That damned hind. Of all the worthless things."

My sister and brother, who had been trapped by the dogs behind the stag-king, reared up. The male kicked a hound so hard the dog flew several feet through the air before landing in a broken heap. Both of the deer bounded away, flying over the other barking hounds and trampling on the wounded one.

My king stood over me, his eyes flashing like blue flames, and he snorted in furious breaths. He appeared unwounded. He took a step toward the Marquise as the hounds wheeled around in confusion. Her horse began to prance away.

There was another boom like a canon, but this time it was no musket going off; it was true thunder from the sky. We didn't see the lighting strike, but in a matter of moments, black clouds had gathered and thickened, and the air around us darkened as though time had turned backward and the approaching sunrise had reversed course into night again.

My king, too, changed and blackened as the sky did. He tossed his head and reared up on his hind legs, and then his body lengthened and flattened and he stood upright. He took on the nightmare form I remembered from the night by the standing stone with Séléné: the bleached-white mask of the antlered skull covering the upper half of his face, cruel red lips showing beneath, the tall, gaunt, sinewy hunter's form, the black clothes and boots, the leather gloves with fingers crusted wine-black from old blood, a bow and quiver of arrows slung over his back, and a white horn and long sheathed knife at his waist.

Flee, oh flee, I wanted to tell my friends, but I was voiceless, and my shoulder throbbed with heat and dull pain. Blood dripped from a hole in it onto the ground, and I realized I was wounded. The life was flowing out of me.

The Erl-King raised the bone-white horn to his scarlet lips and blew. My broad ears heard the shrill sound it made, though the humans' small and mushroom-like ears couldn't. The call was answered at once by such howls as to make any man or beast's blood run cold. The Erl-King's eyes glowed silver-blue from behind his bone mask as the wolves heeded his summons from the depths of the wood.

Flee, oh flee, I pleaded silently. To my immense relief, Aurore and the Scotsman turned their horses away at once and began to gallop back toward the manor. The hounds whimpered and streaked away after them, blurs of brown and black fur. Through the stands of elms and alders, between the rough bark of the trunks, orange eyes gleamed from far off, but their roaring howls were so loud it was as though the wolves were already upon us. The horses pranced as if the ground were the molten mouth of hell burning their hooves. And yet – what madness was this? – Thérion tried to dismount from Hadès's back. He swung one leg up and over his saddle, clinging with both hands to the saddle horn, with one foot still in the stirrup and the other free, as Hadès bucked and reared, trying to throw him off. In a movement like a dancer's twirling leap, Thérion braced himself against Hadès's flank and pushed off with feet and hands out of reach of the windmilling hooves, flew through the air, and landed on the ground, rolling to break his fall.

Donatien's horse threw him and bolted away into the woods. Donatien fell flat on his back and lay still with his mouth half-open, like a child's discarded doll. Hadès galloped after Donatien's horse. The Marquise and the Abbé struggled to keep their seats, to regain control of their mounts and turn away, but now the wolves had surrounded us. These were no ordinary gray wolves, but nightshadow horrors, blacker than the clouds covering the sky, with the thick shaggy pelts of bears and the bulk and length of wild boars, and eyes that glowed amber like sparks rising from a bonfire.

The wolves went first for the horses' throats. They leapt and sank their great jaws into the neck-flesh and tore it open with powerful wrenches and gushes of blood, first the Marquise's horse, then the Abbé's. The horses screeched with a noise like shattering glass. The Marquise wailed and swung her musket like a club, battering down a wolf on her right and one on her left, as the horse toppled to the ground under her, the butt of the gun thumping and cracking against flesh and bone. But they were too many for her, too strong, too fast. One clamped its jaws onto her arm that held the musket, and she shrieked as the gun slid from her grip. The rest of the wolves fell on her as her screams grew hoarse and ragged. I closed my eyes and turned away.

When I opened my eyes again, the Abbé's staggering horse collapsed before me. The Abbé jumped from the saddle with astonishing spryness and began to run while the pack was busy with the Marquise. He was almost out of sight by the time they had finished with her. Through the woods came the sound of a horse galloping to meet him. It was the Scotsman, returning to rescue whomever he could. One of the wolves broke away from the kill, his jaw dripping blood, and streaked through the woods after the Abbé. The wolf reached him a moment after the Scotsman did. Gripping the Scotsman's outstretched arm, the Abbé got one foot into the stirrup and the other foot over the horse's back, and his thin hips slid into the saddle just behind the Scotsman. The Scotsman kicked the horse's flank and jerked the reins to turn and gallop away, but just as the horse sprang forward, the wolf bounded up and snapped his jaws onto the Abbé's leg. It was too far away for me to see exactly what happened, but after a brief struggle, the horse tore away at full speed. The Abbé had kept his seat and still clung to the Scotsman, his arms wrapped around the Scotsman's waist.

The Erl-King towered over the scene, the horn still in his gloved hand, surveying the work of his wolves. They had finished with the Marquise and the horses, and now they began to sniff the air and advance to where I lay, padding toward me with their heads low to the ground. They smelled my blood.

Thérion had gotten back up onto his feet after his rolling tumble over the ground. He drew a long knife from the sheath on his belt and stepped forward to meet the wolves, half-crouching, moving sideways with the knife poised to jab and slash. He meant to protect me at the cost of his own life. Three wolves crouched across from him, about to spring on him.

The Erl-King raised the horn to his lips again and puffed two short shrill blasts on it.

The wolves fell back at once. They turned their tails to us and loped away, slowed by their full bellies, back through the trees, leaving trails of dribbled blood behind them.

Thérion ignored the terrifying figure of the Erl-King, as if he weren't there, as if the ogre were invisible to him. He fell to his knees before me. With one hand he stroked the fur on my forehead, much as he used to smooth back the hair from my brow when I was a woman. He sheathed the hunting knife and reached out to hold my medallion, rubbing his thumb over the embossed figure and the letters that spelled *CERNUNNOS*.

"I know this medallion. My Violaine carried it with her in her pocket. Her clothes were scattered in the clearing by the standing stone, as though she'd taken them off herself and they'd been blown all around in the wind. How did you come to have this round your neck? Did she put it there? It would have needed a human hand to get it on you." His voice was so low it was barely a whisper. "Are you her? Has my Violaine's spirit gone into you?"

I nodded my head. He drew back, startled. The Erl-King still stood over us, watching, his hands on his hips, but didn't move.

"Did you just nod?" Thérion whispered.

I nodded again, twice, so he couldn't mistake it.

"You're Violaine?"

I nodded.

"Am I going mad?"

I shook my head.

"Can you really understand me? Blink three times in a row if you understand what I'm saying."

I blinked three times, as deliberately and steadily as I could so he would know it was no mere coincidence.

He threw his arms around my neck and burst into tears. For several long minutes, he shook with weeping. The wound in my shoulder throbbed and burned as if seared by a hot iron poker.

"Oh, Violaine, thank the Fates I've found you, but you'll bleed to death if we don't bind up your wound. I love you more than my life. Stay with me, please."

His tears wet my face, and I, too, began to weep. I wiped the tears away with the back of my hand, and then gazed at the wet skin of my hand in wonder.

"I'm a woman again," I gasped, as though I had been holding my breath all the time before. "Your tears. It was your tears that changed me back."

I sat up now on the ground, naked, with my hair loose and blowing in the wind of the storm on its way. Thérion's arm was around my good shoulder, and the medallion was still around my neck. My right shoulder was covered in blood from my wound, and I couldn't lift my right arm. With my left hand I held up the medallion and examined it. There was a dent where the musket ball had bounced off it. If I hadn't been wearing it, the ball would have pierced my chest, entered my heart, and killed me in an instant. My skin under the medallion was marked by a round purple bruise the size of an apple. My shoulder wound still spurted blood, and now that I was sitting up, a bright red rivulet seeped out of it and down my rib cage. I felt faint and nauseated.

"My God," said Thérion. "Lie down, you're losing too much blood. I can't believe you're you again."

"You have more magic in you than you even knew," I murmured as he lowered me to the ground. I blinked, struggling to remain conscious, though his face was dimming before me and stars were shooting at the edges of my vision. Thérion tore off his jacket, hurriedly unbuttoned his waistcoat, and pulled off his linen shirt underneath. He bunched up the shirt and pressed it to my wound.

"You can't die. Stay with me."

"Will you take care of Valentin and Aimée? And Father and Edmée too?" I tried to keep my eyes open, to look into his beautiful gray-blue ones. But now I saw a second face leaning over me. It was the masked, horned face of the Erl-King, the red lips a gash in the pallor of his face. But I wasn't afraid of him. He smelled of lily of the valley.

"Darling, it's your ancestor, the *roi des aulnes*. He's right next to you. Why don't you look at him?"

My love's face went pale. "You see the Erl-King?"

"Can't you see him? He means us no harm. Didn't you see how he saved us? He sent his wolves after them. He knew they were hateful and meant to hurt us. Won't you talk to him? He's your grandfather's grandfather."

Thérion groaned. "Please, Erl-King." He looked away from where the Erl-King knelt, toward the forest. "If you're really here, don't take her from me. I know you want her. She's beautiful and good. But let me keep her. For the sake of our shared blood. I promise to protect your forest as long as I live, and our children and children's children and their children after them will protect it and honor you. Only let her live. Take what you want from me. Take my magic, my sight, my money, my lands. Take my years that remain, take the breath from my lungs, but let her stay."

The Erl-King's gash of a mouth didn't twitch or twist, but he removed his stained leather hunting gloves, set them on the ground, and reached out a bare waxen hand with skeletal fingers. The nails were long and sharp and lacquered black like talons. He stroked my cheek, tenderly, and passed a fingertip over my upper lip, then drew it back across my lower lip. He ran his taloned thumb and fingers lightly from my jaw under my chin down to the notch above my sternum. He desired me, I knew it. He was loath to give me up.

But he turned to Thérion and placed a hand on each of his shoulders. He pressed the red gash of his mouth against Thérion's forehead. Thérion closed his eyes a moment.

The Erl-King turned back to me. He spread out the fingers of one hand and pressed his palm down over the wound on my shoulder. Like a flame snuffed out, the pain ceased to burn me, and I felt life and blood coursing through my body again. He moved his palm to the bruise where the musket ball had struck my medallion and pressed it there too, and it stopped aching.

I sat up. The Erl-King picked up his gloves and put them back on as he rose to his feet. He turned his back to us and strode off without any gesture of farewell, back into the heart of his forest. I watched his antlered head moving through the trees until he was too far away for me to see anymore.

XX

Dr. Guillon managed to save the Abbé's leg, at least down to the knee. Below the knee he was forced to amputate. The bones were too splintered to set and the flesh too mangled to heal. He performed the operation in the back room of the Jacquenod's tavern. The doctor only came regularly once a week to the village from Thônes, so it was a great piece of luck that he was there when the Scotsman and Thérion drove the wounded into the village in the carriage.

Donatien didn't wake for two days. When he did, we discovered he was paralyzed from the waist down. He had broken his back, Dr. Guillon said, and would never walk again. Dr. Guillon took charge of both patients and arranged to bring them to a sanitarium in Annecy to recuperate further under the care of nuns. Thérion entrusted M. Fréret, the village wagoner, with the task of ensuring that the wagon with the hounds and the dog-boys returned safely to Donatien's manor near Dijon, though Donatien had said he didn't want them anymore and didn't care what became of them.

Since there was no undertaker in Maisnie-la-Forêt, Thérion sent for one from Thônes. It was surely no pleasant task for the undertaker and his assistant to gather the Marquise's remains from where the wolves had scattered them in the forest amongst the bloody carcasses of the horses. However, it had to be done for the law to be satisfied, and to give her a proper burial.

During the inquest that followed in Thônes, the witnesses all testified in agreement with one another: the hunting party was attacked by wolves of a species of unusually great size and ferocity. No one spoke of the Erl-King. I was the only one who had seen him so far as I knew, and I wasn't called upon to testify. Officially, I had stayed behind in the manor that morning and had seen nothing of what occurred.

Donatien and the Abbé agreed with that part of the story, too. It wouldn't do to admit that Donatien and the Marquise had set the hounds on me, driven me into the woods in the middle of the night, and left me to die. Aurore and the Scotsman believed I must have been beside myself with terror and grief, that I had removed my own clothes and left them by the standing stone and wandered alone for two days in the woods before coming upon Harlequin at the scene of the attack, after the wolves had gone. I didn't tell them the truth. By the time we had found each other again, back at the manor, I was still barefoot, my nakedness covered only by Thérion's bloodstained shirt, but my wounds were gone, healed over without a scar as though there had never been a lead ball lodged in my shoulder.

No one had seen what became of the enormous stag with the silver eyes. He had been there when the shots were fired and then was gone like a vanished mirage, and then the wolves had come. Perhaps the pack had been drawn by the scent of blood from the fallen hind. Perhaps the silver-eyed stag had even been some ghost or spirit of the forest who had led the hunters to the wolves. The wounded hind, too, seemed to have disappeared mysteriously afterwards. Nothing was found of her but her blood on the ground where she had lain. If she had been dragged off by a beast later, one might have expected to find tracks and marks of it in the soil. The magistrate reasoned when he concluded the inquest that she must have limped away to die elsewhere.

The priest in Maisnie-la-Forêt held a service for the Marquise in the village's small chapel, though her remains were to be repatriated to French soil and interred in her parish churchyard in the family plot in Burgundy. We attended the service, and there Thérion was reunited with his nurse from when he was a little boy – the same woman who had told Aurore the tale of the *roi des aulnes,* now bent over with age.

As for Ulysse, Séléné, Tristan, and Clio, Aurore told me they had all left for Paris the morning after Donatien arrived with his hounds. They had been appalled to see me beaten and driven off, and Clio had wanted to get away from Donatien and the Abbé immediately. Aurore had stayed and gone out with the hunting party in the hope of finding me in the woods or hearing some word from me, and the Scotsman had stayed for Aurore.

Thérion had suffered as a damned soul in the lowest circle of hell, fearing me dead and tormenting himself for failing to defend me from Léonore and Donatien. But Aurore's hopes had roused him from his paralysis and he too had gone out with the hunting party.

"I knew what Léonore was," he told me long afterward. "And even so, I never imagined she would strike you and follow through on her threats. I didn't know what to do. I froze, and then I fainted like a child," he choked out bitterly. "When I came to and the others told me what had happened – after that I hardly cared if I went to prison, or if the wolves tore me to pieces."

I forgave him easily, knowing how overcome he must have been, and remembering my own mistakes in trusting and pitying Donatien. One thing I've learned is that genuine encounters with evil in real life don't often go the way of romantic stories and fairy tales. However brave and virtuous one might be, one is seldom prepared for the shock of seeing a friend or companion cross the line into cruelty. One freezes, one fails to defend oneself and others against it, and evil can all too easily prevail if one's virtue and courage aren't helped along by luck, or the kindness of friends – or the forest god who took pity on us. My beloved's strength and courage were those of an artist, not those of a knight; I told him I was glad enough of a lover with a kind heart and a broad and brilliant mind, who mastered my body through his devotion to my pleasure, who freed my spirit with his generosity and humility.

The morning after the funeral service, we left Boisaulne for Paris by way of the tunnel in the grotto under the spring, the four of us in Thérion's carriage drawn through the old underground quarries by his horses, with the Marquise's remains in a casket in back.

Thérion brought Léonore's casket and the report of the inquest from Thônes back to her father in Paris's Faubourg, south of the Seine, while I stayed with Aurore at her house in the Ville. The Paris that Aurore showed me over the next three days was vast, fascinating, odorous, and rat-ridden. The grand cathedrals and palaces, the elegant *hôtels particuliers* and parks and squares overwhelmed me at first. I didn't know how Parisians could find their way through the tangle of *passages* and *rues* that crisscrossed and curled out from the main streets, with no snow-covered peaks in the distance to guide them.

After three days, Thérion returned to me, a free man.

A year later, we sleep late in the velvet-draped bed in Thérion's study at Boisaulne, warmed by the ingenious octagonal iron stove, though it's near freezing outside and snow is on the way. At my insistence, we've installed the same type of heating stove in most of the rooms, so the château is warm and cozy even in the depths of winter, and we live more comfortably than the French king and the ladies and gentlemen of his court in their drafty palaces at Versailles and Fontainebleau. Through the open door, from the other end of the floor, the harmonies and occasional discordant notes drift in of Valentin and Aimée playing their fiddle and harp, accompanied by Madame Grasset on the harpsichord.

Tomorrow afternoon my love and I will be in Paris for Séléné's *salon*, in the new rooms where she and Ulysse have set up housekeeping together. We look forward to congratulating Clio on her latest portrait commission, for we've just had a letter from her, brimming with her usual excitement and charm, and telling us how the Marquise de Véquy saw the portrait she had made of Aurore and arranged for a sitting at once. The following afternoon we'll go to Aurore's, since the period of mourning for her late husband has passed now. To remain near Aurore, the Scotsman has obtained a post as secretary to a British diplomat in Paris, and he calls on her almost every day.

We'll have news to share with our Paris friends: Thérion and I married properly last week, in the little chapel at Maisnie-la-Forêt. I'm not showing yet, but from the signs of my body I expect our baby to arrive in the Lenten season before Pâques, and Thérion wanted to be able to give the child his name.

We won't see Tristan in Paris, so I'll write to him today with the news. His last few books made such a stir they were condemned, first by the French authorities and then by the Swiss. He and his laundry woman had to flee their falling-down house outside Paris to take refuge in a Prussian territory north of Genève. Even so, Tristan has promised that if he can travel again by next summer, he'll join us once more at Boisaulne, where there are no longer any rules forbidding talk of families or children.

I don't expect we'll always live this happily together, Thérion and I. Though we love each other dearly, our life together is no fairy tale. Sometimes Thérion still falls prey to fits of despair, forgetting he no longer needs to wear masks within masks within masks to hide his true self from me and the rest of the world. Sometimes he struggles with drink, especially when his dreams are troubled by nightmares of Léonore and the daughter he lost. We searched for the child's mother, Renée, and learned she had died six years ago in the workhouse where Léonore had her imprisoned.

I have faults and struggles of my own. I doubt Thérion's love sometimes, fearing it will fade as we grow older together, or in the coming months as my body changes with our growing child. I cry over small irritations and pick fights with him. I too have nightmares. And sometimes both of us are exasperated by the children's mischief, and Thérion rails at them and threatens to turn them out and leave them to their great-great-great-grandfather, the ogre who lives in the forest.

I'm no longer a prisoner of the Castle of Enlightenment. Yet in a sense I remain a captive, bound by longing and anticipation for the nights when my love still comes to me in the dark and teases me with riddles and mysteries, caresses me, and makes love to me. He is still my captive, too, ever eager to do my bidding and give me pleasure. Freed to walk together in the light, we yet remain entangled, body and soul, in the chains of our dark love for one another.

Author's Note

THE VAUDOIS WERE a real religious sect with a fascinating history, but the group of secret Vaudois villages in the mountains near Annecy is my own invention. Some of my ancestors were Vaudois of the Piedmont who encountered traveling Mormon missionaries in the nineteenth century, converted to Mormonism, and emigrated to the United States. I grew up hearing family legends about them.

Several of the characters in the book were inspired by historical figures of the European Enlightenment, though I have liberally added, subtracted, and switched around biographical details and dates. The character of Aurore was inspired by salonnière Marie Thérèse Geoffrin (1699–1777) and to a lesser degree Hippolyte de Saujon, the Comtesse de Boufflers (1725–1800), a close friend of the Scottish philosopher David Hume (1711–1776). Aurore's habit of writing fairy tales is reminiscent of women such as Gabrielle-Suzanne de Villeneuve (1685–1755) and Jeanne-Marie Leprince de Beaumont (1711–1780), who penned different versions of the story of "La Belle et la Bête." Hume, in turn, was my main inspiration for the character of the Scotsman.

Donatien was inspired by the Marquis de Sade (1740–1814), and for the Marquise du Herle I drew on the Marquis de Sade's mother-in-law, Marie-Madeleine de Plissay, Présidente de

Montreuil (1721–1789), said to be his rival in ruthlessness. For Séléné I took details from the life of novelist and salonnière Claudine Alexandrine Guérin de Tencin (1682–1749), though I gave her the unhappy marriage of the brilliant Louise d'Épinay (1726–1783). Clio was loosely based on the painter Élisabeth Louise Vigée Le Brun (1755–1842), while Clio's friend Tristan took some of his storyline from Jean-Jacques Rousseau (1712–1778). Ulysse has a few similarities with rival philosopher and firebrand Voltaire (1694–1778), who lived for many years with the woman of his life, the married mathematician and scientist Émilie du Châtelet (1706–1749).

Some of the Abbé's views are reworded excerpts from the writings of the Savoyard theorist and critic of the Enlightenment, Joseph de Maistre (1754–1821), whom Isaiah Berlin depicted as a proto-fascist in an essay collected in *The Crooked Timber of Humanity*.

Acknowledgments

I'M GRATEFUL TO all those who helped shape the book through their reading and critique of various drafts. Thanks to my wonderful writers group, Caroline Bock, Danielle Stonehirsch, Monica Hogan, Cate Bloom, and Garinè Issasi, who have kept me writing and laughing over the years.

Thanks to Valerie Preiss, who in addition to being an early reader and critiquer went the extra mile to organize a reading of the manuscript by her book club, and introduced me to the concept of literary compersion; and thanks to everyone who read part or all of the book and/or discussed it at the book club meeting, including Amanda Jagusiak, Geoff Kabaservice, Suzanne Turner, Blake Stenning, C. Lee Cawley, and David Plummer.

Thanks to Philip Shade Kightlinger, who besides reading and giving feedback on the manuscript was a patient, encouraging, and supportive sounding board as I struggled to work out plot and character ideas, and who helped me visualize the Erl-King with his sketches.

Thanks to my volunteer readers and friends who gave feedback, including Jennifer Ray, Camille Stanberry Myers,

Mariah Brothe, Carolina Lopez-Ruiz, Ravena Guron, and Helen Spande.

Thanks to Embark Literary Journal for featuring the first chapter of this book as an excerpt in its April 2019 issue.

Thanks to all those in my broader network of writer friends for your inspiration, advice, and showing me what good writing looks like. Thanks to the Virginia Center for Creative Arts for granting me a creative writing residency back in 2013 that helped forge many of those connections.

Thanks to my family and friends for being there.

Thanks to the scholars I never had the good fortune to meet but whose work helped inform my understanding of the historical background. I particularly enjoyed books by Philipp Blom, Robert Darnton, Dena Goodman, Maurice Lever, Joan DeJean, Anthony Pagden, and Roger Pearson (though my embroideries on the truth and any unintentional inaccuracies are not to be blamed on anyone but me).

About the Author

THERESE DOUCET WRITES, parents, and works a day job in Washington, DC, and Knoxville, TN. She studied cultural history in a Ph.D. program at the University of Chicago for four years, and is a former Fulbright fellow, as well as a creative writing residency fellow of the Virginia Center for Creative Arts. Her fiction and creative nonfiction have appeared in literary magazines including *Embark, Hotel Amerika,* and *Bayou,* and one of her essays was listed as a Notable Essay of the Year in *Best American Essays 2011.*

She can be reached via:
Website: https://theresedoucet.wordpress.com/
Facebook: https://www.facebook.com/therese.doucet.9
Twitter: https://twitter.com/Strviolin

OTHER EXQUISITE SPECULATIVE FICTION
FROM D. X. VAROS, LTD.

Samuel Ebeid	THE HEIRESS OF EGYPT THE QUEEN OF EGYPT
G. P. Gottlieb	BATTERED SMOTHERED *(coming Summer 2020)*
Phillip Otts	A STORM BEFORE THE WAR THE SOUL OF A STRANGER *(coming Fall 2020)*
Erika Rummel	THE INQUISITOR'S NIECE
J. M. Stephen	INTO THE FAIRY FOREST
Felicia Watson	WHERE THE ALLEGHENY MEETS THE MONONGAHELA WE HAVE MET THE ENEMY SPOOKY ACTION AT A DISTANCE *(coming March 2020)*
Daniel A. Willis	IMMORTAL BETRAYAL IMMORTAL DUPLICITY IMMORTAL REVELATION PROPHECY OF THE AWAKENING